My Heart
Before You

Laura Langa

For AJ, my love

·PROLOGUE·

"What do we have?" Colin asked the emergency physician after briefly glancing at the tall man lying on the stretcher.

"Sixty-two-year-old male. Awake and oriented. Type A aortic dissection diagnosed by CT scan. Came in tachycardic and hypertensive. I put him on esmelol to lower his BP."

As the ER doc spoke, Kitty, the OR nurse manager, and one of her nurses arrived in the trauma bay.

A quick scan of the bleating monitors displayed that for the moment the man was stable enough to transport. "Okay, we've got it from here. Thank you, Dr. McKale," Colin said.

"Thanks for responding so quickly," she replied, helping them push the patient towards the elevators.

Once they started their descent, Colin assessed the man's pallor, flared nostrils, and hyperventilation, but it was the blueness of his eyes shining with terror that made the back of his throat tighten. From the subtle tan of his skin to his sandy-grey hair, the man closely resembled his father. Colin drew a short, painful inhale as the emotions he'd been stifling for five months threatened to take him down like a rogue wave.

"I'm Dr. Abernan." An unintended quaver crept into his words before he swallowed against the burnt taste in his mouth. "We're taking you to surgery to fix your heart."

As the man nodded, Colin clenched his fist around the cold bed railing, and pushed the stretcher into OR six.

A sensation of gratitude swept his body as he vigorously scrubbed the antimicrobial soap over his hands and forearms. He wanted everything to go well for this man and having Kitty on staff would help that wish become reality. The sharp middle-aged woman always impressed him with her efficiency and experience.

"He's crashing," Kitty called out before disappearing through the swinging door.

Drying his hands, he immediately pushed through the door with his back. "What's happening?"

"Patient's in PEA," the anesthesiologist answered, finishing his intubation.

Electronic lines and beeps falsely displayed a steady cardiac rhythm, but Colin understood that his patient's heart was immobile within his chest.

Kitty helped him gown as quickly as possible as he called out, "Scalpel."

Taking the slender tool in his hand, he began an emergency thoracotomy. The metallic scent of blood spilled into the room as he cut along the man's ribs. The sound of his own focused, steady breaths blocked out the alarming machines. In less than sixty seconds, he could see the chest cavity was completely filled with blood.

"Shit," he muttered under his breath.

Blood poured from the opening he'd made in the man's side. "Suction!"

The OR staff flew around him as he worked rapidly to visualize the heart and lungs in the opening between the man's spread ribs. Pushing his gloved fingers against the slippery heart, he found pressure flowing from the aorta.

"Clamp."

His forearms pricked with tension as he worked as fast as possible, but he couldn't gain proximal control of the bleeding.

"I can't see. Get me another suction canister."

As Colin tried to stop the rapid outflow of blood, he finally saw that the tear in the man's heart went all the way through his aortic valve. Ice swiftly flushed through his veins and settled hard in the pit of his stomach.

"Give me another clamp!" he shouted.

When the scrub tech handed him the instrument, he rooted around futilely trying to bring the two sides back together.

"Dr. Abernan." Kitty's soft voice was barely audible over the incessant cacophony of alarm bells.

Ignoring the tightness behind his eyes and the fact that the patient had clearly bled out, he gestured to the scrub tech. "Clamp."

The small tool landed, heavy, in his outstretched hand. His grip closed rigidly around the instrument for a few heated seconds before he threw it from the surgical field across the room. A metallic crash sounded as it hit the wall, ricocheted to the ground, and slid several feet.

"Damn it."

His scrub tech jumped as the rest of the frigid room collectively held its breath.

Shoving back from the table, he tore off his blood-soaked gown and gloves, throwing them on the floor. "Goddamn it!"

As he slammed his hand onto the OR door, he barely registered Kitty's voice. "Dr. Abernan?"

"I'll call it," the anesthesiologist said as the door swung closed.

A minute later, Colin was smashing out of the side exit of the hospital into the crisp autumn air. Rancid dumpster stench followed him from the alley as he took long strides across the street. He swatted a red maple leaf, mid-fall, out of his face and flung open the stairwell door to his condo building. Taking the stairs two at a time, his legs strained with each angry push of his foot.

His cell phone rang just as he reached the fifth floor. "Abernan," he barked as a hello.

"Hey man, I heard you had a rough time in the OR." Even his best friend's voice didn't ease the tension in his muscles.

"It was a shit case." He fumbled for his keys, missing twice before finally jamming them into the lock.

"Kitty told me you threw things."

"Lots of surgeons throw things in the OR," he snarled.

"A lot of surgeons do, but *you* don't," Max replied, his tone calm and even.

"I'm not allowed a bad day?"

Colin strode into his condo and looked around, not knowing what to do with all the adrenaline rushing through his body. He wanted to run ten miles as fast as he could until this pressure in his arms loosened.

"You are."

After pacing a few more tight circles, he flopped onto the only piece of furniture in his condo. The scent of his father's deodorant wafted up from the soft, leather recliner, stinging his nose. His attempt at an inhale sat trapped in his chest.

"I lost him."

"I know you lost him, but you've lost patients before, and you will lose many more. That's the job. You know this. You've done this hundreds of times." Max paused for a few breaths. "You mean your dad."

Colin couldn't even respond, he was fighting too hard against the tears pricking at the corners of his vision and the congestion at the bridge of his nose. Memories of his father, and *how* he died flooded his mind.

I could have saved him.

Defeat pulled his body forward until his head was cradled in his hand.

"I'm taking the rest of your call today, okay?" His friend's voice was gentle.

Pride bristled in his chest. "You don't need—"

"I'm not hearing it. Let me take the rest of the day. Are you working tomorrow?"

Air pushed from his lungs as he shoved his hand over his head and took off his scrub cap. "No, I was scheduled off already."

"Do you need Monday?"

"No, I'm fine. I'll apologize to Kitty and the staff. I'll head back right now." He attempted to rise, but his muscles fought against his brain's commands.

"Kitty didn't call me to tattle on you, Colin. She called because she was worried about you . . . and so am I," he paused, "Do you want to talk about it?"

He shook his head, his hair gently hitting his temples before realizing Max couldn't see him. "No, I just need time."

"Take it. And let me know if you need more."

A reluctant exhale left his lungs. "Okay."

"Give me report. Did you talk to the family after you left the case?"

"Jesus, no." He ran his hand over his face and sat straight up in the chair. "I didn't even pronounce him."

"It's okay, I've got it. I've got it all. What was his name?"

·CHAPTER 1·

Six weeks earlier

Emilie's lips lifted at the familiar set of scrubs standing in front of her at the electronic timecard system. "Good morning, Ash."

"Good morning, Sunshine." Her friend spun around and gave her a quick hip bump.

It was the second time that phrase had been used this morning; an hour ago, her sister sent the identical sentiment via text. Part of her wished that people would stop aligning her with celestial light, but today she needed the extra positivity.

Earlier when the annoying bleat of her alarm pulled her from sleep, she'd reached for a ghost in her groggy haze. Little actions like this made the reality of her life now harder to accept, making the saliva stick in her throat and her stomach twist.

"I hear that Flo's on the rampage this morning, so heads up."

"Thanks for the warning," Emilie said, quickly swiping her badge to clock in.

She followed the scent of her friend's apple shampoo into the locker room. After grabbing her stethoscope and loading her pockets with all the things she'd need for the shift, she collected her unit phone and assignment from the charge desk.

Her colleague, Annette, met her with a grateful, happy grin, excited to hand over report so her twelve-hour night shift could end.

"Mr. Robert Shaw. Readmit from outpatient cardiac rehab, status-post quadruple bypass . . ." she paused when Flo, in the adjacent charting area, was heard tearing into a newly graduated nurse. Annette rolled her eyes. "Looks like someone didn't get the memo that we don't eat our young anymore."

Sighing a frustrated breath, Emilie made a mental note to give the new grad some encouragement later in the day. "Apparently not."

Though she was still new to cardiothoracics, being a decade out of nursing school, Flo had never targeted her. Barbara, her nurse manager, wasn't overly concerned that the transition would be particularly difficult, stating, "ER nurses make good cardiac nurses." Being on a specialty unit for all cardiothoracic surgery was a perfect fit for her. It met her two goals in regards to returning to work—she wanted to be in some area of specialty care, and she didn't want to step inside an emergency room ever again.

The early hours of her shift had vanished as she'd met, assessed, and given morning medications to all the patients in her care. The rhythmic pinging of the call bell rang overhead when she finally sat to chart. Sneaking a gulp of the now lukewarm french roast from her "Totes A Morning Person" tumbler, she let the bitter taste of sweet dark caffeine roll over her tongue. As her fingers sped across the keyboard, Ash materialized over her shoulder.

"TGIF. It's actually 'my Friday' and it *is* Friday!"

"I love when that happens." She looked up from her electronic chart. "It's my Monday."

"Oh that stinks. I was going to invite you out for drinks with the girls tonight."

"Too bad." She tried to pour regret into her words, but she'd never been good at displaying emotions she didn't feel. The idea of going out wasn't something she could manage right now; she was still getting used to this new city and her new life. Ash had been sweet to always invite her, but didn't push when she kept saying no.

"Then you and I should have dinner at Bo's after work. I'm not meeting the girls until ten-thirty anyway." Ash tucked a strand of her straight, chin-length blonde hair behind her ear.

"Now that, I'll never turn down." Emilie grinned.

"Good. We'll chat then." Her nurse phone rang, and she waved goodbye as she answered cheerily, "5SW, this is Ashley. How can I help you?"

Ash was nothing like her name that brought to mind spent embers, grey and cold; she bounded into Emilie's life full of fire and light. A few months ago at the nursing orientation, Ash plopped into the open seat next to her, and after a quick and lively conversation, insisted Emilie call her "Ash" because all her *friends* did.

The computer dinged with a new order for one of her patients, and she turned her attention to the computer popup. The order was for patient Shaw.

Hose out chest wound cavity before next dsg chng.
11:12am Dr. Colin Abernan

The surgeon wanted her to do what? Mr. Shaw had a severe wound infection, and he was currently attached to a poorly draining wound suction device, but to hose out his chest? Annette said that when she and her aide had changed the dressing overnight, the wound smelled so rotten that the aide almost lost her lunch.

Since she didn't recognize the name signed to the order, she pulled up the physician directory and left a page. A minute later, she received a call back on her nurse phone.

"This is Dr. Abernan. I received a page to this number."

"Hi, I'm the nurse caring for patient Robert Shaw in 516. I'm calling about an order you just wrote to 'hose out his chest.'" She paused, waiting for him to explain himself.

"Yes, what about it?"

"You want me to remove his dressing and wash out his wound in the shower room?" She knew she was new to cardiothoracics, but she'd never heard of anything like this, and it seemed wholly unsanitary.

"Just put the shower nozzle into his wound and flush it out." The sound of rapidly clicking computer keys indicated that he was typing as he was talking to her.

Her jaw stiffened. "I'm sorry, doctor, but I'm going to need you to come and give me this order in person. I don't feel comfortable completing this without speaking with you face to face."

She heard a huff of breath. "I'll be there in a minute."

The phone cut out as he hung up on her.

Ten minutes later, a taut male voice pulled her from her chart. "Are you the nurse for 516?"

Pinning her shoulders back, she pushed off from the high computer chair to stand in front of the tall man in surgical scrubs and a white coat. "Yes, I am. I apologize for calling you to the floor, but this order sounds unusual, and I've not done anything like this before."

Surprisingly, he didn't seem irritated. "I understand. It is unusual, but in cases like this, the best thing is to get rid of all the exudate and start from scratch. I've also ordered a slew of antibiotics to hang."

Some of the internal armor she'd put in place loosened. She was used to dealing with difficult doctors and kept forgetting that the Cardiothoracic Surgeons of Boston, or CTSB as everyone called them, were known for collegial camaraderie.

"So you want me to just put the shower head right into his chest?" She pantomimed putting a detachable shower head into a person's chest.

A barely contained look of amusement quickly passed over his face, lifting his mouth into a slight smile that he straightened before speaking. "Right into the chest."

The subtle warmth in his blue-grey eyes somehow made the tightness between her shoulder blades soothe. "And I'll know that I'm done when . . ."

"When the water runs clear."

"Aren't you worried about introducing new pathogens?"

Shaking his head, a few wayward strands of his wavy hair fell into his eyes, and he quickly whisked them away. "There's nothing in the water that's worse than what's already in his wound."

"Okay." That actually made sense to her.

He pulled a folded bunch of printed papers out of his coat pocket. "Do you also have 512?"

"No, I don't, but the assigned nurse will be listed at the charge desk." She gestured behind her.

"Thank you," he said, eyes reading his paperwork as he headed towards the desk.

Emilie went into the medicine room and found Ash pulling up an antiemetic from its vial into a syringe. "You'll never guess what I was asked to do."

"What?"

"Take Mr. Shaw to the shower room and hose out his infected chest."

Her friend raised a golden eyebrow over her stylish glasses. "You better tell the other aides. Half of them are pre-nursing students. And grab that new grad."

"Good idea," she said, pulling the door open, and striding straight into Dr. Abernan.

She was glad she wasn't carrying a handful of syringes like Ash as her body bounced off the wall of green scrubs. Almost immediately, his hands framed her biceps, steadying her.

"You okay?"

"Yeah, sorry." She brushed back her still damp braid that sprang over her shoulder in the collision.

"It's okay," he said, letting go of her.

A strange sensation of warmth lingered after his hands left her body. Since moving here, she hadn't really been held, even loosely, by anyone. She touched a lot of people every day in her job, starting IVs, doing exams, holding a patient's hand, but not many people touched *her*. The last time she'd received anything but Ash's hip bumps was the fierce, long hug her parents gave her when she dropped them off at the airport.

His pager sounded again, and he glanced at the device as James, her patient care aide, called her name followed by, "You're going to hose out Mr. Shaw's chest?"

The left side of the doctor's mouth lifted slightly as he turned away from them to dial a number onto the wall phone in the nearest charting area.

After getting the shower ready, and gathering all interested parties to observe, she spoke to Mr. Shaw and his wife, explaining the process and what to expect. The Shaws remarked that a doctor had been by recently to talk to them, and she was grateful Dr. Abernan had laid the groundwork for her.

Mr. Shaw was weakened from his surgery and fighting such a bad infection, but fortunately was able to walk with assistance and sit in the shower chair. Like the rest of the staff, Emilie covered her lavender scrubs in a gown, and donned gloves and a facemask with a plastic shield over her eyes. Opening just the front of his checkered, cloth hospital gown, she gently removed the dressing as James warmed the water. A pungent scent quickly filled the small space, and her lips parted to breathe through her mouth behind her mask—a trick she'd learned in nursing school.

There was a one-centimeter gap between the two sides of his split sternum, beyond which his heart was beating. It wasn't an unfamiliar sight to her anymore. With infections like this, the pumping muscle was frequently visible through the unhealed opening during dressing changes. The metal shower head pulsed in her hand as she brought it towards his body. Filling her lungs to the brim, she confirmed with Mr. Shaw that he was ready before pushing all the water into his chest.

When thick, brown-green water spewed out in a rush, several of the peanut gallery stepped back. Her free hand found Mr. Shaw's shoulder as she spoke reassuringly, watching the tainted liquid continue to flow—now a cloudy yellow. After a minute, the water finally ran clear, and she applied a new dressing and put him in a clean gown before returning him to his hospital bed.

Stepping back into the noisy hallway, as doctors, nurses, and aides moved around her in a seemingly well-choreographed dance, she glanced at her watch. She wasn't even halfway through what was starting to be a very busy shift. Another nurse might have been frustrated by this point in the day, but her chest only swelled with gratitude that after everything, she still had this. Her nurse phone rang in her front pocket, and her lips lifted at the sound.

"5SW, this is Emilie."

·CHAPTER 2·

Slowing to a crawl in front of the expansive two-story brick house, Colin pulled into the driveway. The sound of leaves rustling on the large mature trees dotting the front yard met his ears as he stepped from his SUV. Walking up the chevron paver path to the front steps, he inhaled deeply the scent of cut grass and burning charcoal ready for a steak. It'd been a long time since he'd been in the suburbs.

When Kate opened the door wide, her long, loosely curled red hair blew back with the swift inward movement. "Colin!" Auburn eyebrows lifted in excitement as she pulled him into a brief hug. "So glad you're here."

"Thank you for having me." He held out the bottle of Malbec he'd brought and noted her breezy, tea-length dress under her white denim jacket. "You look amazing."

She tossed her head with a laugh. "That's because the last time you saw me, I'd practically just given birth."

Bitterness washed over his tongue as he remembered the reason she'd traveled so far with such a young infant. The sound of her son's tiny cries joining those of dozens of adults as they'd stared at the white lily-covered casket replayed in his mind.

Her eyes widened. "I'm sorry."

A sharp, painful inhale filled his chest. "It's okay," he said, waving his hand as Max barreled down the hallway.

"Welcome to Casa Campbell!"

Being enveloped in his best friend's burley arms felt like grabbing onto a lifeline. Though they usually gave each other one-armed guy hugs when they met for their annual "boys only" camping trip, he found both of his arms tightly wrapping around his friend's smooth oxford shirt.

Standing in the threshold of his best friend's house, the feeling of utter loneliness that haunted him like an unwanted shadow dampened diminutively. Behind him was the adrift sensation of having no living family, and in front of him was the warmth of a relationship they'd both nurtured since medical school.

Max patted his shoulder, encouraging him down the hall. "Let me give you the tour. Kate outdid herself with this one."

After thoroughly exploring the house, they settled in the backyard Adirondack chairs surrounding a stone fire pit. An expanse of grass ended with a tasteful wrought iron fence, providing a boundary from the nature preserve beyond. Birdsong floated above the layered chirps of crickets.

"This is an amazing yard."

"Thanks, man. Kate and I really wanted Owen to have the small-town childhood we both had. We loved this house for its space and when he gets older, he can have all of those woods as a playground," he said, running his hand through his short ginger hair before relaxing his fingers on the armrest.

Colin nodded. Some of his favorite memories from his childhood in North Carolina were making forts in the trees behind his parents' house.

"How was your first week?" Max crossed his ankle over his knee.

Seven days of surgeries, office hours, and rounds quickly flashed through his mind, but the baffled look of two soft brown eyes pulled up the corner of his mouth. "Really good, actually."

"You are going to love working here. Surgeons, nurses, and scrub techs working symbiotically in one big collaboration makes such a big difference." His friend's face lit up with a grin. "Plus, we get to high-five in the halls like the good old days. What more of a reason could you want to make the move?"

Colin felt his lips lift higher. "Thank you again for arranging all this."

"You'd have done the same thing for me had the tables been turned, and it just happened to be perfect timing because John Reddington's planning on retiring this summer. We were about to put out headhunters anyway, so really, you saved a lot of trouble looking for a good replacement."

He'd met with the silver-haired legend earlier in the week to discuss performance expectations. Keeping near perfect surgical statistics would be no problem. He prided himself on being one of the hardest working surgeons at his hospital in Tampa, but the culture shift of mandatory decreased hours to encourage work-life balance he'd need to get used to.

The French door opened, and Kate strode down the deck stairs with a baby on her hip. "I see this is where the boys are hanging out. This little bro just woke up and wanted to join."

The baby had his fat fist in his mouth, happily blowing bubbles and muttering against it. He looked dressed for dinner in a collared gingham romper with an embroidered blue whale on the chest pocket.

She handed their son to her husband. "Dinner's in fifteen, guys."

"Do you need any help, love?"

"No, I've got it. You guys catch up. I'll call when it's time." Kate smiled before turning back toward the house.

Max repositioned his son, so he was facing outward in his lap. "I told you he was getting big. Look how chunky he is now. It's a point of pride for Kate, since breastfeeding was so tough on both of them in the beginning. Of course, he just started solids, so that doesn't hurt."

His friend's mouth pulled into a proud grin as he regarded his boy. Since Owen was often a main topic over the last six months, Colin was well versed in his short life.

"He's a chunker for sure. Everything else going well?"

"Lately, he's been teething, so I'm getting woken up at night like it's intern year, but it's not like he's doing it on purpose." He kissed Owen's head. "You want to hold him?"

Colin shifted uneasily in his chair not having much experience with babies, but not wanting to disappoint his overjoyed friend after all he'd done for him. "Hand the little man over."

The affable baby didn't mind the transfer in the least. He let out a little coo and tilted his head, staring up with deep blue eyes. A small tuft of auburn hair wisped from the center of his otherwise bald head. Looking at the soft warm baby nestled against his chest, Colin couldn't help but admit that it felt surprisingly nice.

They talked about the most interesting cases from the week before Kate opened the back door and told them it was time for dinner. The dining room table had been set for three with a highchair at the end of the table. Max settled his son in it and put a few strawberry baby puffs on the tray, which Owen immediately shoved into his two-toothed mouth.

Kate had prepared a mouthwatering roast; the savory taste of the cooked-to-perfection beef paired perfectly with sauteed Brussel sprouts and homemade bread with honey butter. Max opened the wine and gave everyone a heavy pour.

"Ohhh, this is good!" Kate crooned after sipping from her glass.

Warmth spread through his chest. "I'm glad it complements the delicious meal. Thank you again for dinner."

"You are welcome here anytime. In fact . . ." Her eyes met Max's over the table. ". . . we were thinking we could make this a weekly thing."

He swallowed his bite. "Oh, I can't possibly—"

Max's baritone voice interrupted, "You can and you will. Kate and I have talked it over, and we want you to have a homebase. We know how close you were with your dad, and we want you to know you have people who care about you. That's one of the main reasons that we wanted you to move to Boston, so we could be here for you."

The warmth in his chest abated as squeezing tension replaced it. With all he had been through, he should have been better prepared for the crushing blow of suddenly losing his father, but he wasn't. His father's death had knocked him to the ground so violently, he couldn't reorient himself. It was as if he'd lost a chunk of himself.

They hadn't just been close, they were each other's support system and closest confidant. Or at least he'd foolishly believed they were. What he wouldn't give to go back in time and do things differently. His throat tightened uncomfortably, and he poured wine down it in an attempt to alleviate it.

"Think of them as family dinners," Kate piped in. "We'll work them around your schedules, but there should be a day at least once a week or every other week that you both are off. We want you to know you're always welcome here. If it makes you feel better, you can keep supplying delicious wine as a contribution."

Two sets of eyes watched him as Owen let out a squeal and then hit his fist on the tray of his highchair as if in agreement with his parents.

"Okay, if you're sure." As much as he'd happily be here any night of the week for dinner, he didn't want to impose.

"We are." Kate leaned across the table and squeezed his hand briefly before opening a small container of a pureed food substance and spooning some out for her son.

The rest of the dinner passed enjoyably until eventually Owen became fussy and Kate declared bedtime. Max went upstairs to get their son ready for bed while he and Kate teamed up to clear the table and wash dishes.

"Okay, Mommy. Your turn." His friend reentered the kitchen with a freshly bathed, footie-pajama clad Owen.

When Kate set down the dish towel and held out her arms for their baby, Max kissed her over the exchange, making an Owen sandwich.

A twinge pulled across Colin's chest before his friend held his hand out for the freshly rinsed dish. "How's the new condo? Kate said she found you a nice corner unit."

For ease, he decided to live in the new condo tower a block from the hospital. It had an assigned parking spot in the garage for his car and a really nice gym facility on the top floor. Since running and weight training were how he blew off stress, he anticipated spending a good deal of his newly allotted free time there.

"It's great." Mentally, he made a note to tell Kate when she returned downstairs. "I really appreciate her viewing it for me and organizing the purchase."

Max waved him off. "She was happy to help. Kate loves her job. She gets all jumpy, squealy girl over the really nice properties sometimes." He chuckled. "Of course, not in front of the client."

He smiled at the soapy water sliding between his fingers. "Of course not."

"I'll help you unpack boxes this weekend if you like. I saw we're both off on Friday."

A heaviness settled in his stomach at the idea of unpacking the boxes that filled his empty condo. "That's okay. I've got it. I'm sure you'd rather spend the day with your family."

Only the sound of running water filled the designer kitchen until his eyes flitted up to meet his friend's.

"Colin, you *are* family."

Pale blue eyes held his gaze for what felt like an excruciating amount of time, though it was only a brief second. As he focused on rinsing the last serving dish, his teeth clenched together, helping him keep the dampness that threatened at the corners of his vision under control.

Max cleared his throat, and his voice gained a teasing tone when he spoke again. "So you're actually going to live in this condo, right? No sad bachelor pad like all your other places?"

"My places weren't that bad," he threw back, relieved to be on more familiar ground.

"I've seen freshman dorm rooms with more personality." Max placed the dry dish on the counter and crossed his arms.

"You know the drill, man. Work trumps all. Saving lives takes precedence over decorating."

His friend snickered. "You'll have plenty of time now."

"I guess . . ."

"You know you can order almost anything online now. All types of housewares."

"It would be helpful to have a nightstand for my phone, so I wouldn't have to get out of bed to answer it."

"Watch out world!" An elbow hit him in the ribs.

"You're one to talk. I'm sure Kate made this place look like a home, not you."

"Hey." Max thrust out his chest. "I picked out the Adirondack chairs *and* oversaw the fire pit construction."

"My mistake." He grinned, raising his palms.

"I'm glad you live here. It will be like med school all over again, but better because now we have paychecks."

Max could always make him laugh.

"I'll definitely have time to hang out."

"Yes. Let's do dinner out Friday, just us. I know this amazing steak place downtown. Kate won't mind. She'd be excited to get me out of the house, so she can watch trashy reality TV without me commenting on its stupidity every six seconds."

"Okay, that sounds great," he said, excited by the prospect of spending the evening with his friend rather than being alone in his condo again.

"But seriously, you are going to love the reduced hours. Not at first. It's going to seem really crazy, and you won't know what to do with yourself, but soon you'll discover you've got time for things you didn't before. You know, like hobbies . . . maybe even a girl." Max waggled his eyebrows.

Though he'd dated off and on, his focus had always been on his professional goals first. Initially, it was getting into medical school, then excelling at medical school, followed by getting into a top residency, and becoming a great surgeon. All those commitments took a tremendous amount of time. He could never find a woman who could understand his work hours or his dedication to his career. And since the accident, he'd just shut that part of himself down.

But then there was the memory of the honeysuckle scent of the brunette who bounced off his body in the hall. The fragrance immediately threw his mind to springtime as a boy, riding bikes in the humid air, vibrating with the knowledge that summer was right around the corner and with it, the feeling of promise, of potential.

That same potential, that oscillation coursed through his veins for the brief second his hands held her arms.

Mentally, he gave himself a hard shake. Better not to entertain that thought.

He exhaled tightly. "We'll see."

"Since you're new in town I could always—"

"No," he interrupted. "No setups. And if I ever come to dinner and there's a fifth person at that table, I'll stop coming all together."

The last thing he needed right now was to feel pressured into playing nice when he was barely holding it together during his working hours; something that used to come easily to him.

Max backed off, offering his hands in surrender. "Okay, okay. No setups. I promise."

Kate silently tiptoed into the room, bringing a glowing baby monitor in one hand, and waving a bottle of wine in the other. "Fire outside and I'll open another bottle?"

"Great idea, love." Max planted a kiss on her forehead.

Grateful for the distraction, Colin grabbed three wine glasses and raised them to his hostess. "Lead the way."

·CHAPTER 3·

Pushing her knuckles against the condo door while holding the large mesh laundry bag in her arms, Emilie attempted a knock. A few seconds later, the door pulled back and the scent of fresh flowers tumbled out to greet her. With her cell phone to her ear and a look of apology, Ash retreated to her bedroom leaving Emilie in the foyer.

Stepping farther down the hall, the fragrance of roses and lilies intensified. She stopped at the hall closet to empty her dirty clothes into the bottom part of the stacked washer/dryer and tried not to eavesdrop. Even though she'd been washing her clothes here for months after Ash found out she was going to a laundromat and insisted, she didn't want to impose more than she already was.

"Sorry about that," Ash huffed into the hall.

As she pushed the start button, she registered her friend's tight expression and downturned lips. "Want to talk about it?"

An exasperated sigh escaped over the sound of the washer's large metal drum whirring within its small domain. Ash strode to the tiny table beside the front door and grabbed keys and a wristlet from the bright mandala painted clay bowl. "I'm going to need a milkshake to get through that."

After a brisk walk, they arrived at the popular 1950s themed diner in the middle of the lunch rush. Standing next to her tall friend while they waited outside for a table, Emilie felt short, even though she was taller than average at five seven. Ash's knuckles were white around the electronic buzzer as she shook it and finally started talking about what was bothering her.

"Ethan ditched me tonight. I can't believe he's doing this *again*. It's the third time this month. Of course, he'll send a huge bouquet of flowers and apologize for it tomorrow. Like that helps. My condo already looks like a funeral home."

The explanation for the oppressive odor in the hall clicked in her mind as she said, "I'm sorry, Ash."

Her friend paced back and forth on the sidewalk. "Sometimes, I think there's something wrong with me. I always go after these guys who are complete jerks. He didn't even try to hide the fact that he was at a bar. A woman was purring his name in the background. It's noon on a Friday! Who does he think he is?"

In the short time they'd been friends, she'd witnessed Ash date a few different guys and she definitely had a type— dysfunctional men that looked nice on the outside and held respectable jobs, but were rotten on the inside.

"I know I'm the one making these bad choices, but I just can't help myself sometimes. I'm like a moth to a flame." The buzzer went off in her hand, so they headed inside to the hostess stand.

Her friend had the expression in reverse. Ash attracted the wrong kind of guy like a brightly burning fire because having a heart as golden as her hair, she would do anything for another person. The jerks she dated saw and took advantage of this. Emilie told her friend as such, but only received a weak shrug as they were led to their table.

Ash's forced exhale could be heard over the bouncy beat of "Runaround Sue" as she plopped into a red vinyl chair. "I'm getting too old for this. For this type of guy, though to give myself credit, Ethan's a step up from the truly dangerous bad boys I used to date." A groan preceded her head flopping over the Formica table. "I'm turning twenty-eight in two months."

She opened her mouth to speak, but Ash's raised face interrupted her. "Twenty-eight! I'm closer to thirty than twenty, and I've never even had a long-term relationship that wasn't a complete disaster. I don't even think I'd know what real love looked like if it bit me in the—"

A freckled faced nineteen-year-old appeared at the end of the table with a "Welcome to Bo's."

Her pink poodle skirt, cinched over a plain white T-shirt, swished as she walked away with their order a moment later.

"Have you ever been in love?" Ash's words slapped her in the face.

Air quickly drew into her lungs as her brain rushed to decide the best way to answer that question without revealing too much.

"Yes," she said, as the line of her spine tightened.

"Well . . ." Ash beckoned. "What's it like? How do you know if someone loves you?"

Pressure built between her brows, but she kept her voice steady as she answered, "It's the little things. It's not the grand gestures or showy proclamations, like flowers, but the mundane everyday things that a person does for you."

"Like . . ." Her friend rolled her hand.

Blood drummed in her ears. "Like the little ways they go out of their way to show you that they care. Listening to you when things go bad at work and a patient dies, or getting up early to start the coffee for you before you wake up every morning, or getting up with you in the middle of the night when you need them no matter how tired they are."

A thousand memories threatened to flood back, and she shut her eyes hard in an attempt to stop the eventuality. Her thumb traced repetitive circles on the tips of each finger under the table in a febrile attempt to dissipate the anxiety teasing every synapse in her body.

"It's that." She pointed at the custom-made booth behind the bar top which faced the customer side of the restaurant.

With her friend's attention deflected, a ragged exhalation escaped. "That's what love looks like."

Her gaze followed Ash's eyeline to the elderly proprietors of the restaurant. The couple's matching white-haired heads were bowed in intimate conversation as they sat. His neon pink oxford shirt stood in stark contrast to her simple yellow checkered blouse.

"Do you know why he's always wearing those crazy neon shirts? It's so she can see him when he walks around the room." Emilie paused, feeling her back relax a fraction. "Her vision is so bad she can't see him in the standard white shirt that the rest of the staff wears. When she told him this, he started wearing the bright shirts so she could find him. She just looks for the neon blur in the room. Watch her when he gets up; she'll follow him around with her eyes."

Through the hospital grapevine, she'd learned about Bo and Mary's love story. Bo had worked in the hospital cafeteria, and Mary was a young labor and delivery nurse when they'd met. She would always take lunch from her night shift right before the cafeteria closed while Bo worked the kitchen's last shift.

Over long, late-night chats, they fell in love and eventually married. After the birth of the first of their three girls, Bo decided he wanted to build a place of their own and opened the diner. More than fifty years of business later, the once young man's gamble had paid off.

The restaurant was a family affair; their daughters worked there growing up, and now their grandchildren either waitressed or helped out in other ways. Shannon, their eldest, was the general manager. Even in their old age, Bo and Mary were ever-present at the diner.

The memory of the last time Emilie had been seated at the bar top flashed in her mind.

"I like your scrubs." Mary's voice floated up from beneath delicate white hair in carefully placed curls. "I can't see any of the details, but I like the color."

The teal scrub pants with a matching top adorned with eyelet trim around the neck, sleeves, and pockets was one of Emilie's favorites. "Thank you."

"My name is Mary," she said before extending out her veined, age-spotted hand.

"Emilie." She gripped her hand gently, but not limply, and received a firm handshake in return.

"I wanted to name our youngest Emilie, but Bo said it wasn't Irish enough." She blew out a playful huff. "He's one to talk." Mary leaned in conspiratorially and darted her milky eyes to the side as if to check if the coast was clear before continuing. "His real name isn't Bo. His given name is Killian, but he wanted to have something more 'American' to go by and the nickname stuck." She leaned back in her booth seat. "We settled on naming her Erin. I always liked Emilie though, lovely name."

"Thank you." Something about the old woman's voice soothed the near-constant tension she felt between her shoulders.

"What do you do at the hospital?"

"I'm a nurse."

"I was too. What kind?"

She swallowed the root beer sip she'd taken. "I work on the intermediate floor for heart surgeries."

"Ahh, a surgical nurse. In my youth, all those women were the most severe in the place. You don't strike me as overly serious."

"I didn't used to be, but I find that I am most of the time now." As soon as the words left her mouth, she heard her own sorrow streaking through her quiet admission. She'd been so disarmed by the sweet woman, she'd unintentionally answered honestly.

Mary's soft hand slipped over her own on the countertop. "I meant no offense." She paused briefly. "It may not seem like it now, but all things ease with time. Even the worst things. They may never leave us entirely, but the pain does diminish."

She glanced up to find a comforting tilt of Mary's lips that led all the way to her failing eyes.

A gentle squeeze encompassed her hand before Mary released it to continue rolling silverware into paper napkins. "I'd love to keep chatting with you dear, but you're going to have to eat while we do. Your food is getting cold."

Like a small child being told what to do, she obeyed by picking up her mushroom swiss chicken burger and taking a healthy bite.

"How about I tell you a story while you eat?" Mary paused for a brief moment. "How about how my Molly was delivered in a snowstorm in the back of a cab before we could make it the two blocks to the hospital. I promise it's funny and appropriate for the table. Though I am guessing you could probably change a bandage and eat at the same time if you needed to. Iron stomachs, the lot of us."

A toddler at the table behind them dropped his sippy cup on the floor with a wail, bringing her attention back to the present.

"Are you serious?" Ash's mouth gaped in awe. "I thought he was just an eccentric old man."

"No," she said, shaking her head. "He does it for her."

Her friend's eyes never left the twosome behind the bar. "That's so incredibly sweet."

"That's what you need to look for," she paused, swallowing before continuing. "A grown man that would be willing to wear neon pink just for you, be damned what anyone else thought."

Bo gave Mary a kiss before standing and crossing the black and white checkered floor towards the hostess stand. He stopped to shake hands and clasp shoulders of regular patrons on the way.

"That's a tall order." Ash's gaze followed the older man.

Emilie allowed a breath before she said, "Maybe start with someone who doesn't see other people while you're dating?"

"That seems more attainable." She rolled her spring green eyes. "In *theory*."

Their food arrived, and Ash moaned joyfully over her strawberry milkshake and chili cheese fries.

"I've just made a sugar and carb fueled decision about my birthday. Girls only, and we are going dancing!" She put down a fry and opened the calendar on her phone. "Requests go in next week, so you need to ask November 7 and 8 off. Actually, it doesn't matter if you take the seventh as long as you rally after your shift, but you'll need the eighth off. We're going to close the place down."

Emilie hesitated for a nanosecond but quickly realized that her one good friend here was asking for something as little as to go dancing on her birthday. "Take the eighth off. Got it."

"Yes!" Ash's fist pumped the air. "Oh! I also need to ask you for a favor. Some of the ladies I go out with are real 'party girls.' I usually don't drink more than a glass or two to make sure we don't end up anywhere questionable, but it's my birthday, and I want to be able to drink, dance, and not worry. Do you think you can be my DD? Or DU? Designated friend that makes sure I don't end up with another scumbag guy and puts me in an Uber home when the bar closes?"

A laugh broke from her lips. "You got it."

"Consider it my birthday present."

"Don't be ridiculous," she scoffed.

"No seriously, I would only trust another nurse to make sure things don't go south. Maybe take the seventh off too, since you'll be taking care of me that night." Her friend tilted her head and tapped her slender finger to her chin. "I can pay you in milkshakes."

Emilie laughed again. "Ash, it's your birthday. We'll have fun, but I'll keep us out of too much trouble. I don't mind, honestly. It'll be a blast."

"You're the best." Her friend smiled broadly.

"You're not too bad yourself," she returned.

◊◊◊

Laundry washed, folded, and returned to her bag, she gave Ash a firm hug and walked down the hall to the elevator. After only a few seconds, the ubiquitous ding sounded as the doors opened. Stepping in, she craned her neck around the large bag to push the button for the lobby. The elevator began its descent but then stopped at the fifth floor. She scooted away from the button dial to allow the next passenger to make their selection.

When the doors opened, the scent of him reached her first. He smelled of soap, as if he'd just taken a shower, followed by a hint of something natural she couldn't place, like fallen pine straw warming in the afternoon sun mixed with a hint of salty ocean air. It was an intoxicating combination; the scent of home mixed with the undeniable scent of man.

Peeking around her bundle, she noticed that the hair on his collar was still a bit damp. His skin had a warm golden undertone that suggested it would turn beach boy bronze if given exposure to the sun. A light green striped collared shirt rolled to his forearms topped stone khaki slacks, ending in camel boat shoes without socks.

When he glanced over his shoulder, his blue-grey eyes fixed on hers and flickered with recognition. Immediately, her veins coursed with embarrassment that she'd been surveying a colleague unknowingly.

"Oh, hey . . ." He turned his body halfway around and paused. "I'm sorry. I should be better at names but I'm terrible."

"Don't worry about it. I have the same problem." She shuffled the bag into the crook of her left arm to offer her hand to shake, particularly grateful that she had the foresight to pack her bras and underwear into the center of the bag. "Emilie Hunt."

He stepped closer. "Colin Abernan."

The warmth of his large hand around hers sent a strange, slight sensation up her arm and over her shoulder. His gaze drifted to her wrist and fixed there as he held her hand a few seconds longer than a standard handshake.

He cleared his throat as he let go. "Do you live in the building?"

"No, just doing some laundry at my friend's place." She raised the bag in her arms an inch.

The elevator dinged as the doors opened to the lobby. With the mechanical action, she felt the nervous breath she hadn't known she'd been holding flow freely from her lungs.

He placed his hand on the door jamb of the entrance and stepped deeper into the elevator to let her pass. "It was good to see you."

Seeing the button to the parking level illuminated, she stepped out into the lobby. "You too."

He nodded, sliding both hands in his pockets before the doors engulfed him.

When the softening early evening light filled her vision, she took a deep breath of city air, trying to shake the effervescent sensation that slipped down her spine.

·CHAPTER 4·

Colin refreshed his email screen for the third time and topped off his cup from the coffee carafe on the granite island. He hadn't had two days off in what seemed like a lifetime. He'd spent most of yesterday weight training and finishing out his charts for the week before dinner out with Max.

His friend had grilled him again between bites of steak about unpacking his things. And Colin had argued that the king bed on its new masculine frame with a distressed wooden headboard and accompanying nightstand and lamp were already pretty impressive. Especially since for the last several years, his mattress sat unadorned on a metal frame.

Turning from his perch on one of the barstools that came with the kitchen, he stared at the bare living room. Only boxes littered the hardwood floor besides his father's old recliner. Most of them contained clothes, additional shoes, and odds and ends for the kitchen, but there were several boxes that he'd packed from his father's house. In his haste in moving, he hadn't labeled them.

The other piece of furniture missing from his condo pushed a hole through his stomach. Tension returned in his forearms as he fingered an arpeggio on the countertop. He could be playing out some of the emotions roaring in his chest if he hadn't sold their family piano in the darkest days after his father's death. Balling his fist, he rose from the stool to dispense some of the itchiness that flowed through his arms and legs.

"It's just stuff," he told the empty room.

He opened a large cardboard box, and a sigh of relief left his lungs when he found his own belongings instead of those belonging to his parents. His hiking boots still carried a faint scent of campfire smoke as he lifted them from the box. He removed two coats and hung them in the small closet in the entry. When he returned for his snowboarding jacket, gathering its slick material into his hand, a small wooden box was revealed.

With his free hand, he rubbed the center of his sternum. He hadn't touched his box since before . . . when it used to bring him comfort. Tentatively hinging open the lid, he slid his fingers into a smooth, unsealed envelope and took out a familiar handwritten letter.

Dear Colin,

I want you to know how incredibly proud of you I am. You have always been such a smart, focused, and inquisitive person that I know you are capable of whatever lies ahead of you in this new job. I know that your father will be a wealth of knowledge and comfort to you in this transition as he was always good with being flexible and understanding that change can be good. I love you so incredibly much and want you to know that there is nothing you cannot achieve. You have such a fire and a light to you, you always have, that I truly believe that the world will open itself up to you so long as you put forth a good effort and no doubt you have. I only hope that you are doing something that you truly love, something that makes you especially happy. I love you so incredibly much, my sweet boy.

My whole heart,
Mom

He folded the letter along its well-worn creases and placed the college-ruled page back into its envelope. *When you get the job of your dreams* was scrawled on the front in her beautiful, flowing cursive. Placing the envelope with the many others, he lifted them all to look at the photos at the bottom of the box. There was a picture of his mother with a large smile and a larger pregnant belly, one of his parents laughing at each other on their wedding day, and his favorite, the picture of the three of them in the backyard on a warm day. A younger version of himself was on his father's shoulders as his mother's face tilted up from under her sun hat—the three of them beaming at the camera.

The memory of that day always played clear in his mind like a movie preserved in time. He rode on his father's shoulders as he raced barefoot on the grass chasing his laughing mother—a game his father had created to stop his seven-year-old self from crying when he cut open his leg falling off his bike. He remembered distinctly the sting of his knee, the feeling of weightlessness as he was lifted up, and his mother's eyes squinting shut from laughter under the straw hat she always wore gardening.

He felt the next strongest memory flow in like the tide occupying the space it just vacated—his mother's paper thin, cold hand in his as she drew her last breath.

Words like "ovarian cancer" and "stage IV" and "metastasis" make little sense to a thirteen-year-old boy, but he came to understand the impact of those words over the next nine months. He watched his bright and beautiful mother shrink, which was strange because she was the tallest woman in the neighborhood and always seemed to be a force of nature.

His mother took on every treatment that was available from chemo to radiation to surgery. Wearing brightly colored scarves on her head, she meditated and drank wheatgrass juice. She sat outside on their back deck whenever she could, claiming as she often did that "fresh air could cure anything." One day he came home from school to find a woman dressed in wide skirts and colorful shawls waving a burning plant and chanting over his mother while she lay on his parents' bed. His father said she was trying everything, and if it made her feel better, then who was he to knock it.

His father took an immediate leave of absence from his position teaching at the university once she was diagnosed and despite their best efforts, they watched her grow weaker and smaller. After coming home from school each day, Colin would hold her hand and read to her because it was too exhausting for her to do herself. When she tired of her books, he would play her favorite songs as many times as she wanted on their family piano.

Colin helped clean the house on the weekends, in addition to his chore of mowing the lawn, and though he'd been doing his own laundry for years, he started doing his father's and mother's as well. Sometimes her clothes would be stained with rusty spots that he knew from years of cuts and scrapes was blood.

Neighbors and friends started making meals and bringing their families by more than in the beginning, and both he and his father were grateful for them. The kids at school had avoided him in the first few months, as if their mothers would catch cancer like a contagious disease just from talking to him. They began to come back one by one; their parents having explained what was happening in the Abernan house.

Soon, his mother was on oxygen, a clear tube always on her face like a cruel, inappropriate mustache. A hospital bed was brought into the living room because she didn't have the strength to climb the stairs. An aide started coming by four days a week for a few hours to bathe her, brush her hair, and take notes for her in a notebook. She always requested privacy when Phyllis came to care for her, joking that she needed a little girl time.

His father used this time to take him to do athletic things: hitting balls at the batting cage, playing one-on-one basketball, going for long runs together, trying to dissipate their pent up aggression at the complete unfairness of the situation. The hitting of baseballs was most effective in the beginning, but they ended up running the most. Quietly running, side by side, processing through the day's pain, trying not to acknowledge that for an hour or so they were running away from the hellish existence that was their life.

It seemed as if after her diagnosis, the air in the house was always charged with electricity like before a thunderstorm. Small victories were overshadowed by soul crushing defeats, slowly pushing them closer towards an inevitable and loathed end. When school finished, many of his teachers hugged him too long, blinking back tears as he said goodbye.

One warm summer day, his father had encouraged him to go with some family friends to Wrightsville Beach. When he returned, the energy in the house felt calm, which immediately unnerved him. He found his parents on the couch, his father's strong arms wrapped around his mother's frail body. They told him that it was time to stop fighting, that his mother was going to stop treatments, and begin hospice care. Colin ran straight from the house and kept running for the next hour and a half.

In those final days, he would often wake in the middle of the night and find his father next to his mother's bed with his strong hand woven between her bony fingers, his head on her lap, both asleep. Kind, quiet-footed hospice nurses worked around his mother like soft angels. Doctors came to the house, every time with compassion and a best guess to their never-ending question of "How much longer do we have?"

On a hot and muggy day in August, a hospice nurse asked him to his mother's bedside while he was making his dad a bowl of cereal. In her lap sat an inlaid lidded wooden box filled to the brim with sealed envelopes. Various titles covered the front, *When you graduate high school*, *When you fall in love*, *When you become a father*, written either in her familiar cursive or in Phyllis's tidy block print.

"They're letters for your future." His mother's fragile voice came out more as a sigh. "I have been writing to you since . . ."

She didn't need to finish the sentence; he knew what she meant.

His mother took a deep breath from under her oxygen mask. "My sweet, sweet boy, I love you more than you will ever know." She attempted to raise her hand, but it was already ensconced inside his own. "I wish . . . I wish I could be there. I wish I could see everything."

He didn't dare say anything, not wanting to interrupt her when speaking was already so hard for her, but as she took another breath, he stole the moment.

Tears streamed down his cheeks as his words choked out of his mouth. "I love you too, Mom. I love you so much. I'm going to miss you so much. I already miss you."

A little cough tightened her hand in his. "I know. I miss you too."

She took a long time to swallow before continuing. "Read these as you grow and know that as you become the wonderful man you've already shown me you are, I'm there for you every step of the way in spirit and here in my words. I will always be with you, now and forever."

He lay his head over their hands. The pain radiating through his body was so pronounced and profound, he doubted it would ever go away.

"I want you to keep laughing, okay?" Her other hand softly rubbed the hair at his neck. "I want you to laugh with your dad, and I want you two to take care of each other. He will take care of you. Will you take care of him?"

Colin lifted his face and wiped his tears with one hand, keeping the other firmly over his mother's. "I will take care of Dad."

A relieved smile stretched across her sunken face. One of the hospice nurses had put her in her favorite blue nightgown with a daisy flowered scarf upon her head. Even with all the disease ravaging her body, to him, she still looked beautiful.

"Good. Now, please get your father for me."

He stood in the hall while she talked to his father until he heard his name called. As Coin reentered the room, he could see how tired she was.

"My boys." Her lips lifted once before she closed her eyes. "I'd like some fresh air, please. Fresh air can cure anything."

He and his father opened all the windows to the house and let the oppressive, humid southern summer air enter. They sat for hours listening to the sounds of life: insects buzzing, birdsong, the metallic scream of lawn mowers, cars driving past, kids shrieking with joy jumping into a neighbor's pool, and the sounds of death: the raspy last breaths of the most beloved woman in their lives, their own tears, and the whimper of their hearts breaking. As twilight approached, his mother took her last breath in this world.

Colin missed his mother every day, but had long since learned to live with her loss. Reading these letters always made her seem closer, though there were still a few milestones he hadn't passed. He picked up the envelope labeled *When your father passes* and turned it over.

Heat flared in his chest as his skin flushed with thousands of pin pricks. His father's death could have been prevented. It *should* have been prevented. Exhaling deeply through his nose was ineffectual against the firm set of his jaw and teeth. Carefully, he placed the envelope back into the box and shut the lid before his hands fisted.

There was so much he expected his father to be there for—all the things his mother wrote letters for because she couldn't be. Quick strides took him to his bedroom to find his running shoes before jerky, hard movements tightened the laces to his feet. At least now he knew what to do with his morning. He flung open the door to his condo and raced down the stairs to pound the road for a long, hard run.

·CHAPTER 5·

Slapping the nightstand aimlessly, Emilie searched for her ringing phone. When she finally found it, her sleep-crusted eyes glimpsed Analie's face on the screen before swiping to answer the call.

"Whhhhhyyyyy?"

"Good morning to you too," her sister clipped.

It sounded like she was outside, walking briskly by the click of her heels, probably on campus.

"Analie." She drew out the whiny version of her sister's name as she'd done every time she was annoyed with her since she'd learned to speak. "It's my day off."

As mature as it was to be acting like a sulking teenager at thirty-three, her sister sometimes brought out old habits.

"And you have an appointment in Cambridge in an hour, if I recall." Even though Analie was only a minute older, she'd always been the boss of the two of them, which was usually fine. Sometimes, however, her twin pushed that one minute advantage too far and teetered into mother territory.

Emilie pulled the phone away from her ear and saw the timestamp in the upper right corner read 8:02am. "My alarm was set for 8:10. You just cost me eight minutes of precious sleep."

"You and your sleep."

"Most *humans* need it."

A puff of air was her sister's response.

Analie had probably been up for hours, run four miles, showered, packed her kids' lunches, made breakfast for her family, and dropped her kids off at daycare before commuting to campus. As much as she and Analie looked nearly identical, causing their mother to give them almost matching, rhyming names, their personalities were on opposite ends of a very long spectrum.

A door opened and closed and she assumed her sister was in her office by now. "I wanted to talk to you before you headed out." The authoritative tone left her sister's voice and uncertainty replaced it, pulling Emilie quickly out of her sassy mood.

"Sure, what's up?" She sat up in bed, silenced her impending alarm, and ran her hand through her hair, still damp from last night's shower.

"I was looking at my schedule and was hoping to come visit the first week of December. Do you think that would work for you? Something short. Maybe a long weekend?"

She knew Analie felt guilty about not being able to help get her settled into Boston, even though she'd been teaching double summer sessions.

"Yeah, I'd love to have you!"

She heard an exhale. "Great. I'll look up flights and confirm with you before I book."

"Sounds like a plan."

Her sister's voice softened. "I miss you."

Though they'd talked nearly every day, Emilie missed seeing and hugging her sister. Her lips pulled up at the evidence that she wasn't alone in her feelings. "I miss you too."

"It feels like grad school sometimes, except I'm here and you're away."

"Yeah," she agreed, remembering how weird it was the first time in twenty-two years not to live under the same roof. She fought the heaviness pulling at her shoulders with something light. "It should be a winter wonderland when you visit. Complete with snow I'm told."

"There'll already be snow on the ground in early December?"

"Potentially."

"I hate the cold."

Emilie snorted and rolled her eyes. "You'll be fine. You can borrow my winter stuff."

"*You'll* be fine. *I'll* be cold," her twin rebuffed.

Ignoring her sister's words, she did what any "little" sister would do, and pushed the barb farther in. "I've been googling the weather to find out what this first winter will be like. Come January the snow sticks to the ground for months and doesn't melt until March."

"Then expect my next visit to be sometime in April."

"It's still freezing in April. It's just the snow will have melted."

"You're really trying to win me over on Boston, aren't you, Em?" Her sister seemed to finally catch onto her game because she could hear Analie's smile through her words.

A bark of laughter fell from her lips. Her mind played a well-worn image of her sister's face—chestnut eyebrows raised high on her freckled forehead.

"It's nice to hear you laugh."

The comment sat in the air for a moment. They both understood the darkness that hovered around her, but she felt too light after teasing her sister this morning to give any power to it.

Analie switched the subject with another question. "Are you hanging out with Ash today?"

She rose out of bed and pulled up the covers. "No. She's on shift. I'm going skating after my appointment and then cooking some meals for the week."

"That sounds like . . . a good busy day."

She let slide the implication behind her sister's words. Now that her family wasn't there to make sure she took care of herself, they were worried that she wouldn't.

"It should be."

"All right." Analie's voice switched back to business. "I'm going to try and look up tickets before my first class, and I'll email you the information."

"Okay." Emilie glanced at the time on her alarm clock, rushing to reach her dresser before stopping. "I love you."

Emotion crept into her sister's voice. "I love you too."

"An, I'm fine," she reassured her sister, "but I'm gonna be late."

"Sure, talk to you later," she said.

"Talk to you later, bye."

"Bye."

◊◊◊

Emilie knocked on the door's fogged glass window with two minutes to spare. At "Come in," she twisted the cold brass handle and let herself into her new therapist's office.

The musty smell that accompanied old buildings compounded as she stepped into the room. Nia was sitting behind her large wooden desk in the center room, the space around her computer riddled with folders and papers as usual. She rose and gestured to choose one of the floral wingback chairs set against the wall covered in her many degrees and accolades.

"Good morning." Emilie leaned her gear bag and purse against the legs of the chair angled toward the window and sat.

The sun streamed through the large pane window and brightened the otherwise dim space.

"Mornin'. What's been going on? How have you been?" Nia's brown eyes, a few shades darker than her skin, looked up from beyond her coarse grey curls, which bounced in uneven lines over her red blouse.

Their conversations always started this way, allowing Emilie to steer the dialogue from the start. "I've been good. I talked to Analie this morning."

Nia took up a notepad from the mahogany tea table between them. "How often do you talk to your family now?"

"Usually daily—at least to one of them. We text when I'm at work and talk when I'm home."

Nia nodded. "How's your relationship with your sister?"

"Good. We're essentially back to what it was before." She'd signed all the releases for her therapist back home to submit notes to Nia, so she didn't need to rehash everything that happened.

"Tell me how it was before."

A deep breath filled her lungs. "Like most identical twins, we were inseparable. We had different personalities and ways of approaching our goals, but largely we hit life milestones at the same time. It was nice. We always had a person to bounce ideas off who was experiencing the same thing at the same time. We were more than sisters, we were best friends. Then . . ."

The leaves outside the window rustled in the breeze, and a slight hum sounded from a crack in the pane where rivulets of air snuck through. She let herself be distracted by the subtle murmur in the otherwise quiet office.

"That's what they don't tell you. They don't tell you that initially everyone's concerned for you and focused on you, but then life goes on. Things go back to normal for them, they get on with their lives, the calendar ticks away, but you don't change. Everyone else marches on but you're stuck.

LAURA LANGA

It's like living in a parallel universe where time is frozen only for you. You want to scream out, but you're too trapped to even do that. You try going through the motions, but you know in your core that nothing's ever going to be the same.

"I knew it wasn't her fault, but I just couldn't watch her move on with her life when I was frozen in mine. It was like looking in a mirror and seeing yourself and the life you had, and then realizing it was an illusion. I couldn't look at her for the longest time. I couldn't be around her. I was so angry. We were supposed to move through life together, and she got to move forward and I got stopped."

Nia sat in perfect poised silence, as if a statue of a living person instead of one breathing the same air in the room as her.

"After . . . when I was living at my parent's house, they brought a therapist in to help me cope. For us all to talk. I didn't want to talk to her or anyone. They wouldn't give up on me though, and eventually I started working through everything. I started having a relationship with my parents again, and after a long time, I started talking to Analie. The night she came over for dinner . . ." The tightness in her spine intensified as shame ran down it. ". . . it'd been almost a year since I'd seen her."

She remembered how hollowed her sister's eyes were, equally sorrowful and apprehensive, like she was afraid Emilie would run across the room and attack her. But it was the shock of her sister so changed that knocked the wind out of her.

"She'd cut her hair so short and highlighted it to look more blonde than brunette. We always had matching long hair and never dyed it." She aimlessly fingered the end of her braid. "I realized instantly it was for me. She'd changed the way she looked after thirty-one years of looking the same way, so I wouldn't be looking into a mirror when I saw her. It wasn't until then that I saw all the pain I'd caused my sister . . . my best friend."

She remembered the sheared edges of Analie's hair brushing her cheek as Emilie hugged her, whispering apologies. Her sister simply cried, told her it was okay, and that she loved her.

Quiet resonated in the room for a few moments. The warmth on her face registered before she realized that she was crying. Nia broke her repose and leaned forward gently, holding out a tissue box.

She lifted the soft paper to her eyes. "That was the first day I understood that I wasn't the only one who was hurting. While I was bent on my own self-destruction, I caused those who loved me the most pain."

Her annihilation of their relationship and how she refused to see or speak to her sister for so long pushed at her ribs, squeezing all the oxygen from them. She took a quick gasp to reassure herself her lungs still worked, and reminded herself she'd just bickered lovingly with Analie this morning.

It's okay. We're okay. We're closer than we've been in a long time.

When she remained speechless for several breaths, Nia spoke.

"Thank you for sharing that with me," the older woman paused. "I know that you've already done a lot of work processing what happened to you and learning to forgive your sister for not having experienced the same things as you, but I want you to know that every step you take towards your new normal with her is a good step.

"You may never find that the relationship is exactly the same as before and that's okay. You and Analie are working towards a new relationship, and I am proud of you for allowing her to be part of your life while you build roots here."

She nodded, too tired to answer with words.

Nia assessed her silence as completion on the subject and shifted gears. "How's work going?"

Emilie felt like she was being pulled from mud. The sluggishness in her veins slowly dissipated as thoughts of something positive flowed through her brain. "Good. Really good, actually."

"What about it is good?"

"I feel better having something to do that I know I'm good at. When I'm working, I feel just like I used to before . . . It's a relief actually. For the longest time, I felt I was capable of nothing. Little things like cooking and cleaning for myself or driving a car were such big accomplishments.

"When I started taking the nurse refresher classes to go back to work, I wasn't sure how I'd feel in the hospital environment again, but I knew I wanted that part of my life back. Now that I'm up to full speed, it just reminds me how much I love what I do, and it makes me feel so lucky to be able to help people again . . . I'm grateful to have an area in my life that didn't completely change."

This time Nia jumped right in. "Many things did change for you, but from what you've told me, some things stayed the same. The love of your parents never changed, nor did that of your sister towards you. True, there was a time you weren't able to accept that love, but their love for you persisted through that time nonetheless."

A gentle warmth flushed her limbs. Having their unwavering support made it easier for her to try and start her life over here.

"So your relationship with your family is strong . . ." Nia flipped back a page of her legal pad. ". . . and you're making friends here?"

The contented feeling continued to blush through her body thinking of Ash and their budding friendship. "Yes."

"Good, and what about dating?"

Emilie waited for the familiar flood of nausea to blow through her, but instead twin emotions warred with each other and for once, she was dumbfounded. Normally, when asked this question, all she felt was a visceral, punch to the stomach "no" that quickly forced out of her mouth. But when Nia asked, her right arm felt that same strange sensation when Dr. Abernan held her hand in his.

She rubbed her arm. "I don't . . ." Her mind saw his blue-grey eyes fixated on their entwined hands. "I . . . I'm not ready."

Nia held her gaze for what felt like an exceedingly long time, before pulling back another page of notes. "Tell me about the nurse you work with. Ash?"

Her sigh was audible, and the tension in her shoulders loosened as she switched her attention to a relationship she *was* capable of having. "Ash is great . . ."

·CHAPTER 6·

Six hours of appointments had flown by, especially since Colin had scheduled them straight through lunch, so he'd be finished in the early afternoon. It was still strange not being in the office all day, but he wasn't about to go against the rules as the newest surgeon in the group.

Tossing the messenger bag containing his laptop on the kitchen counter, he looked at the large new boxes that were delivered yesterday. Bookcases for his mother's books and the framed photos that always accompanied them in his father's house—thanks to his reduced hours, he had all afternoon to assemble them.

Restlessness streaked up his forearms. "Maybe a short run first."

After changing into his running clothes, he headed out in the direction of the Commons. Generally, he didn't run there because the paths wound and intersected too much. It forced him to pay attention to his route and dodge people rather than relax into the run and mentally process his day. Today, he didn't feel like thinking about what waited for him in his condo.

He warmed up running down Charles Street and turned left when he entered the park. On this early October day, the park was a blaze of yellow, red, and orange. The sight brought a smile to his face as he relaxed into his quick cadence, the crisp breeze pushing over his exposed skin. This time of year reminded him of the multiple times he and Max camped in the Smoky Mountains, building fires to stay warm and sleeping under the stars.

Weaving through the paved paths, the leaves sounded with a satisfying crunch beneath each footfall. After he crossed to the gardens side of the park and passed the ducklings statue, the long brunette plait of the woman walking ahead of him looked familiar. He gave her a wide berth as he raced past, but glanced quickly to his right to confirm that it was the nurse who he'd run into in his building a week ago.

Emilie.

Usually learning the names of all the support staff he worked with was a challenge, but the minute she spoke her name, it seared into his memory.

She had a large leather shoulder bag on her left arm and dark sunglasses. A cord climbed from the purse and diverged at her chin with earbuds resting in the center of her ears. From the brief pass, he could hear that she was on the phone with someone.

Colin decided to loop this smaller side of the park again, and when he came full circle, he found himself looking for her quilted green barn jacket. She was several yards away, strolling very slowly through a tree-lined portion of the park. The cord from her purse was put away, and she was gazing above at the mesmerizing foliage. He slowed his pace, so he could observe her serene grin as her face tilted towards the color-wrapped branches above her.

Without warning, a man in a grey hoodie pushed past her and grabbed for her purse. She clutched at the long strap as it slid from her shoulder, stopping the mugger from taking off with it. Pushing hard against the ground, Colin closed in on the two of them as the man yanked, lurching her forward.

He was practically upon them, yelling, "Let go of her!" when she swung her right arm around and blasted the mugger's face with pepper spray. His momentum collided with the attacker at the exact moment she pushed the trigger. Immediate and intense pain blunted his senses as he and the man hit the ground. He grappled blindly to grab and hold the man's leg, but the mugger broke free and took off sprinting.

He pushed himself up quickly and coughed, doubling over by the unexpected agony of his face on fire. His eyes burned incessantly, and the sensation crept into his nose and mouth the more he gasped for breath. Grabbing the edge of his shirt, he wiped futilely at his eyes and face. Soft muttering that ended in the word "strong" entered his ears before he felt Emilie at his side.

"Oh my god, Dr. Abernan!"

The muscles of his eyes forced them shut, so he could only hear her, not see her. Two hands landed on his shoulders before their cool touch moved to the sides of his face.

"Open your eyes."

He wished he could obey her command, but it was impossible.

"I can't," he groaned.

"I've got a water bottle. I'm going to try and flush your eyes."

Colin felt the pressure of the water splash over his eyelids before it ran down his face to wet his shirt. The expected relief from the inferno he was experiencing did not come. In fact, the water made the pain so much worse. Now, he felt burning and a severe pinprick sensation like he was being stabbed by a million hypodermic needles. A soft cloth smelling faintly of honeysuckle hastily swabbed his face before it was pressed over his eye sockets.

"It's my scarf."

Grunting against the blaze, he pushed the scarf away from his face and found his voice. "Rubbing makes it worse."

Her hand was on his shoulder again. "I live four blocks from here. Can you walk?"

He managed to nod and felt her take him by the elbow, pulling him to walk beside her.

"I am so sorry, Dr. Abernan. I didn't see you until it was too late. I was just trying to get that guy to let go of me." Her words raced out.

His voice was starting to strain as tears continually streamed from his eyes and snot ran from his nose. "I know."

After what felt like the longest four blocks of his life, she helped him through a door and put his hand on what he realized was a stair handrail.

"I'm on the third floor." She sounded apologetic.

They climbed the stairs together, and she helped him through another door before settling him on a plush sofa chair. An attempt to open his eyes revealed a blurry room with a brightly illuminated yellow blob in front of him and what might be a kitchen to his right. Groaning, he rested his elbows on his knees and tentatively touched his head.

The inferno that was his face was improving at least a little. All the tears and mucus he expelled onto the street while walking had helped flush out the mace. A waft of honeysuckle and a shadow drifted in front of his closed eyelids before laying a hand towel over his left knee.

"I know you don't want to rub your face, but in case you'd like it later." She paused. "Can I make you a cup of coffee or something? Tea?"

Unease flooded into her voice. His decreased sight seemed to amplify his hearing—the shouts of small children in the street below, the rustling of dry leaves, and her quiet breathing dominated his experience.

With his pain regressing, his brain began functioning again, and he realized that he was sitting in a colleague's house, rudely dripping body fluids over her furniture in his sweaty running clothes. He made another attempt at vision, blinking at the figure in front of him. Her fuzzy silhouette was backlit from the window, giving her a rectangular-shaped yellow halo.

He closed his eyes as he sighed through his nose. "I apologize for the inconvenience, but since I still can't see, I assume I'll be here a while. Coffee, black, would be great."

There was a pause, and for a moment all he heard was silence.

"Are you apologizing to me after I maced you?"

The tone and rhythm of her voice changed. Even with his eyes sealed shut, he knew she'd spoken through a smile.

Before he could answer, a restrained chortle softly broke into a small pearl of giggles before quickly dissolving into completely uninhibited bright laughter. The sound of her transition from the smallest to largest laugh was delightful to his ear. It was a melodious roller coaster that was completely infectious, and he found himself laughing so hard his abs contracted tightly, and his eyes watered profusely again.

She tried to collect herself and attempted to speak only to have incoherent, high-pitched staccato syllables escape her mouth. This lack of speech only intensified her tumble back into hilarity and made him laugh so forcefully, he shook as no sound escaped him. After a long while, they eventually calmed down, both threatening to start again with spilled giggles and audible sighs.

He wiped his face with the soft hand towel, finding it no longer as painful to do so. "I haven't laughed like that in a long time."

Opening his eyes, he saw a less blurry Emilie sprawled on a loveseat adjacent to the chair he was seated in.

She sat up straight. "Neither have I."

Rising from the couch, she crossed behind the kitchen island. "Let me get you that coffee. How much can you see now?"

"Shapes, but the edges are blurred. Things are coming back into detail, but slowly. At least I can open my eyes."

He heard her pour water into a coffee maker and smelled the roasted beans as she poured their pulverized bits onto a fresh filter.

"That's good," she said calmly, before her next words rushed out. "I just thought of something. Are you on call right now?"

"No. No. I was in the office this morning, but I'm done for today." Now that his vision was returning, he could see what a mess his shirt and shorts were. "Could I use your bathroom?"

"Yeah, do you want me to walk you to it?" She was already coming around the kitchen island.

Colin held up a hand. "Just point me in the direction."

"First right," she said once he stood up and positioned himself facing the short hallway.

Splashing some water on his face felt like tempting fate, but luckily it felt cool and slightly soothing. He attempted to use the towel she gave him to clean up his clothes, but quickly realized it was pointless.

When he returned to the main living space, a mug of coffee was steaming on the island. Emilie stood leaning her hip on the counter, balancing on one bare foot with her other pressed against her calf. She was blowing into a handcrafted ceramic mug with a dragonfly painted on it. The casual stance was charming and distracting at the same time.

"Feeling better?"

He blinked. "A little," he said, placing the refolded towel on the island.

She nodded to the counter. "What's printed on the mug?"

"It's the old PBS emblem." He picked up the mug and took a sip of the burning hot liquid.

For once he didn't welcome the familiar sensation. There'd been enough burning for one day.

"Good. What color are my eyes?"

Her focused chestnut eyes were surrounded by hair slightly askew from the last half hour's events. She had the same small freckles across her nose and cheeks that dotted her hands and forearms. He wondered if she knew she had a cluster just past her right wrist that looked like Ursa Major, or that her skin held the perfect mix of softness and warmth, which had made it hard for him to let go of her hand in the elevator.

"Brown," he said evenly, resisting the urge to clear his throat.

"What time is it?" She pointed to the digital microwave clock behind her.

A grateful exhale left his lungs at the diversion. He squinted. "3:17."

"I'd say your vision is back. How do you feel?"

Colin felt like someone had smashed his face with a sack of bricks then poured gasoline over him and lit it on fire.

"I'll survive. How are you?" With the distraction of extreme pain, he hadn't addressed the fact that she was almost successfully mugged in a city park in broad daylight. The whole ordeal must have frightened her.

Darkness flashed through her eyes for the briefest second. He wasn't sure if he saw it at all, his vision was improving but not perfect, and the microwave clock numbers were blurring now.

She took a deep breath. "I was scared, but on the bright side, I've still got my purse and now I know carrying pepper spray in the city isn't overkill."

"You took both of us out easily," he agreed.

"Yeah, and he didn't have anyone to help him after. I hope he's having a shitty afternoon." The vengeful smile that crossed her lips as she sipped her coffee slightly surprised him, even though it was completely warranted. He'd wanted to pummel the mugger after watching the few seconds of his attack on Emilie.

A quiet strength emanated from her, which was immediately and intensely attractive. Mixed with her subtle girl-next-door beauty and this sense of camaraderie and absolute comfort in her presence, he was having a hard time keeping his thoughts professional.

Get a grip. You're not the kind of guy who hits on his support staff.

He took a big gulp from his coffee mug. "Thank you again for the help and the coffee, but I would really like to get home and take a shower."

"Oh, sure. Do you want me to help you downstairs?" She set her mug down and went back into nurse mode.

That helped. When she acted like a nurse, it helped him forget that dark look in her eyes that made him want to wrap her in his arms, or how her unabashed laughter had lit his chest from the inside out, or that they were in her cozy apartment. Alone.

"No, my vision is back." He turned towards the exit. "I'll manage just fine. Thank you."

Emilie followed him and opened her front door. "You're welcome, Dr. Abernan."

He stepped onto the small landing and ignored his brain's command to walk down the stairs. Instead, he turned around. "I think after macing me, you can call me by my first name."

"That seems reasonable."

His mouth pulled into a broad, playful grin. "Colin."

"Colin," she repeated, a slow smile spreading on her gorgeous lips.

Pushing against every cell of his body screaming to lean forward, he turned and descended the stairs as her door closed behind him with a soft click.

·CHAPTER 7·

Emilie pulled the cold air into her lungs, crossing one leg over the other as she swiftly rounded the corner. The frigid breeze created by her own movement around the rink stung her cheeks. Being the first one on newly cleaned ice was always so satisfying. She loved the feeling of her skates cutting through the slick topmost layer, creating a path proving that she was there. While finishing her warm-up, she covered that line over and over again until the ice blurred into a slight slush.

After two minutes of edge work to warm up her ankles, she settled at one end of the rink. Taking a second to look over the halogen light-soaked expanse before her, she exhaled slowly. "Go" resounded in her mind, and she sprinted to the other end of the rink before fully stopping and racing back to the start.

She pivoted and started out again, this time stopping at the blue line before pushing hard against the edges of her skates back to the beginning. Over and over she went as the distance between her starting and stopping points decreased. She allowed herself a quick minute at the end to catch her breath before starting over again.

Emilie needed to be here today—needed to remind herself that it was her brain that sent signals to her legs to push against the ice. Too much had happened in the last week. The last three shifts had really tested her knowledge and mental strength as each shift brought not only a swamped day, but a tragic code. Seven days ago, she felt completely thrown when a certain handsome face had popped into her mind while telling Nia she wasn't ready to date, and two days later she blasted said man's face with pepper spray.

She'd acted on impulse defending herself that day, but the second imminent danger was gone, her heart had slammed in her chest like a wild animal trying to escape. Her body had trembled on it's own accord, not slightly as if shivering in the cold, but violently. Anxiety had teased at every cell. Even her mantra "You are strong" didn't help.

And then something happened that had never occurred before.

The sound of Colin's rough breathing gave her something to focus on. It was like a switch had been flipped, and she suddenly became Nurse Emilie—tasked with caring for the considerate man who she'd accidentally inflicted damage upon, not falling apart like she'd done so many times before.

Pushing away visions of that moment in the Commons, Emilie focused on slick ice below her. The burn in her quads helped bring her concentration back to the rink, back to this moment. No sooner than she'd regained control of her mind, a tendril of frigid air snaked over her right temple.

Emilie squeezed her eyes shut tightly for a breath, futilely trying to block the memory, but awareness pinpointed over the exact spot where she'd once pressed cold, circular steel. A day after months of drinking herself into a stupor trying to alleviate the near constant physical pain caused by an emotional trauma. The day she pulled the Colt 45 from the high shelf in the closet and turned its surprising weight in her hands, examining the inert piece of metal with dangerous potential.

Her heart had raced as she'd slowly brought the barrel to her skull, not wanting this path, but not knowing how else to exist. At first, she had mistaken the unrelenting pounding on her front door as the sound of rushing blood in her ears. After she'd left with the welfare police officer that day, she had to live with the knowledge that it was her family who later cleaned and boxed up her townhouse—finding the gun where she'd left it on the filthy, unmade bed.

Emilie slammed the wall with her skates and huffed her hard breaths against the plastic inches from her mouth. Her flushed and panting face reflected back at her.

Your memories don't control you.

"You are strong," she breathed to her mirror image and pushed off the wall.

There were days during her detox at her parents' house when she would wallow in her misery. Her mother would nervously flit around her not knowing how to help as she'd spend hours doing nothing but sitting on a porch chair in the backyard, living in her sorrow. Not just feeling it, but breathing it, eating it, letting it soak into her skin. It had encompassed her.

There were other days when she'd stomped down the stairs, let the cabinet slam after getting her coffee mug, and throw herself onto her chair at the table. One morning after performing her unspoken but very audible commentary on how she felt that day, her father, who had been watching her from his seat at the kitchen table, set his mug down and said three words to her that would help her more than she could have known at the time.

"Get your skates."

She'd petulantly sat in the passenger seat of her father's sedan as he drove them to the ice rink where she learned to skate as a little girl. As an adult, skating was something she did for fun in the winter with her sister and father.

Once they were laced up and warmed up, he unceremoniously stopped her at the red line. "You know the drill."

She did, and she tore into the first set faster and harder than her body, weakened from months of misuse, was ready for. Surprisingly, her father didn't complete the drill with her. When she was a kid, it was always a game. He skated next to her and Analie, every time beating them because he was older and stronger, but giving them something to shoot for, someone to chase.

Instead, he slowly skated back and forth, watching her. When she finished the first set, her heart beating harder than it had in forever, he looked her over and said, "Again."

Nodding, she went through the whole thing a second time. Neither of them ever mentioned the drill's carelessly titled name again. The word which so many people threw around like it was nothing. Exercise induced physical exhaustion wasn't the tiniest bit close to the reality of the word—what it really felt like to welcome death of your own choosing.

Two young teenage boys and their laughter spilled onto the ice bringing her attention back to the rink. She finished the leg she was on and started skating fast circles now that she wasn't alone. The local schools must have let out, and she knew the public session would crowd quickly. She got off the ice about twenty minutes later when the little kids trickled on with their parents.

As she unlaced her skates, she glanced at her phone in her gear bag, her lips rising at her father's missed call icon. After the episode in the park and then having to work three shifts back to back, one if not all three of her family members called every day to make sure she was okay.

Today she was okay. Today she'd let herself sleep until nearly noon after yesterday's brutal shift, and treated herself to a late lunch with Mary before coming here. As always, the sweet woman's stories and company settled her.

Emilie slid her phone into her pants' pocket to call her father back on the walk to the T-station. He'd given her something more than a chance to expel the anger she felt on those days he brought her to the rink. Her father gave her the first glimpse of control, that if she could control her legs, maybe she might eventually be able to handle the emotions flooding her body. He gave her something to hold onto when she felt like absolutely nothing was up to her.

Standing, she threw her bag over her shoulder and headed to the exit. The musty scent of used rental skates intensified as she neared the front.

"Hey, Emilie. Get it all in today?" The middle-aged manager of the rink was behind the counter instead of the teenager she'd shown her membership card to earlier.

"Yeah. Didn't even knock over any small children this time."

He barked the coarse laugh she loved.

"Ya know, we've got a really good women's hockey league if you're interested." His Boston accent slipped into his words.

She chuckled. "I'm terrible at pretty much everything but skating, but thanks for thinking of me."

"If you ever change your mind."

"Thanks, Norm." A full smile pulled at her mouth.

He grinned. "Till next time."

As she pushed through the exit, the faintest breeze stirred the air and rustled the leaves in the trees ever so slightly. It pressed light kisses on her exposed skin in an almost imperceptible way. She allowed the fresh air to cleanse away the last of the latent emotions still lingering in her veins. As she walked down the tree-lined sidewalk, she took a moment to enjoy the exhibition above her.

Growing up she woke every day to the view of leaves, bark, and earth surrounding her parents' house. She would stare at the leaves, mentally recording their shade for every season: the bright neon green new baby leaves in early spring, the dark, confident broad leaves of summer, the beautiful pageantry that was fall, finishing with the spindly branches in winter, sad and forlorn for having lost their clothes but waiting patiently to get dressed up again.

Most people had a favorite, but she loved them all equally.

She let out a content breath before pressing her phone to her ear.

He picked up on the first ring. "Hey, kiddo. How are you doing?"

Warmth spread across her chest at hearing his voice. "Good, Dad. How are you?"

·CHAPTER 8·

Pushing through the stairwell door to the fifth floor, Colin grabbed the hem of his T-shirt. When he'd wiped all the sweat out of his eyes, a familiar redhead stood knocking on his front door. Her long hair piled high in a messy bun wasn't what gave her away as much as the pudgy baby strapped to her back in some kind of backpack/child-carrying apparatus. A bright orange beanie covered Owen's head with a green, fabric stem from the center that matched his long-sleeve orange onesie with built in feet.

Colin should have expected one of the two of them to check in on him today, but was still surprised to see her in person this early. "Hey, Kate."

She spun around. "There you are!"

Owen stopped mouthing the cloth strap of the carrier to squeal a hello. When she stepped back to allow him to open the door, he caught sight of the large reusable shopping bag in her hand. From the smell of it, homemade pumpkin muffins were stored inside.

"To what do I owe the pleasure?" Colin put his keys on the hook on the wall as he led her inside.

"I thought I'd bring you breakfast," she said, setting the bag on the counter and her diaper bag on the floor. "It's pumpkin season, so I made muffins. Since Max is the *one person* on earth that doesn't revel in the awesomeness which is pumpkin spice, I thought I'd share them with you."

He tried to hide the grimace that wanted to race across his face. The real reason she was here was because yesterday Max covered his shift after he threw a tantrum in the OR, pitching tools across the room and storming out of the case after his patient had bled out.

Hanging up his call with Max, Colin immediately found his laptop and emailed an apology to everyone who witnessed his outburst in the OR, and made a mental note to apologize in person the next time he worked with each individual. After he closed the lid to his computer with a long exhale, his legs took him to his father's chair. Lowering himself into the comforting worn leather, he sat thinking long after the sun had set through the windows surrounding him.

He needed to work through this. The last time he'd lost someone he'd loved, he and his father had clung to each other like shards of broken hull in a shipwreck. As long as they were together, they'd get through. This time he had to do it alone. Avoiding the emotions he'd been stifling for the last several months was affecting his work. After everything that had happened, his near-perfect surgical record was all he had left.

Slowly rising, he opened box after box until he found his father's photos. Removing the bubble wrap revealed a picture of the two of them deep sea fishing his senior year of high school. Their faces beamed while holding their fishing rods, posing for the picture on the back of the boat. He waited for that burnt taste to flood the back of his throat, for his stomach to drop, but instead he just felt heavy. The strength required to drag his sand-filled limbs to the bookshelves he'd assembled weeks ago was overwhelming, but he forced himself to do it. First with this photo and then again and again.

After he had unpacked all his father's things and his mother's books, he wandered into his bedroom and dropped onto the mattress. Turning away from the twinkling night sky, his gaze fell on his bathroom and closet. Resting on the waist-high shelf was the small wooden box. A long ragged exhalation left his lungs as he pushed himself to standing.

When your father passes

The letter stared at him from the top of the stack. He picked it up, broke the seal, and unfolded the creased paper.

Dear Colin,

I stopped and started over and over trying to write this letter. I can hardly fathom the fact that I am losing him now than to try and help you when you lose him later. I am sorry if I fall short. I hope that when this happens that you two will have had a long life together. I can only imagine how you must feel now. I wish I could take away all your pain. I don't know who you have in your life right now, but I want you to know that you will always have me. I am always with you even when you feel like you are completely alone. I am here, loving you, and looking after you. Read this letter as many times as you need to remember that. There will be a day when even having lost both of us will feel okay. You will always miss us and you will always love us, but there will be a time in your life that you will be able to come up from the sorrow that surrounds you now. Most importantly, I want you to know how much your father loved you. He loved you more than anything in the world, my sweet boy. We both love you so incredibly much.

My whole heart,
Mom

His vision blurred as he finished the letter and fat wet droplets splattered his mother's handwriting. Colin pushed the water from his face and rubbed the letter to the front of his scrub top to dry it. Unexpected pain crushed at him like a sternal saw slicing him in half. He momentarily lost his breath, gasping in short, inefficient inhales as his legs went from under him. Collapsing to the floor of his closet, his shoulders shook as he finally cried the tears that he'd held in for months.

Colin cleared his throat. "That's thoughtful of you to bring them over. Thanks."

If Kate caught his embarrassment, she ignored it as she strode into the kitchen and started opening and closing empty cabinets.

"The plates are still in a box somewhere."

She gave him a look that clearly said, *Really Colin?* before moving to the coffee maker. "Actually, the muffins are a ruse. I'm really here to help you unpack your essentials. I just need another cup of coffee first. This one got up three times last night." She tossed her head back to indicate Owen, whose chubby hands reached for and missed her bun by an inch.

"Kate." He laid his hands flat on the island. "I'm sorry Max got pulled away from you and Owen because of me, and it's not that I'm ungrateful for your company or your delicious cooking, but haven't I already inconvenienced your family enough? Don't you have work?"

Having started the pot of coffee, Kate moved to her diaper bag and pulled out a fluffy green baby blanket. She ignored his first question and only answered the second. "I'm a realtor, Colin. I make my own schedule."

Turning and resting his back on the island, he said, "Then mothering."

She laid the blanket on the ground, unhooked a buckle on the contraption Owen was latched into, swiftly swung him from her back to her hip, and sat him in the center of the blanket. After handing her son a teething toy that she pulled from the pocket of her black skinny jeans, she arched an auburn eyebrow in his direction. "What do you think I'm doing?"

He couldn't help the insolent sigh that escaped his mouth. She was trying to make him feel better, but it only made him feel worse that he'd made such a mess of things yesterday.

"I'm sure that you and Max probably just sit side by side and communicate through grunts and somehow that makes the both of you feel better, but I'm a woman and a mother. I make things better by *doing*." Kate crossed the room to stand in front of him, and he got the distinct impression she was resisting the urge to put her hands on her hips. "So go take a shower, you stink, and let's unpack this condo. You've lived here six weeks, and you don't know where your plates are."

He opened his mouth to speak, but she interrupted him, her expression and voice softening as she spoke. "If you want to talk about it while we work, I'll listen, but you don't have to. I just want you to know that we care about you, and we're here for you."

It felt like the balance of the world was upended. He was the one who was supposed to help people, not the other way around. Kate's eyes watched him carefully as his words struggled to coordinate into a response.

"Why don't you get cleaned up," she said gently.

Normally a pro at the five-minute speed shower in order to get to work on time, he found himself lingering under the hot water, not wanting to face his friend's compassion. Her presence was a reminder not only of his mistake in the OR, but of his inaction which was the reason for all of this in the first place.

When he returned to his living room in jeans and a sweater, Kate was standing near his bookshelves looking at the pictures he'd set up last night. Stacks of dishes, drinkware, and other kitchen items littered his countertops. Empty cardboard boxes were folded down ready for recycling next to the entry hall, and the two boxes of clothes sat next to the doorway to his bedroom.

As she crossed over the fireplace to the second set of shelves, he caught sight of Owen asleep in the center of his blanket. His little arms were raised over his head with balled fists as his whisper breath slipped through tiny slack lips. A strange tug resonated at the base of Colin's chest.

"He's the cutest when he sleeps," Kate half whispered.

His eyes snapped up, and he cleared his throat softly. "That puts a wrench in the unpacking doesn't it?" he whispered, pointing to her sleeping son.

She waved her arm for him to follow him as she padded behind the island. "I put all your kitchen things out so you could pick which cabinets and drawers to put them in. I didn't want to organize your kitchen for you. Then you wouldn't know where anything was," she spoke softly, pointing to the two boxes by his bedroom door. "Why don't you put those away instead?"

As quietly as he could, he picked up the two boxes and placed them outside his bathroom. Kate tip-toed in his room with a brimming coffee cup and silently closed the door. The coffee's delicious aroma made him wish he'd grabbed a cup for himself. He started putting shirts on hangers when Kate's evaluating hum prompted him to ask, "What?"

"I have a close friend who's also an interior designer. She helped do our downstairs living areas and dining room. She's laid back and really easy to work with. You just have to meet with her once for her to get an idea of your style, then after that maybe approve some choices over email. She'll do all the rest."

"Thanks for the offer, but I don't think that's for me."

"Then let me take you to some of the nicer home good stores, so you can fill these empty walls. I get you're a minimalist, but they need something."

His eyes closed with an exhale. He knew Kate felt she was doing the right thing by forcing him to set up his condo, but he needed time to make those strides on his own—to decide for the first time in his life what he wanted home to look like. Leaning out of the closet, he saw Kate perched on the old wooden chair by the window, blowing into her mug.

"I think unpacking all the boxes is enough for one day."

"Suit yourself," she said, crossing her legs. "When you're ready, I can get a discount at—"

Her sentence was interrupted by an unfamiliar ringtone sounding loudly from the kitchen followed by Owen's piercing cry.

"Shoot," Kate said under her breath and leapt from the chair.

After hanging up the rest of the clothes, he broke down the two boxes and entered the main area to find her strapping Owen to her back.

"I've got to head off. One of my mom friends is having an emergency." She stuffed the blanket back into her diaper bag.

His chest buoyed, feeling an opportunity to help after she'd done so much for him. "Can I help?"

"Not unless you're secretly a locksmith."

His shoulders sank. "No."

"That's good because my locksmith, Ben, is the jealous type and doesn't like competition," she joked as she picked up her bag and slung it over her shoulder. "Besides, you've got to finish organizing the kitchen and eat those muffins."

Before he could argue, Kate gave him a quick hug and headed towards the door. "I'll see you Tuesday for dinner."

Simultaneously relieved and disappointed, he lifted a hand to her retreating form. "See you then."

She paused and turned around. "If you need us, just call."

"I will."

Gesturing to the items on the counter, she lifted her eyebrows at him.

"Okay, okay." He dutifully picked up a dish and put it away.

When the sound of his front door shutting echoed in his silent empty condo, his resigned sigh followed it.

·CHAPTER 9·

"Hey, Emilie. Can you do a dressing change on 514 for me?"

Her lips lifted at the sound of the familiar voice behind her. "No hosing out chests, right?" She flipped around to find Colin's mouth curve upward in a slow smile.

"Not today."

"Good." Her grin widened.

Since their literal run in at the park a month ago, working with Colin had been something she looked forward to, though it didn't happen every shift. At first, he'd poked at her by hiding his eyes in his hands when he walked by in the hall, and she'd have to stifle her erupting laughter. Other times, they'd chat a little bit before one of them was invariably pulled away.

"I've ordered silver impregnated gauze for the next change since his wound isn't healing as quickly as I'd like." He tucked his hands into his white coat pockets.

Being a heart transplant patient on immunosuppressants made Mr. Stowe more susceptible to infection in the laceration he acquired after he'd lost his grip on his tree shears.

She glanced at her watch; her next medication pass wasn't until two p.m. "Sure. I can do it now."

"Thank you." His eyes crinkled nicely at the corners.

Her gaze was caught up in them for a moment—today they were bluer than grey.

"Sure thing." Emilie made herself move towards the medicine room to gather her supplies.

A few moments later, she was entering her patient's room. "It's time to change that dressing, Mr. Stowe."

"All right, darling." He didn't look up from his car magazine.

The unforgiving hospital light bounced off his bald head as his bushy eyebrows attempted to take up as much space on his face as possible. She gently lifted his leg, which was propped up on pillows, and put a drainage pad underneath it.

Donning her gloves, she said, "I'm going to soak the old dressing first to make it easier and less painful to get off."

"Works for me, sweetheart." He glanced at her. "Did you see that heifer that was just in here? I can't believe she's the new coordinator. "

Camila, the transplant coordinator, was a little overweight but was a compassionate and hardworking woman. She spent hours working tirelessly, helping coordinate care, medications, and supplies for the transplant patients.

"Camila is great at her job," she said. "It doesn't matter what she looks like."

He snorted. "I don't understand what's with ladies these days letting themselves get so fat. It's disgusting. If they just pushed a broom around their house every once in a while, they could keep their figures."

She glanced at his rotund belly.

You should push a broom around your house.

Letting his obnoxious, sexist comments roll off her back, she went right on working, removing the old soiled dressing and irrigating the wound before packing it with silver impregnated gauze.

"This is looking a little better," she said, trying to change the subject.

She put an extra absorbent 4x4 gauze pad over the whole thing, and started taping quickly so she could leave.

"Just shameful. That's what it is," he paused. "Not you of course, honey, you're damn near perfect."

Out of nowhere, his hand leaned over the railing and slapped her bottom, *hard*. It made a loud popping noise as the sting radiated from the impact point. A startled gasp escaped her mouth as she reeled back several steps toward the doorway.

Two bodies moving down the hall stopped and course corrected towards her. She flipped her head to see Colin striding briskly towards her with her charge nurse, Bettina, on his heels. Emilie knew they must have seen what happened. Colin's jaw was set tight as his hand clenched into a fist the closer he got to the room. Quickly, she held up her arm with her palm flat to the both of them, and they stopped in their tracks just beyond the door.

Swallowing against the sour tang in her mouth, she slowly turned to face the man in the bed. "Not only was that incredibly disrespectful and inappropriate . . ." She glared at him. ". . . that was incredibly stupid."

"Oh pumpkin, it was just a harmless tap—"

Now, it was his turn to get a palm in his direction. "I am not your pumpkin, honey, sweetheart, or darling."

The muscles in her shoulders tensed, and she had to intentionally push them down. "Unfortunately, the staff here has to put up with the things a patient says in order to do their best to heal them, but the minute you put your hands on one of us, that's grounds for immediate dismissal from the hospital. I can call security right now and have them turn you out on the pavement whether or not your antibiotic treatment's done or your wound's doing better.

"The doctors and the administration would completely back me up. You might just find yourself without care, and we'll see how that wound does without medical attention. Maybe the wound gets better." She forced a casual shrug. "Maybe it gets worse and you lose the leg. Maybe the infection gets into your bloodstream, and you become septic and *die*."

She was bending the likeliness of outcomes, but it felt damn good to see fear creep across Mr. Stowe's smug face.

Her eyes fixed on his. "What you have to ask yourself is, do you want to behave, or do you want to die?"

On that she turned on her heel and stormed out of the room, ripping her gloves into the trash as she did so. She grabbed a handful of antibacterial wash on the wall and ducked out of the doorway, rubbing her hands together furiously. Colin and Bettina sidestepped into the charting area just outside the door next to her.

Bettina let out a low whistle. "I'm impressed."

As her heartbeat slowed and her breath returned to normal, she noticed the look of surprise on Colin's face morph into a barely obscured grin of pride.

"Yes," he added. "Me too. He'll think twice before doing that again."

The whole ordeal quickly played over in her mind, and she shuddered now that the adrenaline was fading. She could still feel the impression of his hand on her skin. Swallowing hard against the extra saliva in her mouth, she said, "I hope he *never* does that again."

Colin pushed his lips together as he straightened to his full height. "What can I do?"

It was unclear if he meant to help her or to hurt Mr. Stowe.

"Nothing, Dr. Abernan," Bettina answered. "He's just a dirty old man."

At that moment, Colin's pager sounded, and his face twisted in frustration as he unclipped it from his waistband.

"I've got just the thing for him," Bettina said before calling into the nursing station. "Hunter, come here a minute, please."

Bleached-blond hair, five days of black rough stubble, and serious dark eyes looked up before folding his notes and putting them into his chest pocket. Coming to stand next to them, Hunter was an inch or two shorter than Colin, but much broader. His left arm was inked with an ocean full of life—sea horses and squid intertwined with dolphins and starfish chasing through the waves. On his right arm, tall reaching trees rooted at his wrist and grew upwards to where birds flew free over his massive bicep. An RN badge was clipped to the V of his scrub top; the picture of him looked more like a mug shot than an employee ID photo.

"How can I help, Bettina?" His words came out in a deep rumble.

"You're going to take this patient from Emilie, and she'll take one of yours for the rest of the shift. The man was inappropriate with her, and I think he's done having female nurses for the remainder of his stay."

Colin's pager went off again and before he could even clear the screen, it sounded a third time.

"I've got to go." His eyes focused intently on hers with a pained expression. "Are you okay?"

The same unusual sensation she felt when he touched her zinged through her body as she locked her gaze with his. Connection reverberated through her in an odd, resounding way, even though they were four feet apart. She heard Bettina answer before she could make her mouth form words.

"We've got it from here, Dr. Abernan," she said. "Thank you for your kindness, as always."

Only when she nodded did he reluctantly turn and stride off the floor. She felt her eyebrows pinch in confusion watching his retreating form.

What was that?

Bettina's instructions broke her spell. "Okay. Give each other report. Just let me know who you swapped, and I'll change it on the board. I'm going to make a note in the scheduling for the next shift that Mr. Stowe be only cared for by male nurses."

Muscles held out his hand. "I'm Hunter, by the way. I work across the hall in the ICU most of the time, but they needed an extra body over here today."

Shaking his large hand, she tried not to feel child size. "Emilie. Thanks for doing this."

"Seriously, no problem. I'm sorry he was giving you trouble. No one deserves to be disrespected like that," he said, shaking his head.

She felt an aggravated breath leave her nose. "Honestly, if I was at a bar or something, I'd still be pissed, but that's life as a woman sometimes. Here it felt different. *Wrong.* It felt like such a complete personal invasion happening where I work. I'm a professional here, not an object."

"I completely get it." He nodded. "It makes you feel dirty. You're just trying to do your job and should be treated with the respect your skills and education deserve."

"Thank you!"

Immediately, guilt ran through her for mentally referring to him as "muscles" a moment before. Pulling out her notes and a pen, she asked, "Who do you want to give me?"

·CHAPTER 10·

The night sky was visible through the hospital lobby's glass atrium ceiling as Colin crossed the tiled floor to the automated exit doors. His afternoon surgery had taken much longer than he'd anticipated, and it bothered him that he didn't have a chance to head back to the floor and check on Emilie before she left for the night.

He'd seen before that she could handle herself. She'd obviously done it again that afternoon, but something in the way she shuddered in the hallway hit him on an elemental level. It had taken all of his restraint in that moment to not gather her to his chest.

Colin didn't have a way of getting a hold of her now, and it would be completely inappropriate for him to ask the night charge for her phone number with CTSB's anti-fraternization policy. Even though Kitty and the OR staff had been forgiving of his blowup a month ago, he didn't need another strike against him.

His naturally quick clip slowed as he passed the closed gift shop, and the lobby's black lacquered grand piano caught his eye. The only other person in the large space was a janitorial staff member vacuuming in a far corner. The nerves in his fingertips twitched as he checked his watch. Nine o'clock. It wasn't that late.

Changing course, he stepped onto the low platform and sat comfortably on the bench. A sense of peace fell over him as he lifted the fallboard and let his fingers flex over the blocks of black and white. It had been so long since he'd allowed himself to connect with this side of himself.

The delicate rise and fall of Chopin's Nocturne Op.9 No.2 resonated in his fingers, flowed up his arms, and into his body as he swayed slightly with the pressure applied to each key. The scent of the wood filled his nose as each flex and pause of the music created a conversation from one hand to the other. Some phrases were quick and urgent, other's slow and reserved, the tempo his to command.

Though he hunched just a bit as he played, he felt lighter than he had in months, focusing only on the tactile sensations of his fingers and the vibrations singing from the piano's heart. He let the keys resound louder through the third repeat of the melody before finishing with the soft humble end. The final chord tapered out as if gently set down for a long peaceful rest. His fingers hovered over the keys for several seconds before a voice brought his attention back to the room.

"That was lovely."

The cleaning woman stood at the base of the platform. She glanced at him through her thick glasses as she tucked a short strand of black hair behind her ear. He hadn't noticed that the sound of the vacuum had stopped while he played.

"Thank you." He closed the keylid. "It was my father's favorite."

A brief pause hung in the air while all the calm he'd just experienced was shattered by a simple true statement. The thing that gutted him was his use of *was*. His throat tightened, and he had to remind himself to take an inhale.

"I can see why." The woman smiled at him. "I like to work when they have the pianists playing during the day, but I'm taking my turn of night shifts, so I've missed the music. That was nice to hear. Thank you."

When she walked back to her cart of supplies, he rubbed his hands over the front of his legs trying to dispel the unease flooding his forearms. Pushing back from the piano bench, his phone buzzed in his pocket.

Nicole: *Still coming for drinks?*

That's right, Nicole had asked him to join the single surgeons for drinks. He'd heard that things got a little rowdy sometimes, especially if the residents tagged along, but those who worked hard under extreme pressure tended to really let loose when given the chance. Maybe a night out to let off some steam was exactly what he needed.

Colin: *Just leaving the hospital. Where are you meeting?*

As he stepped out into the darkness to walk to his condo building, the thirty degree November wind slapped his face.

He reached down to zip his jacket up when his phone buzzed again.

Nicole: *Speakeasy place downtown that Andrew recommended called Password.*

Nicole: *We'll head there 10ish*

Colin: *See you then.*

◊◊◊

After a quick shower and changing clothes, Colin exited an Uber and walked to what looked like a service entrance to the building with a dimly illuminated sign marked "Password" above it. The door was painted with white block letters "What's the" with a series of question marks growing subsequently smaller trailing down the door.

He walked down a short hallway that led to a half level of stairs before arriving at the main entrance to the bar. A waitress with double Dutch braids wearing a crisp, black short-sleeve oxford carried a tray of drinks past him as he searched the room. Every wall displayed exposed brick with dim Edison bulbs hung from pendants. Penny tile covered the floor over which eclectic brown leather chairs and low tables were arranged in seating areas.

"Colin!" Nicole held her arm out to motion him over towards the large, wooden bar. "We're just ordering."

After saying hello to his other colleagues Karen and Justin, and meeting Nicole's newish boyfriend, Andrew, he leaned over to the bartender and ordered an Old Fashioned.

"How was your trip?" he asked Karen, remembering she'd just returned a few days ago from hiking the Inca Trail.

"I think my quads will forever be sore. I'm in good shape, but I completely underestimated what climbing that many stairs every day was going to feel like." She took a sip of her French 75. "The ruins were worth all the pain though. It's one of the most incredible places I've ever been."

She pulled out her phone and narrated while flipping through some pictures of the trip for everyone to see. Tinny electronic funk versions of 1930s songs floated from the speakers as the lights dimmed even darker and flickered.

The conversation flowed easily from each person's favorite vacation spot to their worst travel experience as they finished their first round. After everyone ordered a new set of drinks from the attentive bartender, Justin asked, "Any interesting cases this week?" and unfortunately for Andrew, they dissolved into talking shop for the better part of an hour.

Eventually, Nicole and Andrew broke off to a seating area in a secluded corner. Karen had turned on her stool and was chatting up an intense looking corporate lawyer in a full three-piece suit who had offered to buy her a drink. He and Justin were discussing the differences of this job from their last when two attractive women sauntered over.

The first was rake thin with wingtip eyes framed by long, glossy hair; her navy bodycon dress left little to the imagination. Her friend had shoulder-length, wavy cinnamon hair and was wearing a green mini dress that showed off her curvy shape. The two laughed to each other as they approached.

The black-haired woman placed her manicured hand on his arm. "I love your accent."

Colin knew his slight southern lilt exacerbated when he drank. Intentionally pronouncing each word clearly, he pointed his drink towards Justin. "You should hear his." He hoped to transfer her attention off him given he'd always preferred his women a little shapelier, like her friend with the hazel eyes.

"Hello, Ma'am." Justin touched his hand to his head as if to tip an imaginary Stetson, giving his Texas accent even more thickness.

"Oooo you sound just like a cowboy." The brunette saddled up beside Justin.

After learning their names were Bree and Katherine and that they worked in a personal relations firm downtown, he and Justin bought them vodka martinis, and they had a lively conversation about the different places they were from. Bree poured the attention on thick, keeping at least one part of her body attached to him as they chatted. About an hour to close, she shot a look to her partner in crime before stretching her body and faking a yawn.

"I'm getting tired, boys, and I need to be up early in the morning." She directed her gaze coyly at him. "I only live a few blocks from here. Why don't you walk me home?"

Justin winked at him. "That sounds like the gentlemanly thing to do."

"Will you?" She tilted her head.

"Of course."

She had been flirting with him senselessly for the last few hours. Over that time, each caress reminded him how much he missed a woman's touch and since he couldn't hold the one he wanted to, finding a little comfort in the arms of another even if it was just a doorstep makeout didn't seem unreasonable.

"See you on Monday, Kat." She shoulder hugged her friend before they left the bar.

Bree leaned heavily on his arm chatting the two blocks to her apartment complex, and gestured to the building when they arrived. "Why don't you come up?"

By this time, he couldn't see a reason to say no. He nodded a hello to the doorman as she took his hand and led him to the lobby elevator. Bree shimmied around him to push the button marked fourteen and as soon as the doors closed, she pressed him with her body and crushed her lips on his.

He'd been with a few forward women in his life, but no one this direct. Frankly, it was refreshing not to make all the decisions at the moment. All he did today was make choices, often life or death choices, and give orders telling others what to do.

Her strong perfume stung his nose as he widened his legs so she could press between them. When he returned her feverish kiss, letting his fingers graze her protruding shoulder blades, she wove her hands inside his blazer, and pulled them closer.

As soon as they were in her sleek apartment, she pulled off his jacket and made fast work on the buttons of his dress shirt. Her vodka stained tongue swiped wildly in his mouth, and he felt himself returning her unrestrained kisses. It had been so long since he had been with anyone, and she was so very willing. She stopped him at the foot of her bed, flipped around, and pulled her long hair over her shoulder.

"Unzip me." She tossed a heated look over her shoulder, the two fingers of her raised hand pinching a condom between them.

He did as he was told, and they collapsed onto her silken bed in a tangle of limbs.

◊◊◊

Bree stretched her body, propped up on one elbow, and winked. "That was just what I needed."

Putting his hands behind his head, his body still reverberated from their athletic activity and the copious alcohol he'd consumed.

She slid from beside him, her strappy heels clicking on the hardwood floor as she swaggered to a tall dresser. The obnoxiously sharp sound alerted him to the fact that she'd left them on the whole time. An annoyed breath left his lips as she grabbed something off the dresser before picking up his shirt, pants, and boxers. She stood over him completely naked and unashamed as she held out his clothes to him— on top of the clothes pile was a business card.

"That was great, really, but I *do* have to get up early in the morning."

He kept his face even as he sat up. "Of course." After running his hand through his tousled hair, he took the clump of clothes from her outstretched arms.

"There's my card if you ever want to meet up again." Bree cocked her hip. "I work crazy hours, and all my time goes into my job. You get it. You're in finance, right?"

He was about to correct her, but she kept talking, "If you ever need a release again, I could probably work you in, Carl. You were fun . . ." She pushed a twisting hand through his chest hair as he started to button his shirt. ". . . and hot."

Not even trying to correct her on his name, he just let a fake smile cross his face and stood. She gave him a kiss on the cheek before heading towards her ensuite bathroom.

"I'm going to get cleaned up. Make sure the front door shuts, okay?" She tossed one last hooded glance over her shoulder and closed the bathroom door.

As he gathered his blazer on the way out, he dropped her card on the hallway table. There had been a few one-night encounters in his youth, but he never pushed a woman out of his bed like that. He couldn't say that he was truly hurt; he'd gotten what he had wanted out of the interaction after all.

When he exited the building, the doorman gave him a knowing smirk. Colin stepped into his Uber and was silent on the ride home. Something nagged at him. He found himself irritated when he should have been excessively happy having just had sex with an attractive woman, but everything about tonight gave him a sour taste in his mouth like too much bourbon burning at the back of his throat.

He didn't want to do this. He didn't want to be the guy that had meaningless one-night stands. He didn't want to hold women like Bree in his arms. He wanted to hold one chestnut-haired woman whose laughter lit up his chest from the inside out.

Not that what he wanted mattered anyway. The stigma of getting involved with someone from work, a nurse no less, was not something he needed right now.

He pushed the thoughts away as they arrived at his building, thanked the driver, and exited the car. As he walked through the revolving door, he heard women laughing from within the elevator as the metal doors closed. Letting out a loud exhale, he headed towards the stairs.

·CHAPTER 11·

"Cauliflower Dove!" Ash butchered the lyric at the top of her lungs followed by *dern nert nert nert nert* as she mimicked the rhythm of "California Love" with nonsense words.

Emilie laughed and then shushed her inebriated friend as the elevator doors opened. Ash tossed her keys with a "Here ya go" as they walked down the hall. Lurching into her condo as soon as the door was opened, Ash kicked one teal ankle boot off in the entry and another in the kitchen.

Emilie directed her shoeless friend to the bedroom and pulled back the covers. "Hop in bed and let's sober up a bit before you go to sleep."

Ash flopped into her bed, sat against the headboard, and pulled the blankets to the armpits of her nude, sleeveless mini-dress before giving a sloppy salute. "Yes, ma'am."

When she returned with a glass of water from the kitchen, Ash had only slipped down in the bed a little bit.

"Emilie! How did you know I love water?" She took a big gulp and ungracefully wiped her mouth with the back of her hand. "It's sooooooo good."

Another chuckle burst from her lips. "Yeah, water is wonderful. Sleep is also wonderful, and you'll be doing that as soon as you finish a couple more glasses."

"Please, may I have another?" Ash giggled.

Emilie took the now empty glass and refilled it in the adjoining bathroom sink before returning it to her friend's outstretched hands.

"Thank you for everything tonight. You . . ." Her friend pointed emphatically while chugging another glass of water. "*You* are the best. I had so much fun tonight. Best birthday ever!"

A grin lifted her mouth as Ash hiccupped. "I had a great time too."

When the group of screaming twenty-somethings in long coats, bare legs, and clicking heels quickly engulfed Ash's body at the start of the night, Emilie wasn't sure she'd have a good time. But it ended up being the perfect thing to take her mind off being sexually harassed at work and the odd connection she felt with Colin in the hall that had her brain spinning circles the rest of her shift.

As soon as the throng of women had entered Kitty O'Sheas for '90s Night and a thick baseline thrummed into their chests, she did something out of character and ordered shots for all of Ash's friends. When the parroting of "Happy Birthday, Ash!" caused cheers from everyone around them,

Ash's delighted face made any nerves she had over the evening completely worth it.

"Really? Did you? I wanted you to have a good time." Her friend's hand dipped, but she quickly regained control of the glass before setting it on the nightstand.

She felt her grin widen. "*Really.*"

"Okay, good." Ash tugged her pink sparkly "Birthday Girl" sash over her head and set it on the bedspread. "I don't know what happened, but I know I want you to be happy."

When Ash lifted her arm, Emilie saw the tattoo for the second time. The first time was when they were dancing in an unspokenly declared girl's only dance-circle as "Jump Around" blared from the huge speaker. When all the women raised their hands and jumped, Emilie had spotted a small semicolon tattooed on the upper inside of Ash's right arm. Though her body had gone right on jumping, mentally, everything had slowed down and froze.

"Do you want to tell me?" Ash's soft voice pulled her from her memory.

Emilie looked up to find that this wasn't a drunken question.

Reflexively, her shoulders tensed immediately, but her mind wearily urged, *Tell her. She'll understand.*

Silence filled the room for several weighted seconds.

"I was a wife and mother."

The minute her words were out of her mouth, her heart slammed in her chest, and she had to take a deep breath to calm the tight compression she already felt around her ribs.

Ash sat up straighter in the bed, but said nothing.

"My husband's name was Braden. He was a police officer who patrolled the area near the hospital where I worked. We met when he brought a patient in the ER. I was an emergency nurse before I worked here." She swallowed against the thick saliva in her throat. "After we met, he started stopping by the hospital just to visit on days I was working. One time he even brought the ER staff donuts. Everyone had a good laugh at the irony of that." She allowed herself a tiny grin at the memory.

Her husband's face flashed before her eyes. His smile had been the first thing she'd noticed about him—perfect glistening white teeth and how his smile showed in his dark eyes. He was always finding the upside in a situation and helping others with his good sense of humor. People were almost instantly at ease with him, even when he was in uniform. His patrol partner used to jokingly call Braden "the whisperer" because he could talk almost anyone down to reason.

"We started dating. Seeing each other as much as our two crazy schedules would allow. My family loved him. Everyone loved him. After two years, he asked me to marry him. We had a long engagement and lived together in a little townhouse by the beach."

A familiar memory played of her stepping on the small balcony, the cool morning sea air combing through her hair as she stared out onto a peaceful morning ocean. The first rays of sunlight barely peeking over the top of the sharp line of sea above which pink blended with coral while blue wisped with white. A hot clay mug warmed her hands as

Braden's strong arms wrapped around her waist. She leaned back into his solid chest, smelling the salt of the ocean, the bitter aroma of the coffee, and the sweet scent of him.

Emilie drew her arms around herself. "We didn't start trying for kids right away. Our jobs were so chaotic, and we knew we'd have to slow things down. A year after my sister had her son, we decided to start trying casually. We loved being an aunt and uncle and spending time with our nephew made us talk about starting our own family. We didn't really worry about it when it took a while, and eventually we found out we were pregnant a few months after my sister announced they were having their second."

Unlike her sister who seemed to be the magical unicorn of pregnancies, she had a very hard first trimester being pregnant. She'd been nauseated every day and often didn't want to eat. It wasn't until late in the second trimester when she began feeling better that she understood the joy of being pregnant.

The look on Braden's face as he gently laid his hands on her naked belly and felt their daughter kick for the first time was perpetually etched in her heart. She'd laid her own hands over his and pressed to deepen the contact with his daughter's strong feet inside her. Wonder and sheer joy overtook his features as she watched his eyes jolt up to meet hers before he gave her one of the best kisses of her life.

"Braden wanted to find out the sex of the baby, and my sister's too neurotic not to know, so we found out that we were both having girls. My sister and I were so excited. We knew our children, even though they weren't technically twins, would always have a best friend."

At their joint baby shower, their mom had covered the entire ceiling of the living room with a draping crosshatch of pink streamers. She'd set two wingback chairs together for them to preside over the festivities like two swollen queens. Analie was almost bursting at the seams being two months ahead. They drank sparkling pink lemonade and ate tiny vanilla petit fours and bathed in the happiness of their lives at that moment.

An involuntary shudder tingled down Emilie's spine. If only she'd known. She'd been so blissfully, stupidly unaware that anything was going to happen. Tears pricked her eyes, and tension gathered at her temples as an invisible hand pressed down on her chest, making her breathing shallow.

When she spoke again, she moved her arms to hug her flat belly. "Lucy was born a day late, March 24th. She was a beautiful baby who stubbornly refused to come out, though I pushed for hours, ending us both in an emergency c-section.

"I wasn't prepared for the love I felt for her. I was overcome by this serene peace of being her mother and my absolute unwavering love for her. All the pain and stress of the delivery washed away the first time I held her. It's so strange because you love your husband so much, but the love for a child is truly indescribable. Braden felt the same way. He was completely smitten with her."

She'd been surprised at how completely confident she felt at holding and nursing this new baby like it was the most natural thing in the world. Her daughter's miniscule wrinkled fingers gripping and releasing air as she nursed contentedly, her lips and nose flared. Braden standing over her shoulder, kissing her hair, telling her she was the best mother.

He'd taken to fathering just as easily, getting up every time Lucy cried, changing her and bringing her to bed so she could nurse her. His broad shoulders swayed back and forth on the monitor screen as he sang to their daughter before placing her so gently back into her crib for a few hours rest.

Liquid fell from Emilie's cheeks and hit her wrapped arms. "She was such a good baby, and we were so completely happy to be a family together." She glanced up, finding Ash silently listening with moist eyes.

She trembled as she felt her neck tighten against her words. "When Lucy was eleven weeks old, I went to meet with my manager about my schedule since I had one week before I was to come back part time."

A tight breath filled her lungs. She swallowed against the bitter taste in her mouth and forced her strained voice to say the words.

"Braden had taken Lucy with him to the grocery store to pick up a few things. They were driving home midday when a powerline repair truck crossed over the double yellow line and hit Braden's car head on." A choked sound escaped her mouth. "The driver was drunk on the job."

"They brought them to my ER. I was sitting in the office when the charge ran in and told my manager to keep me in there. I took one look at her face and I *knew*. I just knew. I ran to the trauma bay and found Braden open and broken, ten people working hard to save him."

The trauma bay had been a blur of yellow protective coats yelling commands, answers, and numbers to each other. What normally would have been something she knew as familiar and routine, suddenly she saw for what it was, grotesque and tentative. Clear plastic tubes spilled from the bed connecting to a variety of different machines. The oxygen canister hissed as blood poured from what seemed like an innumerable amount of wounds. A cacophony of electric and human sounds pierced her ears like a stabbing ice pick. Her eyes fixed on Braden's dangling, limp hand bouncing with the effort of each pounding chest compression.

Hard tears streamed down Emilie's face, as she stared at the awful picture in her head. "I kept trying to get to him. Three people had to hold me back. I screamed and screamed. They went round after round. Longer than they should have because I was there and who he was, but he was gone."

She felt a shift in the bed as Ask spoke through her own sob. "Lucy?"

"She died on impact. Her infant seat couldn't save her small body from the accident."

In a swift flow of movement, she found herself encased in Ash's arms, her tears staining the sequined fabric of her friend's party dress. Wrapped in her friend's embrace, she surrendered to the heaviness she felt. They sat there for a long time, Ash's lengthy limbs supporting and rocking her as she cried.

Eventually when she calmed, Ash released her from the comforting bind and sat beside her on the edge of the bed, rubbing her back. "Why don't you stay here tonight?"

She felt her head bob in agreement but didn't remember telling her muscles to do so. All she wanted to do now was to lie down.

Ash carefully stood and went to her dresser. "Here are some comfys. Why don't you change, and we'll just bunk up for the night?"

Taking the outstretched clothes, she silently went through the process of getting ready for bed.

Once they were settled, Ash reached for the light, then stopped and turned to her. "If you ever need to talk about it again, or need me to take a shift if you're having a hard day, or literally anything . . . I want you to know that I'm here for you."

Words were beyond her, but she found herself nodding.

Ash's green eyes watched hers for a moment. "Okay." She turned off the lamp, and they laid in the silence.

The soft sound of her friend's even breaths soon followed, but Emilie knew from experience that she wasn't sleeping tonight.

·CHAPTER 12·

The unrelenting wind of the Gloucester beach whipped at Colin's face and hair, cold seeping through his jeans from the chilled sand. He interwove his hands over his knees and leaned back to soak in what little sunlight was permitted through the extensive network of grey stratus clouds. Being as frigid as it was, he was the only one on the beach save an elderly couple walking fifty yards away with their dog at the water's edge.

"I miss you, Dad." A long ragged exhale left his body. "I miss you both."

The memory of the last time Colin had been to the ocean washed over him.

Wading into the surf up to his knees, not caring that the tide was wetting the edges of his shorts, he pushed deeper into the waves with his father's urn in his hand. When the water started to pull at his legs, drawing him in before the next wave overtook him, he tossed the ashes in a large arch. The remains of his father mixed with the salt air in a dusty cloud before finally joining his beloved wife's in the sea.

It had been more than a year after his mother's death before he and his father honored her wishes to always be able to touch a beach by forever living in the ocean. A month after that, Colin opened his first letter from the wooden box written in Phyllis's tidy print, titled *When you miss me* on the envelope.

Dear Colin,
   Go to the sea and talk to me. I miss you, my sweet boy.
   My whole heart,
   Mom
P.S. Take your father with you.

He remembered being a fourteen-year-old boy telling his dad they needed to drive down to the beach to see Mom. His father never balked or asked any questions; he just drove them and then sat next to him in the sand. Colin spoke to the ocean as if she was standing at the water's edge listening to his every word. When he'd said everything that weighed on his soul that day, they sat in silence for a long while before his father slowly started speaking. After that day, they would both come to the sea to talk to her.

Rubbing his hand over the day-old scruff of his unshaven face, Colin listened to the crash of the waves, the caw of the seabirds, and the eolian tones from the wind bashing the beach posting behind him. "Here I am again." He tried to clear away the tightness at the back of his throat. "I always knew I would be eventually, but I thought we'd have more time."

He pulled the collar of his jacket around his neck and jammed his now icy hands into his pockets. "I just wish . . ."

Tilting his head up, he stared at the changing cloud formations. "I mean why?" His hands fisted in his pockets. "Why didn't you tell me? I could have helped you. I could have *saved* you."

The wind blasted his ears in response and he glanced at the sand around his boots, allowing his head to hang heavy. The knowledge that he could have prevented his father's death had the circumstances been different ate at the pit of his stomach. Not for the first time, he felt helplessness surge because in the end there was no changing the past.

Taking a deep breath, he lifted his head to watch the black-backed gulls floating effortlessly on the thrashing gusts of air. "Sometimes, I feel like I'm blowing in the wind. That I'm lost."

"At least I have Max." He ran his hand through his hair before returning it to the pocket. "And Kate," he amended. "They've really taken me in. We have dinner all the time, and they had me over for Thanksgiving last weekend. They keep calling me family . . ."

The elderly couple crossed in front of his view, their calm black lab trotting slightly ahead of them as their heads bowed in conversation. Colin waited a long while after they passed to continue.

"CTSB gives me all this time off. I don't know what to do with it . . ." He cleared his throat again. "I've been running a lot more. I'm working on making my condo look more like a home, though it doesn't feel like one. Not like your home . . ."

The salt spray hit his face with an unexpected sting due to its icy temperature. The misty droplets sprinkling his cheek would have been a welcome sensation during a warmer month.

"I didn't understand the reason behind the hourly reduction and actually started to resent the policy until one of the partner's told me why John set up his rules."

He'd learned that John Reddington's only son had followed in the family tradition, going to medical school and being admitted to a top residency program for cardiothoracics. When John had a harder and harder time getting a hold of his son, he attributed it to the rigors of training, knowing that this time would pass for his son as it did for him. He knew his son was sleep deprived, working a hundred hours a week often in thirty-six hours shifts, and mentally exhausted from the constant "pimping" that the senior surgeons would subject the residents to—calling them out when they were at their most fatigued and berating them in front of the rest of the staff.

Unfortunately, his exhausted son believed he wasn't good enough and took his life, leaving a single note, "I'm sorry, Dad." Around the same time, several other residents ended their lives under similar circumstances and reform over physician working hours became a national issue. All the techniques that had been imposed on his son, John had inflicted on residents in his care and the partners in his practice over the years. After that he stopped conducting things the way "they've always been" and started making immediate changes.

"I know that for the people with families, the reduced hours make a big difference." Colin had seen how attentive his best friend was with his son. "It's just a big shift for me . . . Max says I should start dating."

Emilie materialized before his eyes as if she just stepped out of the sea in her pastel scrubs. A mermaid of soft brown eyes and waving chestnut hair. Her fair skin scattered with tiny dots like sea stones sprawled carelessly along a sandy beach.

"There's this woman I work with. A nurse. She sprayed me with mace." A breathy chuckle left his lips at the memory. "It was an accident, but since then we talk whenever we're working together. There's something about her. She's beautiful and smart and funny, but there's something in her eyes that stops me every time I see it. Some darkness that seems stuck. I wish there was something I could do about it."

Imagining that he could rub his thumb over the delicate freckles of her cheek and watch the shadow in her eyes fade brought a shiver to his body. As much as he wanted to touch her, he also wanted to understand her, to find out why her eyes glinted.

"It's not like that will happen though. CTSB has a policy against it, and it probably wouldn't work out anyway . . ."

Part of him wanted to say that he was too busy for a relationship, but he knew that wasn't an excuse anymore. His body jolted with sudden understanding that it was more than that. On some level, he always used his career as a shield to keep from getting close to the women he dated. He'd seen firsthand the damage a profound love could do when one of the pair unexpectedly died. His father never dated again after his mother's death, never wanted to, saying that he'd had the love of his life and that was the end of it.

What if I loved like that and lost?

He stood briskly to shake off the overwhelming feeling and stamped his feet to free the sand attached to them.

"Don't I know you?" a male voice spoke from behind him.

Colin turned to find an elderly couple steps away. The man held the woman's gloved hand, and his other arm wound around her body. Her free hand held the leash of the sweet dog that sat patiently, regarding him with a cock of his head.

With both of them bundled against the brisk weather in hats, scarves, and gloves, he didn't think he knew them until he saw a peek of a neon green collar from beneath the man's navy peacoat. "You're Bo."

The old man's bright smile wrinkled the entirety of his face. "You're usually dressed in your medical scrubs, but I recognize the face. You come in with that red-headed fella."

Colin felt his mouth lift in a grin as well. "Max. Yes, we work together."

"Have you met my lovely wife, Mary?"

Holding his hand out to the woman, he said, "I don't believe I've had the pleasure, though I've seen you at the restaurant. Colin. Nice to meet you."

Mary held his hand firmly in her gloved grip. "Lovely to meet you." Her eyes held the cloudy telltale of cataracts.

"What are you doing all this way north?" Bo asked.

The lab nosed his hand, and Colin gave his ears an affectionate rub. "I had the day off and thought the drive and seeing the beach would serve me well. What are you two doing here?"

"My sister lives up here. She couldn't take the buzz of the city anymore, so we come up once a month to visit," Mary answered.

The dog barked and pulled a bit on his leash towards the parking lot.

"We'd better get going. It was good running into you, son." Bo took his arm from around Mary and held it out.

Shaking the man's gloved hand, he said, "Good to see you too, and nice to meet you, Mary."

Bo returned his arm around Mary and helped her navigate the plankwood walk back to the road. The dog bounded up the walkway and jumped into the opening rear hatch of their crossover. Bo gingerly placed Mary in the passenger side before heading to the driver's side and putting the car into gear.

Colin inhaled the familiar briny scent of the ocean and felt his chest lighten.

Before him was an impeccable example of two people in love who spent decades of their lives together. Just because his family had seen tragedy didn't mean that it was an automatic for him.

He turned toward the sea and the sky once more. "I love you both," he said, allowing his gaze to settle over the horizon before fishing his keys from his pocket.

·CHAPTER 13·

A slight line of grey light peeked through the folds of the blackout curtains and woke Emilie from her warm slumber. She turned away from the window to find an almost perfect reflection of herself on the pillow next to her, except for the distribution of freckles. The tips of Analie's hair were still a shade lighter than their natural color—a leftover from when she'd dyed it. A large chunk was draped over her forehead, and the rest spread in messy knots across the pillow as she snored softly.

Shifting her weight towards the edge of the bed, Emilie silently slipped out. Analie tossed lightly, and Emilie froze for a few breaths, only padding to the kitchen when her sister settled again. Once she had a steaming mug of coffee in between her hands, she nestled onto the cushioned bench of the triple paned bay window seat. She'd moved some of the throw pillows from her loveseat here to make it an even more inviting place to sit. After a scalding first sip, she placed her coffee on the kitchen table beside her and gazed out the window down the street.

"Her elm," as she'd referred to the lovely mature American Elm tree outside her window, had long lost its serrated, tear-shaped leaves and now stood naked in the brisk December air. Its branches reached to the clouds as if trying to grab the last fleeting bits of warmth from the sun before winter truly set in.

Today the sky was completely grey as far as she could see. She assumed it would be overcast the whole day, which always gave her the uneasy sensation of being trapped under a grey blanket or that she resided inside a snow globe. A sigh left her lungs as she laid her forehead against the cold windowpane.

"Is there another cup of that?"

Turning from her gloomy view, she found a disheveled Analie wiping sleep from her eyes. Her sister yawned and stretched her sweatshirt covered arms towards the ceiling exposing her midriff for the briefest moment. It was another funny difference between them. Analie was always cold and often slept in a sweatshirt, pants, and socks, while Emilie was always hot, opting for a tank and shorts. Before sliding out of her room this morning, she'd grabbed her bathrobe and slippers, so she was comfortable next to the chilly window.

"Mugs are above the coffee maker." She pointed towards the kitchen.

Analie stumbled her way across the wide plank hardwood floor into the kitchen, grabbed a ceramic camp mug with

"Let's escape to the woods" printed on it, and filled it to the brim. "Sweet nectar," she whispered into the cup.

Sitting opposite on the bench, her sister wove her sock-clad feet underneath her extended legs. Companionable silence stretched between them as they watched the movement on the street below and took tentative sips of their coffee.

"My weather app says it might snow two inches later today." Analie pushed the hair from her long, wavy bob behind her ears.

"I wouldn't be surprised. We had a dusting last week." She took another sip, feeling her body and mind to wake up for the day.

"I'm surprised I slept in," Analie said to herself, staring into her own mug.

"We were up late last night . . ." It felt like high school all over again, chatting with Analie until early this morning after she'd met her at the airport late last night. ". . . and you finally had your favorite teddy bear back."

They often slept together as kids, even though they each had their own bed. Frequently at night, Analie would sneak into her bed and hug her like her own personal living stuffed animal. She couldn't count the amount of times she woke up being "the little spoon" growing up. Their mother said that they were always on top of each other in the womb and shared a crib as infants, so it made sense that they preferred sleeping next to each other.

"Mmmmmm, you're right. Plus, your back's less hairy than Scott's, which makes you a better 'lovey.' No hairs tickling my nose and waking me in the middle of the night."

A chuckle left her mouth. "I should hope not!" Her sister had the only relationship that she was aware of in which the wife spooned the husband.

Analie smiled wide over her encircled coffee mug, the steam lifting and dancing in front of her brown eyes. Once when they were tweens, they sat on the double vanity of their bathroom and tried to find any appreciable differences between their eyes, but were unlucky in their search.

"What time is it?"

Emilie craned her neck to look at the microwave. "10:34."

Analie exhaled a dismissive breath. "I must truly be on vacation. Normally, I would have been up five hours already."

"Yeah, yeah, Miss Overachiever. Regale us with your accomplishments." She rolled her eyes.

A tossed pillow narrowly missed her coffee cup.

"Hey! Priorities. Don't spill my coffee!"

"Apologies." Analie took another sip. "What's on the itinerary today?"

"There's no itinerary." She felt a cat-like grin cross her lips, watching her sister's eye twitch. "Didn't you say you were on vacation?"

Her twin nodded slowly, no doubt a feeling of unease brewing in her stomach. Analie's natural state was in motion.

"Relax." She let her grin widen. "I have some plans, but I didn't want us to be overscheduled. It's more of a rough outline of possible activities that we can choose to do if we feel like it."

"Like . . ."

"Ice skating . . ."

Analie's lips lifted as she set down her mug and started finger combing her hair.

". . . walk through the Christmas lights in the Commons, eat at Bo's. I haven't looked, but we can see if there's any tickets left to the Holiday Pops, or we can always hang out and talk."

"I *do* like to talk."

"You?" She mock gasped while flattening her hand to her chest. "The person who pursued a career that specialized in talking *at* others, often without interruption? I wouldn't have guessed."

"Lecturing colleague students isn't *talking at*, it's teaching." Analie's brows lifted.

"Sure. Whatever you have to tell yourself."

Her sister picked up another pillow and held it aloft in a threatening way. "I'll use this if I have to."

She chuckled. "I'll be good."

The pillow returned to the bench. "What do you want to talk about?"

"How are Liam and Penny?"

This was something she had to relearn after her world turned upside down. At first it was getting used to seeing her sister again. Then it was being okay with seeing her children.

Initially, Analie had only brought Liam over with her for visits. Absorbed with her grief and self-destruction, she'd completely forgotten that when she cast out her sister, she lost contact with her nephew as well. It had taken Emilie a long time until she felt ready to see the little girl who was supposed to be her daughter's best friend.

Across the bench her sister tensed, no doubt running through the possible ways to answer that statement without upsetting her. Her family was all still used to walking on eggshells around her.

"It's okay, An. We worked on this before I left, remember? It's important for you to share your life with me as I share mine with you. We have to have more honest interactions with each other."

A loud click from the heater system echoed in the room followed by the reassuring rush of warm air being pumped through the vents.

Her twin exhaled slowly. "They're good. Liam loves first grade. He's such a big little man now, it's funny to watch. Just the other day, he decided that he was going to do all the dishes by himself after dinner. I had Scott supervise, of course."

"Of course," she said. "And Penny?"

Analie held her breath for a moment and then let out in a fast exhale, "Honestly, Em, she's horrible."

She snorted at her sister's frankness. Analie had always held back the truth before since Emilie didn't have her daughter; it seemed heartless to complain about Penny— even when she was being challenging.

"Liam was never like this at three. He was a bit of a handful at two, but I just attributed that to the fact that I was pregnant, and he was adjusting to our family growing. She's a downright nightmare sometimes. Full tantrums, not only at home, but the store and occasionally at school. She's taken to dressing herself in the craziest assortment of clothes you can imagine, and we can't say a single thing or another tantrum will ensue.

"Scott and I stand outside her bedroom in the morning and rock, paper, scissors for who's going to wake her up that day. She always ends up screaming and crying over something the moment she's awake. It's exhausting."

The idea of two grown adults huddling in fear outside of the bedroom of a tiny three-year-old had her laughing so hard. Her sister raised her eyebrows and patiently waited for her to stop.

"I'm sorry," she gasped for air. "I'm sorry. Just the idea of the two of you hiding from Penny is funny."

"Well she's not the sweet little thing you remember from before you moved over the summer." Analie crossed her arms.

She wiped the corner of her eye. "Do you think it's switching her to preschool instead of daycare?"

"No. Mom and the teachers say it's just her 'being three.' I'm holding out hope that things will change with her birthday next month, but apparently according to Mom, I was the same way at that age until I was five." Her sister let out a defeated breath and tilted her head towards the dark-stained exposed beams of her whitewashed ceiling.

"You've always had an opinion."

It was Analie's turn to mock gasp. "Who me?"

They giggled easily for a moment before her twin put her empty coffee cup on the table. "If we're being honest, I have to ask. How are you doing? Like really doing."

"Actually, I'm doing really well. There's times when I feel like the old me, but at the same time it's a new me. Does that make sense?"

"Yes."

Picking up her mug, Emilie drank the dregs from it in one swallow.

"Have you had another panic attack since you were mugged in the park?" Analie pressed.

"*Almost* mugged." She pointed with her mug before setting it down. "I pepper sprayed that jerk, remember?"

"And some guy from work if I recall correctly."

All of a sudden, she was assaulted with thoughts of Colin, but not just thoughts. Textures. The way he leaned past her to grab a stethoscope from behind her computer last shift, and she could smell that comforting pine and sea salt scent of him. Pulling her plush bathrobe tighter around herself, she tried to ignore the prickling sensation running up her arms.

"Em, answer seriously. Are you okay?"

She blinked to focus back on her sister. "Yeah. Some days are harder than others. Work has been a good constant. It's so gratifying to be able to help others again, to contribute. I thought I'd be lonely on my days off not having someone to live with after living at Mom and Dad's for so long, but I actually really like having my own space to decompress."

Her sister nodded. For as much as Analie liked to talk, she was a really good listener.

"I spend my time off trying to make new connections with people here and continuing the healthy habits I built at home. I've befriended the most adorable elderly couple, Bo and Mary, they feel like a twenty-year foreshadowing of Mom and Dad. They own the fifties diner I'm always talking about, and I usually have lunch with Mary once a week."

Mary's amusing anecdotes about her life allowed her to share a truth or two about her own. The wise woman always listened patiently and had just the balm that she needed.

"I also spend time with Ash, who's very excited to meet you by the way. She's actually off today and said she'd be free to meet up whenever. You guys will love each other. I can just tell."

"I can't wait to meet her," her twin said. "Do you want to have lunch with her today? You can show me the diner, and I can meet her at the same time."

She stifled a snort. Analie was always the queen of multitasking. "Sure."

"And you're still meeting with Nia. She's been a good fit?"

Emilie sighed as she ran her hands through her hair. "Once a month like clockwork, and yes, thank you for the tenth time for setting her up for me. She's wonderful."

"I'm not trying to irritate you, Em."

"I know." She let out a careful breath. "I know."

"I just worry."

She reached forward to rub Analie's leg. "I know. I'm actually doing really well here. I feel stronger than I have in a long time."

Her twin's worried face relaxed as a smile overtook her features. "I'm glad."

She felt her lips mirroring her sister's expression before a memory flashed in her mind. "You should know before we meet her, I told Ash . . . everything."

Analie's eyes widened. "Everything, everything?"

She dipped her head in confirmation.

Silence fell between the two of them as the wind gently swayed the branches of her elm just outside the window.

"Ash took it well."

Analie pulled her knees to her chest and hugged them. "I'm glad you two are close enough to confide that, and that you're feeling strong enough to talk about it."

"It was really hard. It's always really hard, but it feels like every time I tell it, a layer lifts. I know that sounds weird."

"It doesn't sound weird."

Quiet fell between them again for several long seconds.

"I'm sorry, but if we are going to keep chatting, can we move over there?" Analie pointed to her white, brick-trimmed gas fireplace, which stood as an anchor to the open concept living room. "I'm freezing by this window. What is this, single pane?"

The laugh that burst from her lips was just the one her heart needed in that moment.

"Why don't we get ready, and I'll text Ash and see when she can meet up with us?"

Analie beamed. "Look at *you*, planning things. I'm so proud. Okay. I just need to grab a shower first."

"Yeah, you do." She popped up from the seat carrying her empty mug towards the sink. "Don't think I couldn't smell those stinky feet through those woolly socks."

This time her sister's tossed pillow hit her square in the back of the head.

·CHAPTER 14·

Colin tipped the bartender for his Manhattan before wandering to one of the many high-top tables covered with fake snowflakes and lit votive candles. Pushing back his shirt cuff and jacket sleeve, he checked the time.

"Hey, man."

Max was behind him wearing a similar well-tailored black suit, but sporting a holly boutonniere and dancing Santa tie. Kate's long-sleeve, dark turquoise floor-length dress only made her fiery hair more striking.

"Hey. You guys made it."

"Yes." She drew out the word on her exhale. "I'm so glad Allyce found a friend of hers to babysit for us after she spiked a temperature this afternoon. I mean I hope she feels better and everything, but I didn't want to miss the party."

Max squeezed Kate to his side. "I was ready to start knocking door to door so I could keep my date night with this hot mama."

"It has been a while since we've been out." She nuzzled her forehead into Max's newly grown auburn beard before resting her head on his shoulder.

Colin tried to ignore the hardening of his stomach at his friends' easy display of affection, and took a long draw from his glass.

"Did you just get here?" Kate asked.

"Yes. Have you guys been here long?"

"About an hour or so. It's picking up nicely now." Max pointed his drink at the crowded room.

The swanky top floor martini bar CTSB rented for their annual holiday party was decorated in a mix of Christmas and winter themed adornments. Outside the large pane windows, the cityscape twinkled under a gibbous moon. The whole staff seemed to be in attendance: surgeons, physician assistants, nurse practitioners, residents, nurses, and office staff—anyone affiliated with their group.

Kate gazed over his shoulder. "They *really* got into the spirit this year."

The residents were gathering at the table next to them. Each male resident had a full three-piece suit made from a holiday print. One was red with reindeers, another blue with swirling snowflakes, and the third green, red, and white candy cane striped. One of the female residents was wearing a long, green dress fully decorated with ornaments and wrapped in tinsel. On her head was a star tiara; she was the picture of a Christmas tree herself. The other wore a long, red bandage dress completely covered with battery operated twinkling strands of lights.

"Those suits are great! What do you think, love? Should we do that next year? You'd look lovely in lights." Max winked at his wife.

Taking her raised eyebrow as a no, Max moved on, nodding to an upright piano in the corner. "Do you still know 'Piano Man'?"

Colin felt a grin rise at the memory of when they were in medical school, and Max found out that he'd minored in piano in college. He explained that he mostly played classical music when Max asked if he knew any popular songs. A local Irish pub just off campus had a piano near the bar and silver-tongued Max convinced the manager to let him play one night. "Piano Man" went so well that they had their pick of the ladies that evening. Max insisted that he learn several more songs for their next night out.

"I remember it."

"What do you think? One more time for old times' sake?" His friend waggled his eyebrows.

He ran his hand through his hair. "I don't know, Max."

"Are you guys talking about how you used to troll for girls at that Irish bar by playing songs?" Kate sipped her martini impassively.

A bark of laughter fell from his mouth. "You told her about that?"

"Oh yes, he told me all about your guys' *endeavors*."

A waitress walked by with a tray of hors d'oeuvres, and they all grabbed a spinach puff and a napkin, saying their thanks.

"I hope he told you that it was his idea," Colin said, biting into his appetizer.

"If I recall correctly, you benefited from those song sessions as much as I did," Max said. "Besides, it wouldn't be like that tonight. I'm obviously not looking for anyone because I have the best woman in the world right here. It would just be for fun."

"I, for one, would be very interested in seeing this act." Kate tilted her head.

"I'm an adequate singer." Max placed his hand on his chest. "You've heard my rendition of 'Twinkle Twinkle Little Star,' my love, but the real showstopper is Colin's fancywork on those ivory keys."

He blew out a dismissive breath as he took a gulp of his drink and glanced around the room.

How much had Max already had to drink?

When his vision returned to his friends, he found them both staring at him expectantly.

Kate bounced ever so subtly. "Please?"

Max's grin was smug, knowing he'd cave if a woman asked nicely.

A long exhale left his lungs. "*Only* 'Piano Man.'"

"Only 'Piano Man,'" his friend echoed and strode towards the DJ stand.

Kate squealed like a teenager and squeezed his arm with her free hand.

He shook his head, drained his drink, and walked towards the upright piano, unbuttoning his suit jacket with one hand.

He arrived at the same moment the music from the DJ stopped and Max's voice boomed in the room.

"Ladies and Gentlemen. Esteemed colleagues. Our newest member of CTSB, Colin Abernan and I have a long history. We attended medical school together and have been the best of friends ever since. In those good old days, we used to sing and play this song, and I'd love it if you'd all join us tonight." Max arrived at the piano as he finished his last sentence.

Colin flexed his fingers over the keys and pressed into the familiar ebb and flow of the entrance as Max hummed the part of the song traditionally played by the harmonica. When his friend's warm baritone voice sang the first of the lyrics several whoops went up from the group. Colin rocked with the cadence, relaxing into the song he hadn't played in years. Max finished the first verse and swung his arms up to encourage everyone to join in, and the room reverberated with the well-known words.

He smiled to himself, sneaking a quick look around the room. Kate was staring awestruck at her husband, who was obviously relishing in his long since discarded limelight. The rest of his friends and colleagues were swaying and singing along, some with drinks raised shouting out the chorus as it came. They went back and forth finishing the second and third verses before coming to his favorite part. He thundered the keys along to Max's strong voice as the song closed toward the end.

Everyone joined in the last repeat and once he'd played the last chord, the room erupted to screams and cheers. Max took a deep bow, winking at his wife, and then pointed to Colin. He put up a humble hand, standing and moving from behind the piano bench. Max grabbed his arm and held it up like he was a champion boxer who'd just won a match, and Colin couldn't help but laugh at his friend's theatrics.

Eventually, the cheers died down and the DJ started playing a dance mashup of Christmas songs. The three of them retreated to the bar for another round. En route they were given hearty praise from their alcohol emboldened peers.

He turned to his friend after they gathered their drinks and raised his glass. "Well done, Max. That was fun."

"Just like old times." Max returned the toast.

Kitty and a man her age stopped by the bar. "I knew you both could perform in the OR, but that was a surprising delight." She made introductions for her husband in the tweed suit and hands were clasped all around.

"Do you guys know any more songs?" her husband inquired.

Before Max could get a word in, he answered for him. "We had a few more, but those have long since been retired."

Kitty tutted, "Too bad."

The conversation switched to work, and the residents' holiday attire. Kitty gushed over baby pictures of Owen on Kate's phone, brimming with excitement about becoming a grandmother herself in a few short months. Letting his attention wane from the discussion, Colin looked out around the crowded room.

Over in the far corner, a small dance area had been designated and a good crush of people were on it. Towards the windows on the edge of the dance floor, he saw the backs of two of the male residents in their ornate holiday suits. Facing them were two women.

He could see the first easily; she was nearly taller than the men in her high heels. Colin recognized her as one of the nurses from upstairs, Ashley. The space between the men's shoulders widened as they moved around, and he caught a glimpse of the woman standing next to her. His breath caught in his throat, and he resisted the urge to cough.

Emilie was wearing an off the shoulder emerald green mermaid dress that hugged her body before flaring just above her knees. Her exposed collarbone was unadorned, but she wore long sparkling earrings surrounded by soft, undulating curls. A large strand of her mid-back length hair draped over her left shoulder and bounced lightly as she turned her head to address either man as they spoke.

He'd never seen it fully down, the closest was the half ponytail when they'd been in the elevator. It seemed unreasonable for something as simple as hair to be so mesmerizing.

Colin rose like a man possessed. "I'll be right back," he offered to the group before him, setting his drink down and pressing across the room.

Other colleagues stopped him a few times on his passage over, but he kept visual tabs on her while he politely made his excuses from each conversation. After what seemed like an eternity, he arrived at the foursome clasping a hand on each of the men's shoulders.

"Barnes. Shulze. Everyone loves the suits."

"Thanks Dr. Abernan!" The resident in the candy cane striped suit grinned widely. "It was Brian's idea."

Shulze, in the reindeer suit, bowed his recognition in an exaggerated way, obviously inebriated.

"Ladies." He nodded to both of them, trying hard to evenly spread his eye contact between the two in a casual way. "Good to see you outside the hospital."

All he wanted to do was stare at the gorgeous miniscule freckles fanning Emilie's delicate shoulders and dotting their way to her cleavage. With a quick glance to the side, he noticed Shulze losing his battle with the same issue.

"Colin." Emilie smiled at him at the same time Ashley replied, "Dr. Abernan."

Hearing his name through those lips was its own kind of pleasure. Their blissful formation of vowels and consonants seemed heightened since they were painted a bright holiday red.

Ashley slightly arched a golden eyebrow when Emilie spoke his name instead of his professional title. "Enjoying the evening? That was quite the performance earlier."

He controlled the speed of his eyes as they bounced between the women, silently gauging Emilie's reaction, before waving his hand dismissively. "Max likes to have fun."

Shulze slurred, "Dr. Campbell's the best. He always has the funniest jokes. Like the one . . ."

The resident lurched towards the women raising his hand to tell the joke before suddenly losing his footing. He took a few rapid, exaggerated steps forward before face planting into the thick pane window, nearly taking Ashley down with him. Luckily, she sidestepped him just in time before he hit the glass with a loud thunk.

Barnes quickly recovered his friend, taking him by his shoulders. "Excuse us. I think it's time for a glass of water."

"Or several!" Ashley called after them, cupping her hand to her mouth. She let her gaze pass between him and Emilie. "Come to think of it. I'm a bit thirsty. Emilie, what can I get you?"

"I can come get it."

"No, I got it. Same as before?" Ashley asked breezily as she quickly strode off to the bar.

Once alone, they both grinned at each other for a weighted beat, waiting for the other to start the conversation.

He made the mistake of looking her over. Her dress held a slight sheen that was damn distracting as she subtly shifted her weight back and forth. The black heels that peaked from underneath only brought her face closer to his.

"You look . . ." He tried to think of the most professional way to end that sentence. "That's a nice dress."

"Thanks." She dipped her head to look at her dress, and the familiar scent of honeysuckle reached his nose. A pressure hit his chest hard as he inhaled, his eyes slowly drifting closed. Every cell in his body vibrated with an insatiable need to step closer to her.

"Ash insisted I needed a new dress. It's nice to see everyone so dressed up when we all wear pajamas to work each day."

Yes. Work. Co-worker. You work together.

Colin snapped his eyes open before she lifted her gaze. "You're right. It's a nice change."

Jamming his hands in his pockets, he surveyed the room to distract himself.

Her voice brought his attention back to her. "How long have you played the piano?"

He set his gaze on her lined eyes and willed himself not to move it. "Since I was six. My mother thought it would be good for me to take lessons, and I had an affinity for it once I started."

"It must be nice to have a talent like that." Those red lips lifted, dragging his vision down.

He cleared his throat and looked out into the starlit night. "Honestly, I haven't played much here since I sold my piano before the move." His jaw tightened reflexively. "I made a mistake thinking it was a part of myself I could do without."

A pause fell between them, and he knew he'd been too honest in his answer. It'd just come out of his mouth. He glanced back to see that slight shadow glinting in her eyes for a millisecond before she forced her lips up.

"There's always the one in the lobby." She said it as a joke.

He exhaled, relieved that she'd let his vulnerability slide, and smiled back. "That's true."

Suddenly, a blur of buzzed red hair appeared on his right flank with two burly arms suctioning to him with the ferocity of a crazed octopus.

"Buddy! You 'scaped! You 'scaped . . ." Third time's a charm. "You e-s-caped," he said very slowly, sounding it out.

Emilie was trying and failing to hide a giggle behind her hand.

He looked down at his friend's slack face. "Hey there, Max."

Max hung on his body, staring up at him. "Colin. Colin. Colin. Do you know," he gulped. "Do you know that I love you?"

Laughing, he slowly peeled each of his friend's arms from around his torso. Max tilted dangerously back and forth before Colin supported him again under his shoulder.

His friend snapped up his head while poking him in the chest. "Hey. Hey. When someone says they love you, the decent thing is to tell them you love them back. Isn't that right, nice nurse from upstairs?" He pointed his finger at Emilie. "Make him tell me he loves me."

Emilie could hold her amusement no longer, and she let out a long, head-tilting laugh that brightened his soul as thoroughly as a kiss on his brow from his mother would have.

"I think he needs to hear that you love him."

He glanced at his friend's face in the crook of his shoulder and said with sincerity, "I love you, Max. You know that, man."

Max beamed as pleased and satiated as a child who'd just been praised.

"There you are!" Kate came striding up to them, more than a little flustered. "I lost track of him after I went to the restroom. I think I need to get him home."

Seeing Emilie for the first time, she pushed her hair behind her ears. "Oh, hi. We have an infant at home and don't get out much. I think our drink limit may have come down several levels after becoming parents."

Emilie's eyes softened as she gently touched Kate's arm. "It happens to the best of us."

The tension around Kate's mouth loosened as she let out a loud exhale. "Thank you." She turned to Colin. "Can you please help me get him into the car? He's too heavy for me to support."

Max started singing softly to himself.

"Of course. Are you okay to drive? Or do you need me to drive you?"

"I can drive. I only had the one earlier," she said.

Pulling his friend to standing, he heard Kate say, "It's time to head home, Max."

Max let out a petulant, "Awwwwwwwww."

Colin focused back on Emilie and tried to not let the hopefulness seep into his voice. "I'll see you later?"

Those red lips lifted high. "See you later."

After he had Max safely buckled in the passenger side of the car and waved them off, he tried to curb the expectant resonance that swelled in his chest as the elevator made its ascent. Once back at the party, he made several rounds, chatting with other friends and trying not to be too obvious in looking for her. After an hour, he realized with a sinking heaviness that Emilie was nowhere to be found.

·CHAPTER 15·

An instrumental version of "Sleigh Ride" softly wafted down the hall as Emilie donned gloves. Picking up a yellow gown and slipping her arms through the sleeves, she tied the strings around the nape of her neck then reached back to tie the one behind her waist. Colin walked up to the PPE cart and momentarily blocked her view of the room as he reached past her for a mask.

"Hey." His voice sounded distant and distracted, no doubt thinking of the impending surgery he was about to perform.

"Merry Christmas." She placed a simple mask on her face and snapped the elastic around her ears.

"Merry . . ." He glanced at her and paused, his whole body stilling. "Your . . ." His speech stopped again while his eyes focused on the side of her face.

He reached past her ear and grasped a long wayward strand of hair that must have tufted free of her braid between

143

his fingertips. With a slow, fluid motion, he delicately tucked it behind her ear running his thumb along her neck to her collarbone. Then he lifted the neckband of her gown and gently placed the loose end of hair beneath.

Under her mask, her lips parted as she sucked in a quick breath. A strong, tingling sensation traced the path his thumb had taken from the edge of her jaw down her neck. The soft, mechanical swooshing from the hospital room and the Christmas carols from the nurses' station drifted away to complete silence. All she could hear was his breathing.

She became acutely aware of his proximity to her, and how his chest rose and fell as his gaze remained fixed on her collarbone. Her heart beat hard in her chest as she flushed with heat under her gown. For a moment, time seemed suspended. When she swallowed and finally exhaled, he took his eyes away from her and returned instantly to the focused, quickly moving man he'd been only a moment before.

Leaning onto the doorjamb while holding the mask across his face, he spoke to Sierra. "I'm going downstairs to check the heart right now. The harvest team said it's in good condition. Emilie's going to bring you down. We'll talk about the final details in Pre-Op, okay?"

Sierra's "okay" was meek. She was probably a little overwhelmed by the day's activities and the prospect of finally being free of the Total Artificial Heart machine.

Colin leaned back out of the room, his voice retaining it's professional demeanor. "Once the engineer gets here, bring her down. We'll prep her in the OR."

Emilie nodded and he was gone as fast as he appeared, exiting through the unit doors. For a few seconds, she stared blankly at the closed doors frozen in place until she heard a soft "Emilie?" coming from within the room.

"Be right there." She gave herself a shake and entered the room.

Sierra was unique in that she'd had the biocompatible plastic 'heart' that pumped pneumatically through two large tubes placed in her chest almost immediately after she'd given birth. Most mothers leave the hospital after delivering their babies. Sierra went emergently to the OR, and the only thing they could do was remove her failing heart to save her.

Since then, she'd been confined to the walls of the hospital so that medical staff could care for her and "Big Blue," the washing-machine sized device that kept her alive. Her husband and daughter visited the hospital almost every day. Her thirteen-month-old was as comfortable with the nursing and physician staff as she would have been with aunts or uncles, having seen them so often.

Emilie was helping Sierra into a wheelchair when Nick, the engineer, showed up at the doorway and started gowning.

"Merry Christmas, Sierra! You're getting a heart *on* Christmas," he practically shouted into the door.

Sierra lifted her head from her chair. "I still can't believe it."

"Believe it." He made the necessary adjustments, mobilizing the machine. "We're ready. Let's get you to the OR."

Once Emilie was back on the floor, she checked in with her charge nurse, Enid, to make sure the rest of her patients hadn't needed anything while she was gone. She was just finishing typing all the details of the transfer for Sierra's electronic chart when Enid stopped over her shoulder.

"I've put the OR feed on the TV in the breakroom if you want to watch part of it." The stocky, middle-aged woman moved on to tell the rest of the nurses that she had the surgery broadcasted.

Emilie peeked into the breakroom to see the soundless monitor showing a close up of the center of Sierra's chest. They were just starting to scrub her skin when her nurse phone rang with a patient needing pain medication. She went from task to task, busier than expected before things finally calmed down. Slipping back into the breakroom, she found her charge leaning her body weight against the foot that was propped onto a chair.

Enid pointed to the screen. "He's so fast."

Two hands covered in surgical gloves and a scant amount of blood quickly worked on Sierra's superior vena cava reanastomosis. His fingers connected with tiny precise sutures, the receiving ends of Sierra's own vein to those of the donor heart.

"He really is."

For a moment, all Emilie could think about was what it felt like to have those nimble fingers on her neck. The skin he'd touched pinpricked with the memory as it replayed slowly in her mind. Her own hand lifted and traced the path. There was no mistaking that his touch was deliberate.

Somehow, she couldn't lie to herself anymore and pretend that she didn't feel some type of fundamental shift when Colin was around her. She'd told herself that they were work buddies, but talking to him at the Christmas party, she realized her thoughts about him weren't like the ones she had of Ash, or Barbara, or even Dr. Campbell.

If she was honest, even after such a slight encounter, she craved the sensation of his fingers on her skin again. The air in the small break room was suddenly very warm and stifling. Emilie pushed up the sleeves of the Henley underneath her red scrub top.

Enid's eyes were glued to the screen. "What a gift for Sierra, right?"

A crushing weight settled between her shoulders. "I'm happy for Sierra, but as wonderful of a gift this is for her, I keep thinking that there's another family who just lost their loved one on Christmas."

Her charge turned from the screen to her, thinking before answering. "It is bittersweet. I understand how you feel, but in a way that person's living on in her. They are giving her a second chance at life and a first chance at being a mother."

Sierra had never been able to hold her own child without a plastic tube separating them. Downstairs this second, Colin was doing everything in his power to give that chance to her.

Pressure built between Emilie's brows as the pungent scent of multiple potluck dishes littering the breakroom table pricked at her nose. The aroma turned her stomach, and she had to swallow against the sour taste in her mouth.

"Would it be okay if I took lunch?"

"Sure." Enid stepped back from the table.

"I'm just going to hop downstairs to grab a fresh cup of coffee first." She slipped from the breakroom.

Striding off the floor, she walked into the locker room instead of down the hall. Blood thumped in her ears as she heard the click of the door close behind her. Pushing a hand against her chest, she forced herself to take a deep breath. And then another. And another.

She'd never felt like this on shift before, and she had to gain control of herself and fast. Forcing her eyes closed, she fought against the image teasing at the periphery of her mind. A strained gasp choked from her mouth as her legs threatened to give out from underneath her. She backed against the wall, sliding down against it.

"I'm sorry," she whispered to the room as she wrapped her arms around her legs.

Hanging her head between her knees, she wasn't sure who she was sorry to. Sorry to the family who'd just lost her loved one on Christmas. Sorry to Sierra that she didn't get a chance to nurse her baby and hold her without a plastic obstruction always in the way. Sorry to Braden that she'd just relished the touch of another man. Sorry to her sweet baby girl for trying to move on with her life.

Not for the first time, she wished she'd been in the car with Braden and Lucy.

A halting breath filled her lungs, and her arms quivered as she tried to let it out evenly. If she'd been with them, she wouldn't have to try and live without them. Then this treacherous feeling as she tried to start over wouldn't be crushing at her ribs.

"Love isn't a one-time-deal. You can still love those you've lost while feeling affection for someone new. It's not a betrayal of those you've lost to live your own life."

Nia's words from their last session crept into her mind— the ones encouraging Emilie to consider dating again.

The idea of dating had always felt like replacing her husband and child.

But now she couldn't deny the fact that her body *wanted* to be touched.

Bile stirred in her throat again.

No.

She didn't have to do anything. She didn't have to acknowledge the way it felt when Colin's thumb traced down her skin. Ash would have tucked Emilie's hair away just as quickly.

He was just being friendly.

Something deep in the center of her chest whispered *liar*, but she ignored it.

Right now, she had to get off the floor and get back to work. She leaned her head back against the wall and scrubbed her face with her hands. Then she pulled the tie from her hair and carefully rebraided each strand, trying to ignore the sensation of her hair brushing against the same spot Colin had touched. Unable to keep her awareness from her neck, she let out a frustrated breath, tossed her hair out, and braided it over her other shoulder.

She could do this. She could dismiss this feeling.

She'd already been through so much; what was a little more cognitive dissonance?

·CHAPTER 16·

The murmur of conversation and upbeat jazz filled his ears as he opened the front door to his friends' house. Kate had unabashedly lured him out into the freezing mid-January temperatures with an invitation for good food, drink, and company. Admittedly, he was a willing attendee of her winter dinner party since their "family dinners" had dropped off over the holidays. A lightness radiated through his body as he stepped through the threshold, and the delicious scent of beef, butter, and cooked vegetables reached his nose.

Colin left his heavy wool coat on the large portable clothing rack placed in the entry, straightened the cuffs of his dinner jacket, and made his way to the living room. He ordered a cocktail from the small bar temporarily set near the French doors. While the college-aged man in a black silk vest and bowtie stirred and garnished his Negroni, his gaze drifted to the backyard. The light spilling from the house reflected off the snow, illuminating a trio of snowmen lining the back fence. It seemed his friends were really enjoying Owen's first winter.

Mingling with the other attendees, he chatted with people he knew and met those he didn't; the guest list seemed like an even split of people from his work and from Kate's. It wasn't until their hostess stood before them in her lace, long-sleeved navy sheath dress announcing it was time for dinner that he noticed the attendees were mostly couples.

The muscles in his forearms twitched, thinking that his friend might have gone back on his word not to set him up. Once everyone was gathered at the table, however, he saw his coworker, Karen, sitting at one end and his name card resting on a gold charger at the other end of the table. A quiet breath left his lungs. Karen held up her glass in a salute of solidarity from her chair, and a smile broke from his lips, raising his glass to his fellow surgeon.

The dinner was an amazing journey for his taste buds, especially since he'd only been eating frozen dinners or hospital cafeteria food since he'd been here for Thanksgiving. The conversation only slightly outshined the food, bringing with it laughter and camaraderie he'd been missing almost as much as good flavor. After lingering over dessert and coffee, the guests started to rise and give their thanks to their hosts.

"Amazing dinner." He leaned in to give Kate a hug before heading to collect his large winter coat.

"Thank you. I hope the other two will be as successful as this one."

"Other two?"

"We're going to host one every month of winter." Kate opened the hall closet and grabbed her wallet from her purse. "Can you stay for a bit? The bar staff is finishing packing up, and I just have to pay the babysitter. It would be nice to catch up. I feel like I haven't talked to you since the Christmas party."

Though that was precisely the amount of time it'd been since he'd seen Kate, he didn't mention it. "Of course."

He and Max helped the bar company put their boxes into their van, while a teenage girl walked past them to her car just down the street. Returning to the living room, he laid his heavy coat over the back of a wingback chair before sitting. Max relaxed on the eggshell white couch opposite him.

"What restaurant did you cater from?" He leaned farther into the incredibly comfortable chair. Maybe he should let Kate's friend decorate his condo; it'd be worth it alone if she could find him a chair just like this one.

"L'eau. I took Kate there for our anniversary."

"It was really good, even catered. I'd imagined it's even better in person."

"Oh, it is." Kate flopped next to her husband, newly changed into yoga pants and a fluffy, oversized sweater. "I'm so glad tonight went well. I've had the idea of winter dinner parties brewing in my head for years, but finally decided to act on it. You'll find that you lose contact with people you don't see at work over the winter season because everyone just stays inside their own homes."

"We all turn into little heat loving hermits, it's true," Max agreed, loosening his tie.

"I'm not going to lie. This is more snow than I've seen in my whole life, and we are only a month in. I can't imagine it being on the ground through March."

"Sometimes April." She tucked her bare feet under her.

"You're kidding."

"Unfortunately no, my friend. I'm sure you've got some snow gear, but when you have another day off, you probably should buy some more. And good boots if you are going to keep walking to work every day." Max snickered as if Colin was a mad man.

"I live a block from the hospital, of course I'm going to walk."

His friend muttered under his breath. "We'll see."

"Cold sinks in fast, Colin." Kate's face took on a worried parental look. "Just don't make the trek in your scrubs. Wear winter gear or snow clothes and change when you get to the OR."

"Okay, I'll do that." They were, after all, veteran New Englanders, and this was his first real winter. "Thanks for the advice."

"The best advice would be to find someone to keep you warm on the long winter nights." Max wrapped his arm around his wife and squeezed her to him.

Kate playfully hit her husband in the chest. "Max! Leave him alone. He'll find someone when he's ready."

"So when he's *seventy*?"

"Colin's more of a gentleman than you are. He's probably taking his time finding the right woman."

"First off, I was a perfect gentleman when we started dating . . ." She arched an auburn eyebrow. ". . . well, almost a perfect gentleman. Secondly, he's not even looking. This is why I think we should set him up. Amanda from your office seems nice. Who knows, maybe they'll hit it off."

"He's probably looking for someone who likes him for him, not someone who specifically asked me to set her up with one of my husband's 'doctor friends,'" she scoffed, using finger quotes.

"So he's a talented surgeon. Should we hide that fact from the world? Anybody can Google him."

Colin cleared his throat loudly, bringing to his friends' attention that they were not at home alone having this discussion but conducting it in front of him. Two sets of eyes blinked at him.

"I can see this is not the first time you've had this conversation. Thank you for your concern but I'm *fine*." Adding as an afterthought, he slipped into old habits. "I'm too busy with work for a relationship anyway."

"Oh no you don't. You can't use that excuse anymore. I know exactly how many hours you work, and there's plenty of time . . ." Max smiled at this wife. ". . . to find a wonderful, smart, incredible woman who you love and respect."

Kate turned and gave her husband a quick kiss. As the two grinned at each other, momentarily caught up in their affection, a pressure built in Colin's chest that came out as a single dangerous word.

"Actually . . ."

He gripped his teeth together tightly. Both of them would jump on the hopefulness in his voice like hammerheads on fresh chum.

"Actually?" They said in chorus.

He let out a groan and flopped back in his chair, covering his head in his hand. Instead of facing the questioning firing squad like he expected, the two of them started whispering to each other excitedly as if conspiring against him. Clips of phrases slipped to him. "No, don't, you'll scare him off." "I don't know, I'd never seen her before." "Which one?"

"Guys, this is worse than a thirty-six hour shift." He sat up with a long exhale. "Get on with it."

Kate straightened herself slowly and seemed to be mentally sorting through a list, as if she only had one question to ask the President of the United States. "Is it the brunette in the green dress from the party?"

His mouth gaped momentarily before composing himself.

"How did—" came out at the same time Max asked, "What brunette in a green dress?"

At that second, Owen's computerized cry screeched through the baby monitor on the coffee table between them. Max snapped it up and turned the volume down, having a wordless conversation with Kate.

When Max stood to help his son, Colin did the same. "I had a great time, really, but it's late. I think I should be going."

"Oh no, you didn't answer the question!" Kate shot up and pointed her finger at him.

They stood at a momentary standstill for a handful of seconds before Owen's increasing cries tumbled down the staircase and broke them from their deadlock.

Max pushed past his wife towards the stairs. "Don't let him leave."

"I think it would be best if you sat down." She motioned to the chair.

"Really?"

This was insane, even for them.

Kate's expression softened. "I've known you for four years. I know that's not as long as Max has, but in those years, I've never seen you with someone you really cherished. You hold your heart so protected it's hard for anyone to get through. I know that life has been harder on you than most, but don't you think that's even more of a reason to find someone to love?"

He was silent for a moment trying to think of how to explain why he lived the way he had for so long. How for years he'd been terrified of the idea of finally letting his guard down. But now that he'd met a woman he wasn't just willing to, but really wanted to try a real relationship with, she wasn't interested.

"It doesn't matter. She doesn't see me that way."

"How do you know that?"

Max quietly stepped into the room, taking silent inventory before sitting on the couch.

Colin didn't want to explain his huge mistake. That when he'd seen Emilie's long, beautiful strand of hair astray, he finally had an excuse to do something he'd wanted to do for such a long time.

It was a perfect little Christmas gift.

Part of him thought maybe it would be an opening had she responded differently—leaned in, said something, touched him back. Once his brain focused back on reality and not the warm, silk-like quality of her skin or how he was nearly as out of breath from the brief contact, he'd seen she was frozen like a startled deer. He'd acted on impulse and hadn't realized until he saw the shocked look in her eyes that he'd been so inappropriate.

In the last three long weeks, she seemed to distance herself from him at work, and he couldn't blame her. It was a classic human resources nightmare—doctor hits on nurse. He'd been half expecting John to call him for a meeting to discuss his second indiscretion.

His eyes darted around the skillfully adorned room, looking for anything to focus on beside the people in front of him. "I just do, okay?"

Kate shook her head as she sat. "I'm good at reading people. I can tell if a couple is going to put in an offer, or if they love one house but are trying to play it safe with something less desirable. The woman you were talking to at the party looked pretty into you from where I was standing."

"She did?" A surge of adrenaline pumped through his veins at the thought before he remembered what Kate saw didn't count. Emilie's actions spoke the loudest.

"That's what I saw, though I *was* a little distracted at the time." Her eyes shot daggers at Max.

"What?" He leaned away from this wife. "Who are we talking about anyway?"

Kate let out an irritated exhale. "I don't *know*. I don't work at the hospital, and I didn't get formally introduced to her because you were two seconds from passing out in the middle of your holiday work party."

"Oh. Right." He ran his hand over his buzzed head. "Sorry, Colin."

"Don't worry about it. It doesn't matter, and even if she did like me, which she doesn't, I'm pretty sure John wouldn't be happy about it."

Max furrowed his brow. "What does John have to do with you liking someone?"

This time he let out the frustrated exhale. "She works for the CTSB."

"Oh shit." His friend's eyes widened before his brows furrowed again. "Wait, who is it? Both Natasha and Eileen are married with kids. I know you're not that man."

"She's not one of the surgeons." He rubbed his forehead, wishing this conversation never started.

His friend tilted back his head as loud barking laughter shook his fiery beard. Only when Kate slapped his chest and shushed him, pointing to the stairs did he clap a hand over his mouth and compose himself.

"The anti-fraternization policy is only within CTSB." Max grinned widely. "Between surgeons. Not between us and *hospital* employees."

"Wait, what?"

Both of his friends tried to hide their smiles as they exchanged a glance.

"You should ask her out," Max pushed.

Colin's head fell into his hands.

"It's not going to hurt your career to ask out a woman."

"I don't care about how it would affect . . ." he began to protest and then stopped mid-sentence.

He'd always cared if something had affected his career. Why all of a sudden was that no longer an issue?

"You *really* like her." Kate's voice lowered several notes.

"I . . ." He stopped. He couldn't deny he liked Emilie. He couldn't dismiss the crushing ache deep in his chest when he walked on the floor for rounds and she hid away in the medicine room.

His eyes slowly closed as he let out a defeated breath. "It doesn't matter."

Silence stood between them except for the faint static from the baby monitor.

"Oh, Colin," Kate said softly.

He scrubbed his hands over his face and stood. "I think I should be getting home. Thanks again for dinner."

"Sure, man." Max rose and followed him to the door.

The icy cold temperature struck him hard as soon as he stepped outside, matching how he felt inside.

·CHAPTER 17·

Emilie sat at her kitchen table over a steaming bowl of hearty minestrone, staring at the deep crossing ridges that served as her elm's protection from the bitter cold. The branches still had a light layer of snow on them giving the appearance of iced cake. Even the idea of skating at the Frog Pond couldn't drag her out of her warm, comfortable condo today. Soon, she'd have to lace up her boots to get to her appointment with Nia, and then to the hospital to help out Jessica by finishing her shift. That would be enough snow tromping for one day.

When she entered Nia's office a few hours later, her therapist was already in a chair with a laptop balanced on her woolen slacks and a pashmina wrapped around her shoulders. The dim grey daylight barely brightened the dark office.

"I hope you don't mind." Nia gestured to the other armchair. "I was doing some work from here. It's a bit cozier than my desk in the winter."

"Sure." Emilie sat down and propped her bag of clothes against the chair leg.

Setting the laptop aside and picking up a notepad, Nia asked, "How have you been?"

"I'm struggling with something."

She'd tried avoiding Colin for the most part when she worked, but it was so much harder than she thought to ignore that subtle sensation of *want* every time she saw him. She'd wake up anxious before every shift wondering if today was a day their schedules would coincide. If today she'd need to fight all her normal demons and then this one too.

"There's a surgeon I work with, the one I accidentally maced in the park, and we'd been sort of work friends, but then something happened." She pulled at the collar of her sweater.

Nia tilted her head slightly, but kept silent waiting for her to elaborate.

"Colin . . ." Saying his name out loud unexpectedly took her breath away. "He and I were both caring for a patient, and there was a moment when he took a strand of my hair and tucked it behind my ear and into my collar."

"How did you feel about that?"

One hundred different emotions swam through her head. "That's the problem."

"What's the problem?"

"I can't stop myself from feeling it."

Nia's silver curls bobbed as she soundlessly processed what she'd said.

"What should I do?"

Her therapist leaned back in her chair. "What do you want to do?"

A huff of air left her mouth. She'd been in therapy long enough to know that you're never given an answer to a question.

Nia must have sensed her frustration because she continued, "Are you telling me that you enjoyed a moment of intimacy with another man?"

Emilie's hand mindlessly found her neck. The skin beneath it flushed as her heartbeat sped. Simultaneously, that dip in her stomach made bile rise at the back of her throat.

"I don't want to."

"Why?"

"Because if I move on, who loves Braden and Lucy?"

Nia inclined her head. "You do."

Her arms drew around herself as she felt the familiar weight settle down her spine.

"You will always be connected to your husband and daughter. Even as your grief morphs and changes over the years, they are forever a part of you."

Her voice came out in a hoarse whisper. "I feel like I'm betraying them."

Nia nodded for a moment before speaking softly. "Guilt is a natural response and usually lessens in time. What you need to understand is that it's possible to still have thoughts and feelings about them and be happy in a new relationship with someone else. Loving and grieving can happen at the same time.

"Maybe enjoying this moment with another person is a sign that you are ready to start dating again, but ultimately you decide when you are emotionally and physically ready to have another relationship.

"My advice would be to take it slow and expect to have dichotomous emotions. You might feel simultaneously giddy and nervous, happy and guilty. It's okay to feel both ways. And it's okay not to know the answer to how you'll feel ahead of time. Sometimes, you have to experience something to know. Give yourself grace and do what you feel most comfortable with."

Nia's words slowly sank into her skin. Nothing in this world would ever make her forget the life and love she had, but maybe, just maybe, it was okay to start something new or at least be open to the idea of it.

Letting go of her body, she blinked. "Okay."

Nia's lips curled up before she lowered them a fraction. "Okay. What else has happened since I've seen you last?"

◊◊◊

Emilie swayed with the rhythmic pulsation of the train as it coursed down the Red Line. Leaning her forehead against the vertical rail bar, she thought about what Nia had said.

Was she ready?

She felt like she had finally gotten her life back together, truly together, a year and a half ago. A lot of that was with the help of her family and the fact that she seemed to be continually surrounded by at least one of them. When she started over here, she surprised everyone by not just surviving, but thriving on her own. There'd been setbacks, but she'd been able to tackle each one as it came.

A metallic voice overhead announced Kendall Station, efficiently breaking into her thoughts. When the doors slid open with their pneumatic groan, enough of the passengers left the train allowing her to sit for the short rest of her ride.

Maybe it was okay that she thought about Colin differently than she did her other coworkers and friends. Maybe it was okay that the timber of his voice sent a warm vibrating sensation down her spine, or that his eyes mystified her with their various shades, or that she didn't understand the strange connection she felt with him, but that it made her feel safe.

Sloshing through the sidewalks to the hospital was at least a shorter walk than from Nia's office to the T-station. The dim light was already fading, even though it wasn't yet four o'clock. It'd be dark before office workers clocked out for the evening. The smell of snow in the air reminded her she'd forgotten to check her weather app. Not willing to take off her gloves to check her phone, she made a mental note to do it at work.

After changing into her scrubs and sneakers, Emilie locked everything in her locker and walked onto 5SW. An odd feeling washed over her as she did, as if the unit was charged with a mournful energy. Shaking it off, she found a quick moving Jessica in the medication room.

"Hey, Jess. How are you doing?"

"Good, good. Thank you again for doing this. If you ever need a favor, just let me know." She finished typing in the medications she needed from the Pyxis dispensing machine and the first of several drawers opened for her. "Can you witness?"

"Sure." She counted out the narcotic pills with Jessica before signing her identification number into the machine as her colleague took the two pills her patient needed. "Who are these for?"

"Eaves in room 512." She shut the drawer and another popped open. "I'll give all these real quick before I give you report."

"Okay." Emilie followed her to the room and logged into the computer outside, looking up the orders to be finished on that patient. When Jessica came out, she received a full report on him and the other three patients she would care for until change of shift.

"I hope that your dad enjoys his surprise party."

Her co-worker huffed. "I hope so. He hates surprises, but my mother insisted we do something big for his seventieth. I just hope we don't scare him into a heart attack."

Emilie's eyes widened. "Let's hope not."

A dark look crossed over Jessica's face momentarily before she lowered her voice. "Do you ever eat at that diner near the hospital?"

"Bo's? Yeah, all the time. Why?"

"Mary is here. She had a heart attack early this afternoon. They were able to stabilize her in the ER and brought her up here so that CTSB could discuss options with the family, but . . ." She took a deep breath and then released it. ". . . they don't want any interventions."

Someone had knocked the wind out of her. "What condition is she in?"

Jessica slowly shook her head. "She probably won't make it through the night."

Tears instantly pricked at the corners of Emilie's eyes, and she cast her gaze down as tightness crept from her brows to her stomach and started cinching her arms and legs. It was if someone had just told her that her own grandmother was to die within hours.

She looked up only when she registered Jessica's hand on her sleeve. "That's how we all feel."

Jessica didn't know that she'd spent hours over the last few months not only talking with Mary, but coming to love her. "What room is she in?"

"504. Ashley's taking care of her."

"Oh, good." A relieved exhale left her body.

Jessica nodded. "That's what I said too . . . I hate to leave you like this, but I need to go. Are you okay with everything?" She gathered up her hoodie and water bottle from the charting area.

"Yeah." She forced her lips up. "Have a good night."

Emilie knew that it would be best to round on all her patients and introduce herself, but she was drawn to 504 and the crowd of staff that was outside. Beside three nurse aides, she found her manager, Barbara, in her white coat over frost blue scrubs talking to Ash.

"If they want the chaplain while they wait on their priest just let me know. I'm going to stay. I just need to call the girls and let them know to order a pizza." Barbara turned to walk to her office, pausing to squeeze her shoulder before heading down the hall.

"Hey," Ash said quietly.

"Hey."

Through the small glass window, she saw only the crowd of people around what she knew in the center was a hospital bed. The room was packed with family. An IV pole rose from behind the shoulder of a granddaughter, and the oxygen valve hissed at the wall beside one of the sons-in-law. She glanced at the telemetry monitor above the window to watch Mary's failing heart beat out a damaged rhythm.

"Who is . . ." she started the sentence to see Colin walking slowly out of the room and didn't need to finish it.

Solace rapidly sped through her veins as her hand found her chest with a shaky breath. Colin cared for Bo and Mary and would do everything in his power for them. They'd talked about the restaurant before and the older couple's way of making themselves surrogate grandparents to those who needed them. He knew she often sat at the counter with Mary, and she knew he often chatted with Bo every time he ate there with Dr. Campbell.

His gaze lingered a moment on hers before he spoke to Ash. "I talked with Bo and their daughters. Everyone's in agreement with Mary's wishes."

"Mary's conscious?" The question blurted out.

His sorrowful eyes looked like the sky she had just seen outside. "No, but they all discussed this possibility when she had her first heart attack a month ago."

It dawned on her that while she had a social relationship with the elderly couple, Colin had the dual position of being their friend and their doctor. His mournful frown deepened as he glanced at the beeping pager clipped to the waist of his scrub pants.

"I need to see this patient in the ICU, but I'll be back. Page me if anything changes."

"Yes, Dr. Abernan," Ash replied.

Numbness set in as soon as Colin stepped away from the room. Emilie's fingers found the sides of her crisp scrub top as she wrapped her arms around herself. She needed to keep her breaths even to keep her vision from blurring.

"Why don't you say goodbye?" Ash suggested.

The water gathering at the edges of her eyes threatened to relinquish itself to gravity. "I couldn't possibly intrude. All her family's in there. They need their time with her."

She felt her friend's hand on her back, her thumb gently rubbing between her shoulder blades. "Several of us have already done it. They don't mind. They understand that she had family outside those who were related to her." Ash's tear washed face confirmed that her friend had already taken her turn.

Small, tentative steps led her into the hospital room and the sound of nearly twenty people breathing and quietly crying. Surely, they were breaking a fire code, but there wasn't a staff member in this hospital that would have cast out Mary's family.

Their eldest daughter, Shannon, saw her first and held a hand out. Emilie took it and was immediately pulled into a firm embrace. It was then the tears started to fall, and a shaky breath broke from her constricted ribs. Shannon released her enough, so she could see Mary in the bed. Bo was hunched over his wife from his chair, no doubt too weak to stand.

"Dad," she spoke through a tear strained voice. "Another friend of Mom's is here."

His aged face was slack, eyes dull and wet as he looked up. "Thank you, dear, for coming."

Emilie couldn't believe it. On the precipice of complete disaster, this family was not only kind to her, they were gracious and comforting.

"I wanted to say goodbye," she managed through a tight exhale.

Two granddaughters stepped back so that she could stand beside the bed rail nearest Mary's hand.

She placed her hand over Mary's cool, paper-thin skin and leaned, speaking in a near whisper. "Thank you for talking to me and all the things you taught me. Your friendship is one that I will cherish always."

As she straightened, Bo nodded to her once while softly brushing Mary's curls with his fingers. The second she was out of the room, her patient care aide found her, needing help. She pushed her emotions aside as she was slung back into the busy final hours of her shift.

·CHAPTER 18·

Like all the other staff, Colin was ushered out of the room while the family said their last goodbyes. The priest was saying a prayer over her bed as the family held hands in concentric circles around her. The staff outside the room watched as the telemetry monitor moved from its incredibly slow rhythm to a sporadic beat before resting in a long, solid line. Barbara leaned into the room to notify the family Mary was gone. They held vigil at her bedside for a long time before Bo came out of the room.

"Thank you, son, for being here. It was nice for there to be friendly faces she knew in the end." His weathered, wrinkled face was streaked with wet and dried tears.

Colin opened his mouth to offer his heartfelt condolences, but Bo was immediately ensconced by the rest of his family, ushering him down the hall. Bo's collapsed shoulders disappeared between his daughter's and granddaughter's bodies as a sea of strong women pulled him gently along. He watched until the unit doors closed behind them before sitting to finish the death paperwork with Ashley. She wiped a tear from her cheek before flipping the page of the paper document, so he could add his signature in the necessary place.

"Thank you for being so great with them."

"I loved Mary just as much as everyone here. They actually taught me a lot about love, something I've been working on." Ashley's red-rimmed eyes stared through the small window from the charting desk into the hospital room at her nurse aides as they started cleaning and preparing Mary's body for the morgue.

He followed her gaze and watched as the aides gingerly lifted Mary's frail pale arms and wiped them with soap sudded wash cloths before toweling her dry. Her skin had already taken on the waxy artificial look of the recently deceased. He saw it all the time, the way the body turned from a vital active person into a cavity no longer possessed.

Colin thought about what Ashley had said. The love between Bo and Mary was something of a legend. It was a tangible thing that you witnessed when you walked into the room. You could almost see the invisible line of string constantly connecting the two of them. It hovered over tables and jumped up and out of the way when the young servers flitted around the room, but it was there and present as much as the air in your lungs. He could only imagine that's what it would have looked like to see his parents grow old together. The thought made his saliva catch in his throat.

He blinked his eyes away from the window. "She will be missed by many."

"Yes, she will." Ashley closed the folder cover to the slender paper chart before entering the room to help her aides.

He sat at the computer and finished his charting before slowly walking off the unit. He found himself looking into the nurses' station and glancing up and down the halls, knowing he was looking for her. She'd stayed after finishing her shift like many of the other nurses and aides did, but now it seemed she'd vanished.

His stomach rumbled on its own accord, and he realized that he hadn't had lunch between cases earlier. His watch revealed it was a quarter to nine, and he decided to swing by the cafeteria before leaving. After this emotional evening at the end of a long surgical day, all he'd manage was a shower and to pass out in bed once he got home.

The hospital cafeteria was essentially the same as all the others he'd been in. The same expansive room with different congregations of tables and impersonal chairs. The ceiling that he could touch if he decided to raise his arms and push through the pocked ceiling tiles. A curious mix of smells from fried food to the saccharine smell of desserts all mixed with the undeniable aroma of overcooked vegetables. Today the wafting scents of cumin and curry jockeyed for primary position in his nose.

There were a few families scattered around the room, but he did not see Bo, nor his family. In a corner of the room, Emilie sat alone facing the wall hunched over a cup of coffee. He strode straight to her before pausing ten feet behind her table.

Her right hand twisted the cardboard coffee sleeve absently, and her braid leaned toward her left shoulder, which heaved irregularly. He took a few slow steps forward and stood behind her for a moment not knowing how to start or if he should even be here after she'd so obviously avoided him for weeks.

If she sensed his presence, she didn't betray it; she just continued moving her hand slowly while mutely crying to herself. His forearms twitched as he ran his hand through his hair.

He couldn't see her like this and do nothing.

Taking one final step closer so that he was directly behind her, he tentatively placed his hand on her shoulder.

"Emilie?"

She didn't turn around or look at him. Her right hand stilled while the left one moved achingly slow until it covered his at her shoulder. The scent of her shampoo drifted up ever so slightly when she tilted her head towards their overlapping hands.

His whole body responded to the soft touch of her hand over his and the sorrowful dip of her head. Electricity bolted through him as every single infinitesimal cell in his body quickly communicated the signal to the adjacent cell with nanosecond speed. Synapses opened and closed over and over until it settled in his chest with a twisting ache.

Standing behind her was torture. He hastily grabbed the chair next to her with his free hand and pulled it to sit diagonally to her. Surprisingly, she leaned over and let her body slump onto his. Wrapping his arms tightly around her frame, he tucked his chin to the crown of her head. Emilie nestled into his chest and placed a hand unwittingly over his pounding heart.

Her uneasy breaths and sobs continued while he silently held her, knowing words were useless at the moment. His only consolation was that she didn't seem uncomfortable in his arms.

After some length, she calmed and began breathing evenly. The urge to lift her chin, gaze upon her speckled cheeks, and tip her lips to his strongly vibrated through his body. He momentarily flushed with the heat of the image before he chided himself for even thinking of it. She probably wanted nothing to do with him after he was her literal shoulder to cry on.

She's just distraught. Remember, you touched her and she avoided you. This means nothing.

She stirred in his arms and lifted her hand to wipe her eyes. At the loss of the heat of her hand from his chest, his breath caught. It was as if she had pushed an imprint into him by removing it, like a hand into wet cement. He raised his head and blew out a short, painful breath.

"Colin . . ."

His vision pulled down to her tear-washed eyes. They locked with his for a few agonizing seconds before they flitted to his hair, to his lips, and down to his wet scrub top where her head had been only seconds ago.

He was stunned by his own inability to speak. His body resonated at every point of contact it shared with her as the muscular contractions in his chest sped. If there was movement or noise or light in the area surrounding them, he could tell you nothing about it. His entire being was solely focused on how it seemed that she was holding her breath. Tension ran through his body as he waited for what she would say or do.

Slowly, she pulled herself upright, and he felt his arms reluctantly release her. The pinprick sensation at her separation was only heightened with his anticipation of her rejection. Even with this expected blow, his need to help her burned in his chest like air held too long when diving underwater.

"What can I do?" His voice was huskier and more breathy than he'd expected.

She sat with her red eyes trained on the table before answering. "Nothing."

The simple word knocked him down harder than he'd anticipated. He took a deep breath and released it. A glutton for punishment, he didn't stop. "Can I take you home?"

She exhaled, shocking him with another simple word. "Sure."

They arranged to meet in the lobby in a few minutes to allow each of them to grab their belongings. Only when they both stepped out of the side exit to the hospital into the crisp twenty degree night did he see it was snowing lightly. Each falling snowflake took its turn catching an amber glow as it passed under the arching street lights.

"My car's just a block away in the garage of my building."

"I'd rather walk home tonight." She seemed impervious to the freezing weather as she slowly shuffled down the sidewalk. "If you'd like to head home, I understand."

He took two large steps to catch up with her before setting his pace to match her cadence. "I could use the fresh air."

There was no way in hell he was going to let her walk home alone in the freezing weather as upset as she was.

Misty white clouds of breath puffed ahead of them as they tracked over the mostly cleared sidewalk. Snow had been on the ground for a solid month now, and the piles of cleared snow were getting larger and dirtier. He was grateful that she'd changed, like him, out of her scrubs into jeans and snow boots under her coat.

They walked for several minutes in silence as intermittent gusts of wind stung his face, coercing him to pull his jacket's hood over his head. He thought he heard her mumble something over the swiping sound of his snowboard jacket.

"Did you say something?"

"We're even," she said.

"What?" He furrowed his brows.

"You cried all over my scarf, and I've cried all over your scrubs. We're even."

Watching her forward fixed face slide into a genuine smile warmed him more than a roaring fire would have in that moment.

She took a deep breath and her smile fell. "I was a mess tonight. It hit me harder than I thought. Thank you for being there."

He wanted to say that it was his extreme pleasure and could he please hold her for the rest of the night, but he managed, "You're welcome. Mary will be missed by us all."

"She really will."

They trudged through the newly collecting snow for a few moments in agreeable silence. Their boots crunched and squeaked with each step, compressing the snow beneath.

"Where are you from? Originally?" Her question materialized from thin air, and he realized that whenever they'd talked at work, it had always been about the present. His lack of knowledge about her life before working at Boston General suddenly felt expansive.

"I was born and raised in North Carolina."

He yearned to ask her a million questions to find out more about her but decided against it. Things could go back to the way they'd been at any moment. Right now, he'd just enjoy what he could get.

"I thought you were from the South. Sometimes the way you describe things your accent comes out a little. It's very subtle though. My mom is from northern Georgia. Where I grew up in Virginia, some people had a slight accent, but not everybody."

He chanced another gaze at her face tucked under her hat and hood. As they passed through a shaft of light pouring from a nearby building, he could see that her nose and cheeks were adorably pink from walking in the frigid temperature.

"I try to keep the colloquialisms out of my professional speech." He tightened his hood around this face. "But I grew up in a smaller beach town, so most of us speak with it. Though it's a bit different sounding than a Georgian accent."

"I don't really have an accent. My dad didn't, being from the Northeast, and between the two of them, I just adopted more neutral speech."

"That makes sense."

A slight joy at the comfortable back and forth they used to share bounced around in his body.

"After listening to my mom speak my whole life though, I've been known to drawl a bit more depending on if I am speaking to someone with an accent. I know I shouldn't, but I have a bad habit of mirroring whomever I'm talking to. The minute I say, 'bless your heart,' I know I've gone too far."

"I'm surprised as all get out," he said, completely deadpan with perfect diction.

It was natural for him to tease her, and he hadn't thought about how right now, that might be a really stupid idea. Fortunately, he was rewarded with a swift, playful punch that sent his spirits soaring.

"Stop!"

"Yes, ma'am." He laid his accent on thick.

Another playful punch hit his jacketed arm. "I mean it."

His lips rose so high they hurt for a few long strides, but then dropped when she halted suddenly.

She glanced at the brownstone beside them. "This is me."

He swore he saw disappointment flash over her face, or at least he was going to tell himself that's what he saw. His gaze swept his surroundings as recognition set in. How did they get here so fast?

The urge to reach out to her pulsed so strongly through him, but since they were finally getting back to normal, he wasn't going to chance ruining it. He pushed his hands deeper into his jacket pockets to stave off temptation as she turned to face him.

"Goodnight then. Will you be okay?"

"Yes. Thank you for everything. Truly. I really appreciate it, Colin." As she said his name, she held her hand out as if to touch his arm but rested her hand and her eyes on his jacket just over his heart.

It was if every surgical alarm bell he'd ever heard rang loud in his head screaming, "She's touching *you*." He almost lost all of his restraint not to wrap her in his arms and kiss her with that single simple action. Luckily, she released him as quickly as she'd possessed him and turned to open the door.

Emilie was through the glass entry door and waving from beyond it, ascending the stairs. He took his hand out of his pocket to return the wave before turning to trudge home in the cold. All he could think of as he spent the late hours of a freezing Boston night walking in the falling snow was that it was completely worth it.

·CHAPTER 19·

Emilie woke to a buzzing sound. It took a few seconds to figure out that it wasn't her alarm, but the doorbell. Groaning, she flipped the covers off her and shuffled down the hall to the front door intercom. This had better not be a salesperson waking her up on her day off.

"Hello?" She rubbed her knuckles over her eyes before pushing the hair out of her face.

"Emilie?" The distorted intercom sounded with a man's voice. Definitely someone who knew her. The buzzer downstairs for her unit simply said "Hunt" in neat block letters.

"Yes?" She stifled a yawn into the back of her hand.

"It's Colin." A quick pause was followed by, "Abernan. From the hospital?" He said it as if she didn't know who he was.

Her heartbeat immediately quickened as her groggy brain put together that Colin was at her door, and that she was braless in her pajamas. When he spoke again, she realized that she never responded to him, just stood there frozen with her finger on the intercom button.

"Can I speak to you for a minute?"

She sputtered a response. "Um, uh, yeah. Just wait at the top of the stairs. I'm not dressed."

Why did I say that?

A pause was followed by the sound of him clearing his throat. "Okay."

She pushed the button to open the entry door to the building and ran as fast as she could to her bedroom, throwing on a pair of leggings, a bra, and an oversized wide neck sweatshirt from her alma mater. Pulling the sheets over her bed, she stopped, wondering why she would make her bed when he wasn't going to see it and instead rushed to brush her teeth instead. She quickly finger combed her hair and took a look at her main room.

Generally, she wasn't a messy person and kept her condo picked up, but currently it was in a state of slovenliness. She bustled around the room tidying with the speed and efficiency of a spider untangling a fallen leaf from its web. At the door, she took several settling deep breaths before reaching to open it. While she stretched her hand toward the handle, it dawned on her that he probably heard her running around like a mad woman.

Colin was facing away with his hands on the banister. When he turned to her with a shy grin, her already speeding pulse quickened. It was an endearing look on a powerful man.

She'd only seen him wearing surgical scrubs, workout clothes, or a suit at the Christmas party. As incredibly handsome as he had looked in his tailored suit, he looked completely different in casual clothes.

A blue and grey plaid flannel laced with hopeful thin stripes of yellow was layered over well-worn jeans and scuffed leather boots. The shade of his shirt made his eyes even more striking than normal. There was an easy ruggedness to him that suggested he was as comfortable alone in the woods as he was scrubbed into surgery. A long navy wool coat covered his attire, and he must have driven here since he was lacking the accoutrement of walking in the snow.

It had been three days since he walked her home from work. Three days since she'd cried through his scrubs onto his strong, solid chest. Since she had felt so completely safe and secure in his arms. Three days since she'd felt giddy and light bantering with him as they walked in the falling snow. Wasn't three days the requisite time before calling a girl back after a date?

"Hey." His voice brought her out of her cogitation.

"Hi." She felt a smile tug on her lips before her brain reminded her to explain her appearance. "I'm not a morning person. I usually sleep in on my days off."

He looked as if he had majorly overstepped. "Oh, I'm sorry. Did I wake you up?"

"It's fine. I needed to get up anyway." She looked into her condo towards the microwave clock. She really needed to get a real clock and hang it on the wall; there was no way she could see the time from here. "What time is it?"

Pushing his coat sleeve up, he glanced at his watch. "Almost nine thirty."

She was still standing in her doorway, and he was still on the landing.

"Why don't you come in?" She moved out of the threshold. "I need some coffee. Do you want some?"

"That would be great." His shoulders visibly relaxed.

Leaving him to close the door behind them, she busied herself in the kitchen making coffee. She caught her slight reflection in the kitchen window and wished she'd taken the time to wash her face and properly brush her hair. Colin laid his coat over the same armchair he sat in when he was here last time before joining her at the kitchen island.

"Black, right?"

The grin that pulled at his lips as he said "yes" had her blinking hard. She turned to pull two mugs from the cabinet, keeping herself moving so she wouldn't reveal her nervousness. Today would have been a good day to have used the timer on her coffee maker so that it would have been ready now.

"I wanted to talk to you about something. Something I wanted to mention the other day at work."

Ohhhh crap.

She had misread the situation entirely. Her eyes squeezed shut in embarrassment for a second before strongly walking to the island and placing her hands on it.

"I'm sorry about that. It's just Bo and Mary became like family to me, if that makes sense. I'm incredibly close with mine, and this is my first time moving away from them aside for when I went to college, and even then I had my sister with me. I didn't mean to act unprofessionally in any way. I was just overcome when she died." The last word caught in her constricting throat.

Her eyes drifted to the countertop remembering how small Mary looked swallowed up in a green checkered hospital gown, monitors bleating all around her. A heaviness pushed on her, and she fought to take a deep breath against it reminding herself how Mary had been surrounded by everyone who had loved her—her family by blood and the family she built from those in her community.

"Emilie."

She'd been so lost in her own thoughts, she hadn't noticed him move beside her. His subtle, comforting scent reached her nose as he gently laid his hand over hers. As her skin relaxed at the warm solid weight of his hand, she tried to control her response. He was just being kind like he'd been the other night.

"That's not what I wanted to talk to you about." His voice was low.

She chanced getting lost in his beautiful eyes. "It's not?"

He searched her face. "No, but if you would like to talk about it, I'm happy to listen."

Feeling her heart leap into her throat, she asked, "Why are you here?"

Colin opened his mouth as if to explain in a reasoned manner his presence in her home before his eyes lingered on her lips. She felt herself holding her breath as anticipation surged through her veins. Closing his mouth, he leaned slightly toward her, decreasing space between them. His other hand found her cheek and with the tenderest caress, he tilted her face towards hers.

"For you."

Her eyes fluttered closed, sighing the breath her lungs had held into his lips as they pressed gingerly to her own. All the pent-up tension she'd tried to ignore since Christmas relaxed in an immediate sweeping sensation. Everything about this moment, the heat rising from his body, the smell of his skin, the buzzing of his lips on hers, felt right. Her fingertips tingled as her hands hesitantly raised, brushing lightly against the flannel fabric covering his biceps before pushing her palms flat to grip his arms.

A slight groan vibrated against her mouth as she felt his other arm wrap snugly around her waist. Pressed against him, heat soared instantly though her body. Her lips parted at the surprising pleasure of his strong and solid frame against hers. When she felt the slight touch of his tongue, hers raced to touch, to taste, to savor him. He sweetly explored her mouth, never letting the tender caress of his thumb leave her face.

Her hands wove up his arms, over the skin at his collar, and into his sandy hair. An image of his boyish locks tousled between her fingers as he hovered over her naked flashed through her mind. Shocked by the brazenness of her thoughts, she pulled back.

His body stilled with her hesitation, but he savored her lips one last time before lifting his face. He was breathing as hard as she was, his collar bones rising and falling under her gaze. The coffee machine gurgled in finality before punctuating the silence of the room with a resounding beep. She took a step back from him, staring into his dilated eyes in disbelief.

Moving away towards the coffee machine, she poured two cups of coffee with a not-so-stable hand. When she felt him step behind her, she tried not to lean towards his radiant heat. With delicate hands, he pulled the hair from her shoulder and held it aside as he kissed the side of her neck.

Her body responded instantly.

A low hum escaped from her mouth as her eyes closed, tilting her head away from his kiss to expose more of her skin.

Instead of kissing her again, he reached beyond her, his chest brushing against her back as he gathered up a cup of coffee. After a steadying breath, she turned to find him leaning, legs crossed at the ankles, against the island facing her. She glued herself to the kitchen counter and took up her cup as well.

"I would like to ask you out on a date." He sipped his coffee casually.

Here was the arrogance she'd expected from a surgeon. Only on him it wasn't arrogant at all, just a confidence that was incredibly sexy.

"Would you now?"

"Yes." He grinned with a hint of mischief in his eyes.

Why did she feel so bubbly when he smiled like that?

"I'm not sure. I have a very busy schedule," she teased.

He dropped the act as sincerity swept his face. "If you can find time, it would be my extreme pleasure to take you to dinner."

The implications of his request finally hit her brain. An unexpected tornado of thoughts and emotions overwhelmed her. Was she really doing this? Was she going to commit to her first first date in more than eleven years? A fierce jerk went through her body realizing that this was the first time she'd kissed a man other than her husband since she'd been married. Her stomach flipped, and unconsciously she wrung at the ring finger of her left hand.

The conflict must have read on her face because Colin set his mug down and took a step towards her. He reached out his hand but then placed it firmly at his side. "I'm sorry if I upset you." His hand ran through his hair. "It's just . . . I'd really like to get to know you better."

She knew he hadn't meant to upset her, but it was much too early to explain to him why she was having reservations.

"Can we take it slow?" Her voice came out timidly.

A breath escaped his lungs. "I can do slow."

She nodded and took a sip of coffee to steady herself.

"How about lunch instead?" he countered.

She grinned slightly. "Lunch would be good." Thinking of the business she'd recently passed just outside the Commons, she added, "On one condition."

"Name it." He settled back on the island and took up his mug.

"There's a piano store just south of the Commons. After lunch, I want you to take me there and play something."

The mournful look that had crossed his face when he mentioned not being able to play the piano anymore had stuck a barb between her ribs. She wanted to bring him the joy she'd witness when he'd been behind the keys at the Christmas party. Another part of her longed to watch his skillful fingers and his toned body rock with the music as he played.

"What would you like to hear?"

She hadn't anticipated that question, but the answer materialized instantly. "Your favorite song."

Colin nodded once, his mouth curving upward in a slow smile. "When would you like to go to lunch?"

"I'm off next Friday."

He set his mug back on the counter and took his phone out of his pocket. "That will work. Could I get your number? It would stop me from coming to your home every time I need to talk to you." That teasing glimmer was back in his eyes.

A chuckle burst from her lips before she rattled off her number.

"I'll pick you up at noon? Hopefully, that won't be too early?" The left side of his mouth tugged up.

She narrowed her eyes playfully. "I'll be awake and dressed by then."

Colin opened his mouth as if to say something but closed it and went to gather his coat from the armchair. She followed him to the door, and when he walked through and turned around, anticipation surged through her, catching a swallow in her throat. He leaned towards her, then gave her a very gentlemanly kiss her on the cheek.

His grin was wide when he pulled back. "I'll see you next week, Emilie."

A strangled "See you then" was all she could manage as she watched him stretch his powerful body to gracefully put on his coat.

She was still standing there staring when he turned at the half flight to wave up to her. Raising her hand to wave back, effervescence coursed through her veins. Colin smiled again before disappearing down the stairwell. After shutting the door, she leaned against it, giddy for a breath before the implications of what she'd just agreed to hit her chest with a smack.

·CHAPTER 20·

The leather of Colin's glove pushed against his fingertip as he compressed the small red button next to "Hunt."

Almost immediately, he heard a staticky. "Colin?"

He smiled. Even with the interference, he didn't think he'd ever tire of hearing her say his name. "It's me."

The door buzzed open, and he forced himself to slowly walk up the three flights of stairs instead of taking them two at a time like he wanted to. When he arrived at the landing, he took a second for a deep, settling breath before he knocked. It didn't matter. Once she pulled the door open, his breath caught in his throat anyway.

A snug cobalt blue sweater with a shallow V-neck topped skinny jeans that hugged the curves of her hips and tightly circled her legs, ending in camel mid-calf boots. Her hair was down and curled the way it had been for the Christmas party in relaxed spiraling tendrils. The thing he noticed the most was how her chestnut eyes lit up as they focused on his and those lips curved up in a smile.

"Hi."

"Hey," he said when his breath finally returned to him. "You look . . ." *Gorgeous. Radiant. Stunning.* He settled on a word that was appropriate and hopefully wouldn't send her back pedaling. ". . . beautiful."

"Thank you." She tilted her head down as she'd done at the party.

He wanted to wrap her in his arms again, but he cleared his throat and made himself focus. Today was about getting to know Emilie better and not scaring her off. "Ready for lunch?"

"Yeah. Let me just grab my coat." She ducked into the small closet nearby. "Are we walking?"

"No, I'm driving."

Once on the landing, he gestured to her coat. "May I?"

The corners of her mouth tugged into a shy grin before handing it to him. Once she'd shrugged into it, he debated gently pulling all that thick hair from its wool prison, but she wove her hand behind her head and freed it before he had a chance. He gestured his hand to the stairs and allowed her to walk before him, trying not to be too obvious of the fact he was inhaling her sweet floral scent. When they arrived at the ground floor, he held open the door of the building and then the passenger door for her to a repeat of, "Thank you."

Once he'd settled in the driver's seat she asked, "Where are we going to lunch?"

"Do you like Chinese?"

"Who doesn't like Chinese?" Her voice held that joking quality he loved.

"Just wanted to make sure." A grin laced his lips as he checked his rear-view mirror and pulled into the snow cleared lane.

The restaurant was only a mile and a half from her house, but in winter city traffic, it took twenty minutes. He'd found a garage across the street ahead of time, so she wouldn't be too cold walking outside, though the cold didn't seem to bother her. He'd tightened his scarf and buttoned his coat to his neck, but she let hers gape open as he led her across the street.

The restaurant looked like many of the others in Chinatown. Wood floors with white cloth covered tables in different sizes surrounded by red cushioned and gold trimmed chairs. The ceiling was painted gold with a huge, circular low-profile glass chandelier, and the wallpaper was the same red with gold floral accents. He told the hostess "two" and they walked past a cart of steaming metal containers on the way to their table.

A waitress took a card from their table writing something on it before nodding to them. "Hot tea?"

At their request, she was soon back with two glasses of water and a stainless-steel pot full of steaming Oolong. Emilie turned over the cup on her plate and poured herself tea from the pot before taking the chopsticks from their paper case.

"Have you had dim sum before?"

She rubbed her chopsticks together while craning her gorgeous neck to look at all the different carts. "No, but I like adventure eating."

He almost spat out his tea, stifling a laugh. "Adventure eating?"

"You know, eating something you've never had before." She was watching the six Chinese men in suits at the table next to them serving themselves dumplings from a lazy susan.

"We don't have to eat chicken feet if you don't want to."

"If that is what you normally order, then I'll try it."

This woman is amazing.

He ordered a variety of different things, so she could try a bit of everything, but left off the chicken feet because truly he didn't care for them. As she bit into a piece of shumai, she momentarily closed her eyes and hummed her approval, licking the slick pork fat from her lips. His chopsticks froze in midair, heat rapidly flushing through his muscles as he stared at her. Fortunately, he was saved by the congee cart and ordered her a bowl.

"You said before that you were from Virginia." He picked up a har gow and dipped it into the red chili sauce on his plate.

She took a quick sip of tea. "Yeah, Virginia Beach. You grew up near the beach too, right?"

"Yes." He said around his bite.

"Do you miss it?"

"Yes, but we are right on the water here too. Of course, it's a little different than what you and I are both used to. It's a bigger city, but there are beaches around the city and up and down the coast. I've been told that there's a massive clambake over Fourth of July that CTSB hosts. Apparently, it puts the Christmas party to shame."

Another cart brought them potstickers and steamed pork buns.

"I heard about that too. I've never been to a clambake."

"Me neither."

"Adventure eating!" she declared a bit too loudly with raised chopsticks.

A few of the businessmen glanced over, and they both dissolved into a fit of laughter, trying hard to compose themselves.

"I like how much you make me laugh," he said when they caught their breaths.

The sound of the carts pushing on their steel wheels, many people talking in a variety of different languages, and the clicking of so many small round containers being placed on tables all drifted away to nothing as she said, "Me too."

He mentally shook himself. "Is your family in Virginia?"

"Yeah, my parents and my sister. My mom and dad still live in the same house I was raised in, but my sister and her family live in the next city over. It's kinda like here and the suburbs. They are all different cities, but only fifteen miles away from each other."

Picking up another morsel, he asked, "Is your sister older or younger?"

"We're identical twins."

Glancing up, he found her watching him. "Really?"

She seemed to expect that reaction. He was sure that people found the fact that she had an identical twin fascinating, but likely not for the reasons that were flying through his mind. He didn't think there could be any more beauty in the world, but the universe had made a carbon copy of hers. A blush of jealousy that her sister's husband already had the joy of calling someone like Emilie his own rushed through his body.

She nodded before taking up a spoonful of congee. "Do you have any siblings?"

"No, it was always just me."

After swallowing, she asked, "Do your parents still live in North Carolina?"

He knew this question would be coming, and he was prepared for it. "My mom died of cancer when I was thirteen, and my dad died in May."

She nearly choked on her second spoonful of soup. "This past May?" Placing her spoon down, she reached for his arm over the table. "I'm so . . ." She stopped. "I know there are no words."

He swallowed against the tightness in his throat, allowing his head to hang heavy with a resigned exhale. The gentle weight of her hand on his forearm was more soothing than she would ever know. "Thank you."

Her fingers wrapped and then squeezed his arm before releasing it. "Do you want to talk about it?"

"Not today," he said in a way that hopefully conveyed that he wanted to continue their fun date instead of talking about his misfortune.

Taking his hint she asked lightly, "What are you going to play for me?"

He tried to keep the smirk from his smile. "You'll have to wait and see."

◊◊◊

Colin was lucky to find street parking near the piano store that she directed him to after they finished their lunch. A large sign with a treble clef on it advertised the shop to the street. He held the door open for her as they walked into the building. There was a coat rack by the door, and he helped her out of hers before placing his over it on the rack. An elderly gentleman in a blue suit with a complimenting blue herringbone bow tie approached them.

"Welcome. How can I help you today?" His white mustache rose as he smiled.

"He's here to buy a piano," Emilie stated.

Colin's head snapped to stare at her.

"What kind of space do you have?" the man asked her. "We have mostly grand pianos on this floor, but upstairs we have a few uprights."

The salesman probably thought they were a couple, maybe even lived together. The thought warmed and stirred something in his chest.

Emilie looked at him to answer and he coughed. "Unfortunately, it would have to be an upright." He shrugged. "City living."

They followed the gentleman upstairs to a white bricked room filled with at least ten grand pianos. In the corner sat two uprights: one in a lacquered black, and the other a warm walnut that looked just like his family piano. He walked silently to the walnut one and paused a moment before pulling back the humble wooden bench to have a seat.

"We'll just need a minute," she said.

"Take your time." The old man's footfalls receded down the stairs.

Lifting the fallboard, he gently pushed it back from the white and black keys. He'd forgotten she was behind him until she pulled the black piano bench right next to his. With a little melodic noise, she sat and put her large purse on the other side of the bench, scooting even closer to him. He took a halting inhale, not sure if he could play mistake free with her so close.

"So what'll it be?"

He glanced at her lovely freckled face. "I was classically trained, so it won't be a popular song like I played at the party."

"I like all music. I even contribute to the local PBS station. I used to put classical music on in the car back home to keep me from road raging on all the other incompetent drivers." She braced her hands behind her on the bench and leaned back.

"Sounds like you are an aggressive driver," he teased.

"I'm pretty forgiving of most things, but if you don't know how to drive, you shouldn't be on the road." She pointed to the piano. "You're stalling. This was part of our deal. My lunch company for your favorite song."

He leaned forward, his hands hovering just over the keys before starting with the strong first few bars of music.

Letting his body relax, he felt that lightness he always did when he played this piece. The dominant cadence led into the repeat with the momentary key change before lightening to a hint of his favorite part to come.

Circling through the repeats, he finally reached the counter melody; it sang out so sweetly to him, as if the piano was expressing his innermost soul. A familiar flush resonated over his skin as his right hand delicately held the longer notes while his left hand wavered over and over creating a rolling, undulating balance to the pleading nature of the right.

Gradually picking up the main theme, he increased the volume and vigor, pounding out the joyful notes. His fingers felt as if they were dancing out the next several bars, accelerating rapidly to the end. With a quick, quiet prance of the final two keys, he immediately pulled his hands from the piano.

"'Rachmaninoff's Prelude in G minor.' Nicely done!" The gentleman's voice brought him out of his musical focus and back to his surroundings.

He turned over his shoulder to nod his thanks to the older man, and saw that Emilie seemed to be in a trance gazing at where his hands had been over the keys. It took her several seconds to notice that the salesman was standing next to them again.

When she eventually pulled her eyes from the still subtly vibrating piano, she grinned playfully at the salesman. "It's no 'Flight of the Bumblebee.'"

Colin waited until her eyes met his before letting a smirk lace his lips and turning to the keys. Starting into the rapid song she'd just listed, he continued for about ten seconds, which was enough of the piece to make his point before laughing and pulling his hands from the piano.

"I haven't played that one in a while. I only remember the beginning."

Her open mouth and look of shock said it all.

"With your talent, you really should have a piano at home." The older man winked, seeming to figure out that the woman accompanying him was not someone whom he lived with, but whom he wanted to impress. "I'll be downstairs when you are ready."

Emilie watched the elderly man's wispy white head disappear before turning to him. "I didn't know you could play like that."

He quietly folded his hands in his lap humming with satisfaction. Twice this week, he'd snuck into the hospital lobby to practice before his morning surgery just so he could have this effect on her today. Once a crabby security guard had even kicked him off halfway through.

"That was one of the most beautiful things I've ever heard." Her gaze was transfixed on the piano keys while her chest heaved slightly. Soft brown eyes flitted to his. "Do you know many other songs by heart?"

"Yes." His lips curved high at her surprised face.

Out of nowhere, she punched him in the arm. *Hard.*

"You sneak! You've done this before. I'm sure the ladies love a man who plays piano."

"*You're* the one that brought us here, not me," he reminded her.

She let out an exasperated huff of air. "I thought you would just play 'Let It Be' or something."

As he turned his body back to the piano and lifted his hands over the keys, she grabbed for his forearm. "Don't you dare."

His pulse quickened under her grip, while his gaze fixed on her hand on his arm. Her body froze, seemingly understanding the closeness she'd created in holding him back from the piano. Buzzing energy surged through his body as his focus shifted to how her lips were parted while she took short, shallow breaths. Whether intentional or not, she wet them and he could no longer resist the driving hunger that vibrated through his body since she'd opened the door hours ago.

Placing the hand she gripped on the bench between them, he weaved the other through her hair, kissing her soundly on her freshly moistened lips. Emilie didn't tense or pull back but melted into the hand behind her head while her grip tightened on his forearm. She parted her lips with a delicious sigh, and he deepened the kiss.

The blinding pleasure of kissing her made him forget any knowledge of the world beside where her body touched his. The space between them lit up like an electrical storm, and he had a powerful urge to decrease it as fast as possible, wishing he wasn't balancing them with his other hand, so he could pull her closer.

As her tongue played lightly with his, she leaned slightly forward and finally released his arm. Reaching behind her hip, he pulled her flush to him on the bench. She bounced down a fraction of an inch, as her bench was slightly higher, with an amused sound before weaving her arm around his back. A low groan escaped his throat as she pressed her chest to his.

He was a man of action and no control as she licked the edges of his mouth. Pulling one of her legs over his until she was firmly straddling his lap, he repositioned his hands, exploring her waist. Slender fingers wove carelessly through the hair at the back of his neck as her forearms pressed down on either side of his neck.

Her mouth never left his, and he let his hands float higher, gently fingering the sides of her ribs. When his thumbs barely grazed below her bra line, her breath caught, and he knew in an instant he'd gone too far. Internally, he called himself every word for idiot he knew. She rested her forehead on his, eyes closed, as her breaths heaved.

"We are in a piano store," she said, her voice raspy.

"Yes." He exhaled, trying to catch his own breath while watching her.

"I am on your lap." She pulled her face away, and her glossy eyes focused his own.

"Yes." He was exquisitely aware of her body on top of his.

Emilie slowly moved to stand, swinging her legs off of him while keeping her eyes on his. "This is not slow."

Never taking his gaze off her gorgeous eyes he repeated, "This is not slow."

Breaking their eye contact, she gazed back at the black bench before sitting. With every fiber in his being, he resisted the urge to touch her. Sitting, staring ahead, she blew out a large breath then started to chuckle. The pearlescent sound of her earnest laughter always made him feel light and strangely satisfied.

"What?"

"I think you have to buy that piano now. It's been used."

He thought of the many different ways that it could be used before he dragged his mind back to reality to respond. "I suppose so."

Her eyes and voice were serious when she looked at him. "Will you, though? Buy it, I mean?"

He shrugged. "No, probably not."

"But it makes you so happy."

He wanted to argue that kissing her made him happier than a piano, but she was right. Music was a part of who he was. It connected him to his past, what he'd been through, and his newly forming dreams of the future. An image of a swollen bellied Emilie sitting on the bench next to him while he played flashed through his mind, followed quickly by teaching little fingers beginning scales.

She broke through his vision. "Not to be rude, but don't you have enough disposable income for a piano? You're a heart surgeon, and you drive a Subaru."

A laugh burst from his mouth. "What's wrong with my car?"

"Nothing. I like your car. I like how down to earth you are, but I don't think you should deny yourself this." She reached up and brushed a strand of hair from his forehead.

How is it that she seemed to understand without him having to tell her a word?

As if on cue, the gentleman returned upstairs again, this time leading a mother and her two tween children. "There is one upright left. I believe this gentleman is purchasing the walnut one. Is that correct, sir?"

Emilie smiled brightly and answered for him. "Yes, he is."

·CHAPTER 21·

Closing the washer lid and hitting the start button Emilie asked, "Are you sure you don't want to run your laundry first?"

Ash's voice answered from the kitchen. "No. I'm off tomorrow. I'll get it all done then. Most of it is caked in dirt anyway, so it'll require multiple washes."

"You amaze me. I've camped with friends before, but never done it by myself."

Emilie closed the closet door and turned to find Ash standing in the hallway with two large glasses of red wine. Her friend was in a pair of yoga pants and a hunter green half-zip pullover, somehow making the ensemble look stunning in addition to cozy.

Her shoulders lifted. "I'm used to it. I spent a lot of my younger years running around and sleeping in the desert. Solo backpacking was kind of a natural hobby for me." She took a large gulp of wine. "It was nice to hear quiet again. It's so noisy in the city, even at night."

"I'm still amazed."

"I'm amazed you've been here ten minutes and you haven't spilled the details of your date." Ash arched a golden eyebrow.

Something about the girly way Ash was excited about her date made Emilie feel like a twenty-something dating again, instead of a widow starting over. She wasn't sure if her observant friend did it on purpose, but it allowed her to feel joy over this new situation instead of concentrating on the reason she was dating in the first place.

Emilie pointed with her wine glass. "I was being polite asking about your trip first."

"Uh-huh. Are you sure you wouldn't rather be with Dr. Love tonight?" A sly smile laced Ash's lips.

"No, I want to be here with you. Besides, we went on *one* lunch date. It's a little early to be spending Valentine's together."

"So he's out there breaking hearts?"

"More like fixing them. He's on call tonight." She wondered if he was already at the hospital or maybe somewhere in this building at this very moment waiting for his pager to beep.

"When are you seeing him again?"

"Sunday."

Colin had asked for a second date as soon as he dropped her off, but instead of confirming, she said she'd text her availability later. As much as her body ached for more when he leaned over to kiss her cheek goodbye, she decided to space out their dates in an effort to keep things slow. Next time it would be harder to get caught up in him since she was choosing such a public place for their second date.

"Mmmm." Ash walked to the kitchen where their heart-shaped pepperoni pizza was waiting. Setting her wine down on the kitchen counter, she opened a nearby cabinet. "Do you want me to make a salad?"

"No. I think we can just eat pizza and wine tonight, and not feel bad about it."

Her friend's smile was luminescent. "Agreed!"

Placing a plate in front of them both, Ash opened the box and served them both two slices of pizza. Her friend allowed them each a few bites of greasy, savory deliciousness before she asked, "So are you going to give me all the details, or am I going to have to coax them out of you with more wine?"

Honestly, she'd been waiting all week to tell Ash the details, to have someone to talk about this new step she was taking. So far no one knew but her and Colin. She felt strange omitting the date from her last call with Analie or her parents, but she wanted to see how this all played out before looping her family in.

Ash only knew "Boston Emilie" the woman that, yes, was broken, but also the woman who was building herself back up. Her friend had only seen her as a single entity, not as a wife and mother. Her whole family had seen both.

The biggest problem she was having was that being with Colin was oddly easy. Outside of potentially getting caught making out on top of a piano bench by a mother and her young children, the first date she'd had in over a decade had gone off without a hitch. Something about that seemed wrong. Her brain had run through it over and over, trying to find out why things had flowed so smoothly. The only explanation that made sense was it must have been because they already knew each other from work.

Taking a large gulp of wine, Emilie let the tart blackberry currant taste wash over her mouth before she gave Ash all the details she craved. She recounted how he'd been a perfect gentleman, the delicious lunch, how they had laughed and shared more information about themselves learning all the little things that you do on a first date: likes and dislikes, hobbies, where you went to school, who punched who when you were eleven. Just retelling the afternoon made her lips curl into a smile.

"That sounds like a perfect first date." Her friend punctuated her point by clinking her glass.

The only part that could have constituted as imperfect was Colin's palpable sorrow when he told her about his father's death. The way he bent his head in the restaurant made her want to hold and rock him. Another time maybe he would allow her to listen while he talked about it.

"It was, but there's more to it." She'd been replaying the date in her mind all week, but if Emilie let her mind wander, she found herself focusing on the second half.

Ash bit into her pizza and spoke from behind the back of her hand. "Oh?"

"I told you how he came to ask me out at my condo—"

"Oh yes, you did," Ash interrupted, winking.

She rolled her eyes. "Yeah, yeah, we made out like teenagers. Is that what you want to hear?"

"Yes." Her grin was wide with satisfaction. "At least one of us is."

Unfortunately, Ash met and started dating another crappy guy a few days after her birthday. Before she left for her trip she broke up with him, swearing off men all together, saying if she couldn't make a good choice in a man, she was better off without them.

"Like I was saying, when he asked me out, I felt I needed to feel some control over—"

Her friend interrupted again, but this time her voice was very serious. "You are always in control. If there's any man who makes you feel otherwise, tell me, and I will kick his ass."

Emilie believed her. As sweet as Ash was, she was also loyal to a degree that made you believe she would happily inflict bodily harm on your behalf.

"I know. I didn't mean it like that."

"Good." Ash set down her glass. "Offer still stands."

Her lips pulled up at her friend's protectiveness. "So after lunch, I had him take me to a piano store and play me his favorite song."

"Ooohhh, I see." She slapped the table, laughing. "A little 'Dance, Monkey, Dance!' Aren't you clever?"

Emilie chuckled. "It totally backfired. I mean we did go, and he did play me a song, but . . ." A sigh broke from her throat. ". . . he is so incredibly talented." Her mind played the memory of his long fingers stroking the piano keys with different intensities, coaxing it to make whatever sound he wanted.

"Did you expect something different? The song at the Christmas party was really good."

"I'm not sure what I expected. I guess I enjoyed watching him play at the party, and I wanted to see that again. We talked a bit when you disappeared to 'get me a drink'—" She used finger quotes.

"You're welcome."

"—and he talked about how he hadn't played since he moved to Boston. He just looked so sad about it. I thought if we went to the store, I could see him play, and it would bring him that same joy again."

Ash topped off their wine glasses. "Hmmmm, so what part of it backfired?"

"When he played his favorite song, it changed the way he played. He was magnetic with this quiet focus that was tender and at the same time incredibly sexy . . ."

Colin moved something deep inside of her when he played, something she didn't quite understand. She knew she brought him to the store and asked him to play, but the minute he turned to the keys, she understood that it was as much for him as it was for her. It was a true gift to witness someone doing the thing they loved.

Her friend waited patiently this time as she looked up from her memory. "Then he started showing off. To be fair, I might have instigated it."

"Might have?"

"I might have challenged him to play 'Flight of the Bumblebee' which, of course, he could do." She took an irritated sip of wine.

"I'm not much for classical music, but isn't that a really hard song? It seems fast anyway."

"That's the point. Apparently, he has this huge repertoire under his fingers. I called him on it, and we were joking back and forth." She swallowed.

"And?" Ash seemed to know where this was going.

She buried her head in her sweatshirt-covered arms on the table. "We ended up making out again, but in the store, right on top of the piano bench."

"Nice!"

She leaned up, swatting at her friend.

"What? You of all people deserve a good makeout." Green eyes glinted with earnestness before she lightened them to ask, "How was it?"

"Incredible. It's a little weird for me to feel so instantly comfortable with him, but I do, and when that happens, I just want to be as close as I can get."

"I *bet* you do." Ash smirked.

"The thing is . . ." She felt her ribs tighten instantly as her thoughts shifted. "I never know how I'll feel after. This is all so new to me, and as enjoyable as it is, I'm sometimes racked with guilt after." A slow exhale left her lungs.

When Colin had kissed her the first time, everything felt completely right. Being with him almost gave her temporary amnesia to the pain of her past until it came crashing through later. After he left, she'd paced the hardwood floor of her condo, racing her thumb over her fingertips and wondering if she'd just agreed to something she wasn't ready for. As the days passed, her anxiety about starting over lessened a tiny fraction each hour until eventually he was standing at her door again, looking at her with those mystifying blue-grey eyes.

"This time was different though. I don't know if that's because it was the second time it happened, or I was more comfortable with the idea, or what."

Ash's hand dropped over her own. "You never have to do anything you're not ready for."

"I know, and he's really good at listening if I pump the breaks, so I think that's one of the reasons I trust myself with him." Speaking the sentence out loud was the first time it occurred to her.

"That's really good, Emilie."

It was. It was good to feel safe. It was good to feel safe, but also respected and listened to. She also felt wanted, and on some level needed, though she wasn't sure why.

"Are you going to tell him?" her friend asked gently.

Her stomach flipped involuntarily. "I don't know. Nia said to be up front when I started dating and tell the person where I'm coming from, but what if this never really goes anywhere, and we go back to being coworkers, and he knows my whole life story? For some reason, that just makes me feel vulnerable."

"I know your story and we work together. So does Barbara and she's your boss," Ash pointed out.

"Ugh, I know, I think . . ." She pushed her plate away. "I think I'm just scared to start over in the first place, and I'm not ready to share that part of me yet. There's already the added stress that we work together, and it will be awkward if it doesn't work out."

Ash sipped her wine thoughtfully. "I'm no Nia, but that sounds reasonable to me."

An intense need to shift the focus off of her stirred in Emilie's veins. "Have you been to Bo's since . . . ?" A deep inhale filled her lungs. She hadn't been able to make herself go to the diner since Mary's death. The idea of the space behind the bar where her friend had laughed with her so often being empty set a thorny pit at the base of her spine. "I was thinking of giving my condolences tomorrow and bringing flowers."

"I went before I left. Everyone is still there working. Bo's at the door, and Shannon is running things, but they are obviously heartbroken. I guess when a restaurant is your livelihood you can't just close it down to grieve." Her friend paused, staring off as a clock ticked softly in the background. "If you want to bring flowers, there's a collection of them near Mary's booth. You aren't the only one with that idea. It almost looked like a shrine . . . It must be so hard on them to be somewhere everyday where she was with them and now, she's not."

Ash unwittingly described how every person who'd ever lost a close loved one felt about living without them.

Emilie's head dropped as the familiar heaviness set around her lungs. Running her fingertips over the soft fabric of her sweatshirt, she tried to ground herself in this moment with her friend and not return to any prior ones.

Ash's voice was bright when she spoke again. "Okay, let's shift gears."

When she lifted her gaze, her friend winked.

"We're supposed to be having a fun girl's night in, so for tonight's entertainment, I want as much hot man as I can get. Preferably shirtless."

Surprised by the swift topic swing, Emilie broke into laughter despite herself.

"I don't want to watch a romantic comedy because that would make me weepy, so it's any of the Marvel movies. And yes, I own them all. I'm particular to Thor when he's walking around Earth in jeans and a T-shirt. Yum! Also, the long hair." She hummed. "Or I found the *Baywatch* movie on Netflix. Which is just gratuitous oiled up nakedness of The Rock and Zac Effron. I hear the plot is stupid, but does it matter?"

Another laugh burst from her lips before she tapped her finger to her chin. "Tough choices all around. I'm thinking we max out on hot man nakedness and go for *Baywatch*. Two for the price of one."

Ash hopped off her stool, taking her wine glass to the couch. "Pecs and abs here we come!"

·CHAPTER 22·

There must have been some pact that he secretly made with the sun. It agreed with all its powerful burning fury to give two tiny humans idyllic conditions whenever they were together. Colin lifted his face and basked in the slight warmth on this ice-cold afternoon. It was a strange thing to be so happy waiting on a park bench in the middle of a freezing, snow-covered landscape.

"Hi."

Emilie's voice brought a grin to his lips as he looked at the path. "Hey."

She walked up to him with a slight swagger in her step. "Ready for our second date?"

He loved when she was like this, when a quiet strength emanated from her. He'd bet good money she had no idea how incredibly sexy she was.

Standing, he clapped his gloved hands together. "Absolutely, what are we doing today?"

A slight mischievous twist of her mouth let him know that he was either in for the time of his life or big trouble. Perhaps both. "Ice skating. Have you skated before?"

It was then he noticed that the large bag on her shoulder was not her purse, but an equipment bag.

A twitchy sensation ran down his arms. "Not really." The one time he'd gone skating as a boy hadn't gone well, but he was an athletic adult now. He'd figure it out. How hard could it be?

Colin wasn't sure, but he thought he saw a smirk out of the corner of his eye.

"You're in for a treat then because we get to skate in the middle of the Commons." Her face tilted towards the cloudless sky. "The weather couldn't be better."

"It is nice out," he agreed, despite winter not being his favorite.

"There's a coffee shop a block from where we met. Afterwards, I thought we could warm up and talk." She shifted the weight of the bag on her shoulder.

"Sounds like a plan. What's in the bag?" he asked, half knowing the answer.

"My skates." That deliciously wicked smile touched her lips again as they arrived at the picturesque ice rink.

It was like a sight out of a movie. A low green-rimmed half-wall separated a well-maintained ice rink from the rest of the snowy landscape. He recognized the area as the low-lying pond he'd run past in warmer months. Trees stretched around one side of the rink still covered in the last bits of the snowfall from a few days ago. On the other side of the rink stood a large pavilion where he assumed he'd be renting his skates. Beyond the rink, the city expanded in all directions, the light reflecting off the windows of the expansive buildings.

She led him to the counter to buy admission to the rink and waved him off when he went to reach for his wallet.

"I planned this date, so it's on me," she said in a way that he couldn't argue against.

Sitting to change into their skates, he was surprised when she pulled hockey skates out of her bag. His face must have betrayed his thoughts because she commented, "My dad's from Rochester and played hockey growing up. Even played in an amateur league for fun while we were kids.

"He took me and my sister to the rink with him when we were little and taught us to skate. Unfortunately for him, neither of us showed any interest in playing hockey, but we always loved skating with him. We still go skating every winter." A chuckle bubbled free of her mouth. "The three of us do anyway. My mom wouldn't be caught dead on the ice."

"Your mom and I sound like we'd get along." He grinned.

After they locked all their things away in a locker, Colin walked the awkward skate-restricted steps to the edge of the rink. Several people were taking advantage of the beautiful weekend afternoon turning the circle of the rink over and over.

"Any tips?" He decided to just lay his ignorance bare.

She pushed easily onto the ice before turning around to face him. "Would you like a lesson?"

That teasing smile of hers was going to be his undoing today. "Please."

"You'll have to come on the ice first."

Emilie was clearly enjoying this.

Carefully holding onto the wall with one hand, he placed his first skate on the ice. So far, so good. When the second one followed, he felt the easy give beneath his feet and grabbed the wall with both hands. He swore he heard a restricted giggle behind him before she skated up next to him.

"Get your balance first. Try to keep your weight over the skates evenly and bend your knees."

He studiously followed her instructions.

"Good, now let go of the wall and take a few little steps forward." As he let one hand off the wall, she gathered it strongly in hers.

Normally, he would've reveled in the contact, but he was focusing too hard on not making a complete fool of himself. After a few unsteady, tentative steps, his balance evened out.

"Now, push a bit more with each step and allow your toes to slightly turn out." Her eyes were on his skates.

He did as instructed and received a coo of encouragement. "Good!"

"You're a good teacher." Glancing up to see her face, he nearly lost his balance. Her body steadied him as he groped desperately for the wall next to them.

"Why don't we stick to the wall for the first round until you get the hang of it?"

He nodded, not taking his eyes off the ice in front of him as he let go of the wall again. They pushed slowly along, her stabilizing him when he wobbled slightly.

"How was your week?" he asked.

"Not bad. How was yours?"

His foot slipped, but he was able to recover quickly. "Not to be rude, but I don't think I'm going to be able to keep up a conversation while doing this."

Her joyful laugh sounded in his ears as his eyes concentrated on scratched up ice. "I'll talk then."

They went around slowly the first time with her talking about her week and what she'd been up to. He started to gain ground and move faster, so they moved away from the wall. She let go of his hand, saying it was easier to skate not holding onto someone. Colin would have begged to differ since he liked holding her hand, but it turned out she was right. Eventually, he joined the conversation as they continued doing lazy loops of the rink.

When the crowd started to thin out, he noticed an antsy energy radiating from her. "You want to go faster, don't you?"

"No, I'm enjoying skating with you." It was clear she was being polite.

"Take a few laps. I think I'm doing pretty well for it being essentially my first time. I'll be okay on my own." He chanced losing his balance in turning his head to smile broadly at her.

"You are doing well." Her eyes draped down to his skates and then back up. With a slight puff of air she said, "Like I'd expect anything less from you."

She pushed off and in a flash was already turning the corner of the rink. It was amazing how fast she was. Before he knew it she was flying by with a giggle that set something bubbling inside himself.

Emilie was in her element out here.

She passed him two more times, her legs pushing strongly against the ice. The hood on her jacket flopped down and the hair loose from her knit cap flew in the breeze of her own effort.

When she passed him a fourth time, Colin sped up himself. Reasonably, he knew that he couldn't keep up with her, she had a lifetime of experience to his forty minutes, but something inside him wanted to try. It went well on the straight away, but he misjudged his footing around the curve.

Colin fell hard against the ice, trapping one leg under the other and twisting his ankle at an unfortunate, painful angle. In seconds, Emilie was beside him.

"Hey, are you okay?" Her voice was casual and even; he assumed to protect his pride.

He pushed himself to sit. "You can't learn something new without falling down a few times, right?"

She helped him up, and when he put weight back on his left foot, he tried not to wince. His ankle seared, and he could already tell that it was probably sprained. He pushed to skate again but ended up half skating, half limping in his attempt to keep the weight off his left side—not exactly the impression of strength you wanted to give on your second date.

He gave up trying to be macho and was honest. "I think I might have twisted my foot a bit." Okay, mostly honest. "Do you mind if we take a quick break?"

"Not at all." She flipped to skate backwards, watching his feet as if making an assessment.

"Now you're just showing off." At least his sense of humor wasn't injured.

Emilie carefully observed his attempt at a roguish smile with a slight frown on her lips.

"It's official. We can't be in the park together. Somehow, you always end up injured one way or another." She easily slid off the ice.

Grabbing the wall, he leaned into it, taking the weight off his left foot and breaking into a deep, throaty laugh. Her eyes lit up as she faced him from the other side of the wall. The shade of her cheeks were perfectly pink as she enjoyed a full laugh with him. Their gloved hands alternated on to the wall, and his fingers itched to touch her without all of the paraphernalia of winter shielding their skin.

"You're right. Since I've met you, I've sure taken a beating. I promise things like this don't normally happen to me."

Her lips downturned as she pushed from the wall. "I'll grab our stuff and meet you at that bench," she said pointing while she skate-walked away.

With her attention diverted, Colin moved with a full limp to the bench before collapsing onto it and unlacing his rented skate. It was painful to remove, and he allowed a groan to break from his lips. His ankle was already swelling and turning the beginning stages of purple.

"How's it looking?" She flopped down next to him, putting her gear bag on the floor.

Quickly pulling his sock up to conceal the injury, he shrugged. "I'll survive."

She eyed him for a second then went on unlacing her skates with quick efficient movements. A slightly pleasurable sound escaped her throat as she pulled off her skate that made him swallow hard. Focusing on unlacing his second skate, he tried to keep his thoughts clean.

When they both had their boots back on, her eyes fixed on his. "You still up for coffee?"

"Absolutely."

Pushing up from the bench, she led the way back to Beacon Street. As he controlled the limp in his step, he fell behind in the conversation, giving single-word or nonverbal answers.

They were nearly to the road when she rounded on him. "When are you going to admit that you sprained your ankle?"

"I, ah . . ." He blinked at the irritated slant of her eyebrows before letting out a resigned exhale. "Is it so bad that I don't want our second date to end early because I accidentally fell on the ice?"

Her beautiful freckled skin relaxed under the knitted flower sewn to the rim of her beanie, a wishful nod to a season nowhere in sight. She pushed back a small chestnut tendril stealthily trying to escape at her forehead.

"This is my fault. I was just so floored after watching you play on our first date. The way the music possessed you, and it seemed as if you had a tangible relationship with it. I thought I'd show you something I was good at. Maybe show off a little. It was childish and . . ." She looked him up and down. ". . . apparently dangerous. Are you even going to be able to work like that? It looks like you're in pain just standing here."

His breath quickened in his chest. "You enjoyed the music?"

"*Colin.*" Her gorgeous eyes raised before resting on his. "I basically forced you to buy a piano. Of course, I enjoyed the music."

He stared intently back at her. "You didn't force me to do anything. I wanted to play for you."

That tense spell he'd experienced when he was this close to her washed over him. He wondered if she could feel this static electricity pulling at every fiber of her body too. Maybe she even craved his touch as much as he wished for hers. Completely forgetting the last hour, he stepped forward with his left foot.

Emilie frowned at his unmasked cringe and went straight into nurse mode. "I don't think we're going to coffee. You can hardly walk on that."

Damn it.

"I can manage."

"No, you can't." She dug her cell phone out of a pocket of her skate bag, pulled a glove off with her teeth, and took a few seconds tapping onto it. The glove hung from her mouth while she typed, and he tried not to be envious of a piece of fabric.

"Okay, it'll be here in five minutes." She snatched the glove from her mouth and held it in her bare hand with her phone.

"What will be here?"

They heard a horn honking on the street twenty feet away.

"Are you Emilie?" A man was hanging out of the driver's side of a grey sedan, the Uber sticker visible in the passenger window.

"Huh. One second instead of five minutes. Gotta love that." She called to the driver, "Yes! Thank you. We'll be right there."

In a split second, she repositioned her gear bag crossbody away from him, and tucked up under his left shoulder. "It's okay. You can lean on me."

She wrapped her arm around his back and took a step towards the car, pulling him with her. This wasn't exactly the contact he was craving a moment ago, but beggars couldn't be choosers.

"Where are we going?" They three leg walked to the car.

"Your place, to treat your ankle." Her voice held a business-like quality. "You know for a doctor, you don't seem to know the basics. Rest. Ice. Compression. Elevation."

His face wrinkled. "I know what R.I.C.E. is."

Once they ducked into the warm car, they idly chatted with the man until the small talk whittled away to companionable silence.

Emilie leaned over. "I'm just helping you to get back to your place. I don't want you to get any ideas." Her low voice did exactly the opposite of what her words dictated.

Pointing a hand to his bad foot, he said, "How could I, in this condition?"

A small chuckle escaped those beautiful lips. "I'm serious, Colin."

"Scouts honor." He made the familiar salute.

She rolled her eyes. "You probably were a boy scout."

"Eagle scout," he corrected her.

A huff of breath preceded "Naturally."

"We are here, Miss Emilie," the kind man interrupted their conversation.

"Thank you." She was out of the car and over to his side before Colin could get all the way out.

He gave her a disgruntled look as she closed the car door behind him. "You're killing me with this. I'm supposed to be the one that helps you out of cars."

"Harness your male pride for one day." She acted as his human crutch again, pulling him toward the lobby doors. "You can't be smart, and skilled, and strong, and talented, and sexy all the time."

They skipped the revolving door and went through the side entrance. "You think I'm sexy?"

An irritated huff came from under his left shoulder. "What floor do you live on?"

They reached the elevator bank, and she pushed the up button as he answered, "Fifth." He couldn't help himself. "And talented?"

"I will step on your ankle," she said slowly.

"Okay. Okay. I'll be good."

He was pretty sure he heard her mumble "you better" under her breath.

·CHAPTER 23·

If he was going to keep poking at her, then she was going to leave him at his doorstep. That was the lie Emilie told herself as she helped Colin to his condo floor. Truthfully, she was very curious to see what his place looked like. She always thought you could tell a lot about a man based on how he lived.

They stopped in front of a door. "This one's mine."

Easing himself off her shoulder, he took out keys from his jeans pocket. She rolled her shoulders, grateful not to be his crutch anymore. Colin was as solid and heavy as he looked.

When he entered the condo, he automatically put his keys on a hook on the wall that also had a small wooden slot where he placed his wallet. It was sweet to watch him do this simple daily action without thinking about it.

The short hall he hobbled down was just like the one in Ash's condo, but that was where the comparisons ended.

Emilie hadn't noticed in the hall that they were in the corner of the building.

Windows wrapped around the large room, letting the bright winter sunlight stream in. To her right was the same industrial kitchen that was in her friend's condo, only bigger. Beyond it was a doorway that she assumed led to the bedroom and bathroom. Straight ahead a familiar walnut piano was nestled between floor to ceiling windows. She smiled seeing it in his home, glad that even in their small time together, she'd made an impact on his day to day life.

To her left, two sets of low bookshelves were under another two banks of windows. Between the bookshelves there was a gas fireplace and a wall mounted TV over the mantle. By way of furniture, there was only an old recliner, except for the same counter height stools that came with Ash's kitchen. For what it was lacking in personal touches, it made up for in cleanliness.

Colin seemed self-conscious as she scanned the open concept room. "I didn't know you'd be coming over today. My place isn't really set up for visitors."

"It's okay. Let's get your foot elevated."

He tried to fight her, saying that he could take care of his ankle himself, but she just tucked herself under his arm and helped him across the room. Once he'd sat with a defeated sigh, she pushed the creaking wooden lever for the old chair to raise its footrest. Striding to the kitchen, she opened the freezer side of his refrigerator to look for an ice pack or a bag of frozen vegetables. It was completely empty except for the ice in the icemaker.

What did he live on, sunshine and coffee?

"I usually have microwave dinners in there, but I ate the last one yesterday."

She chuckled at his response. "Okay then where are your sandwich bags?"

"Umm." He stared at her. "I don't have any."

"Plastic wrap?"

His sandy locks swayed as he shook his head.

"A towel, then?"

He seemed relieved to have an answer to that one. "In the drawer to the right of the sink."

After finding the towel, she collected a good amount of ice from the freezer. He'd taken off his boot and sock, and she could see that his ankle was not only swollen but bruising as well.

A frown turned her mouth as she handed him the ice-towel bundle. "Where do you keep your ibuprofen?"

"Emilie, I'm fine. It's just a sprain."

She placed her hands on her hips, and he exhaled, gesturing to the doorway beyond the kitchen. "It's in the medicine cabinet."

A large floor-to-ceiling window was in the bedroom as well, bookended by automatic looking blackout curtains. In front of it, plaid pajama pants were carelessly thrown over the back of an old wooden chair. An odd tenderness rang in her chest at the slack orientation of those pants, one leg splayed over the back and the second draped off the seat almost to the floor.

A king-size bed with a masculine navy comforter and a wooden headboard was situated against the solid wall in front of her. Beside it stood a single nightstand with a small lamp and phone charger. Outside of little touches like the headboard, everything else seemed sterile and impersonal. The bathroom was beyond the bed with the closet. She opened the medicine cabinet and found the medication, trying to ignore the overwhelming scent of him emanating from the closet.

"I'm sorry that the place is a mess," Colin said as soon as she reentered the room.

She chuckled. "It's not messy."

"Incomplete then." His eyes looked so grey as they moved from hers to scan the room. "This is the first time in my life that I've put together something that slightly resembles a home. My apartments always looked like glorified call rooms before. I had a bed and a kitchen and a bathroom. That was all I needed. I worked a ridiculous amount of hours, so it didn't matter what it looked like where I slept. My father's house was always my home," he paused with a deep breath. "That's where all the living happened. I worked and slept at my place. I lived at his."

Her body froze with the medication in her hand, not wanting to move to the kitchen to get water for fear of breaking his focus.

"After my mom died, my dad and I formed a strong bond. He was my dad, but he was also my best friend. He took care of me, and I took care of him. We made things work just the two of us, and when I was accepted to medical school in a different city, he moved with me. He moved with me, changing his job again, when I was in residency. I studied or worked and slept in an apartment by myself, but I would eat dinner with him whenever I wasn't working, and we'd do things together as often as we could."

He glanced at the piano. "Our family piano was always at his home. It looked very similar to this one. He'd have me play whenever I was there to keep me fresh and to remind him of Mom. She was the one who insisted I take lessons and who loved music."

A jolt ran through her that the recliner must have belonged to his father. Possibly also the books and photos on the bookshelves. This man owned nothing that was his own. There was a reason Colin was one of the best surgeons she'd ever met; outside of the time he'd spent with his late father, surgery was his entire life.

His gaze drifted to his hands before his head snapped up with wide eyes. "Wow, I'm sorry. That was a lot. I was just trying to explain why there are no chairs for you to sit on." He winced as if his words had been painful.

Emilie's heart squeezed. Crossing quickly to him, she stood beside the only item of furniture in the room for a fraction of a second before pulling the piano bench next to him. She set the pills beside her, reached for his hands, and was grateful when he let her hold them.

"Tell me more about him," she said, focusing her eyes on his.

He seemed to be warring with himself as to whether to say more or to close the subject.

"He would have liked you," he said quietly to their joined hands.

Letting the words hang in the air, Emilie counted her breaths as she waited for him to say more.

"Could I have those?" He nodded to the pills on the piano bench.

Letting go of his hands, she gathered up the medication and handed it over silently.

"Thank you." He swallowed them without water. "I'm sorry that ice skating was a bust. Thank you for your help getting back here."

"It's the least I could do after unintentionally causing the harm in the first place."

"You didn't cause this." He glanced at his ice-covered ankle. "My ego caused this, as much as I hate to admit it."

She raised her eyebrows. "That's quite an admission."

"I can admit when I'm wrong," he joked with her before his smile fell to something more serious. "And you were right to show off today. It was amazing to see you in your element." He took a deep breath. "I don't think you have any idea how incredible you are."

The look in his eyes almost burned a hole through her. A quick shallow gasp filled her lungs as the pulse of her rapidly beating heart throbbed in her neck. She didn't have the language to answer that, to give an appropriate response, so she steered the conversation back into a lighter territory.

"Admitting fault is a good quality in a man." She wavered at the beginning but tried to keep a teasing tone in her voice.

Colin blinked and lowered his head a fraction. For a breath, she worried she'd upset him, but when he raised his face, a playful grin was set on his lips.

"You know what else are good qualities? Resourcefulness and attention to detail."

His grin widened as her brows furrowed.

Ticking off his fingers, he said, "Resourcefulness: I have coffee, a coffee maker, and mugs in the kitchen. Attention to detail: You take your coffee black so there is no need for a coffee shop, just a coffee maker." Then he lowered the footrest and asked with a sexy confidence that of course she would say yes to, "Emilie, would you please stay and let me make us some coffee, so we can continue our date?"

◊◊◊

Two hours or so later, Colin limped ever so slightly to his doorway to give her a breathtaking kiss before she left. As she rode the elevator down to the lobby, she thought about the afternoon. Something nagged at the side of her heart, and she mulled it over on the short walk home.

Putting away her things and kicking out of her boots, she flopped down on her window seat, pulling Analie's contact up on her phone's screen.

Her sister picked up after two rings. "Hey Em, hold on."

She could hear Penny and Liam squabbling in the background.

"No! Stop it. We've been through this, the two of you have to share. Scott! Help me, Emilie's on the phone." Her brother-in-law addressed the kids in the background as her sister shut a door and let out a huff of air. "Hey, sorry about that. Penny's cranky because she's refusing to nap, so we're all living in her terror reign for the time being."

She chuckled at her sister's description. "I'm sorry, An."

"It's okay, we'll make it through." Analie sighed. "What's up?"

"I wanted to talk to you about something . . ." she paused, taking a deep breath as her stomach knotted.

Her sister waited patiently on the other end of the line.

"I've started dating someone." As she let the words fall from her mouth, it felt like artillery shells falling to the ground, only there was no explosion when her sister registered them.

"That's wonderful!" Her sister nearly shouted in excitement.

"Really?" Emilie's face released its tightness.

"Yes. Why would that be a bad thing?" her sister asked and then answered, "I mean, I understand that you wanted to wait until you were ready, but I don't think it's bad that you're dating. I think it's great."

"Really?" She was beginning to sound like a broken record.

"Yes!"

"Okay." This was going better than expected.

"Who is he?"

Pushing into the plush throw pillows and gazing at her poor winter-stripped elm tree, she answered, "Someone I met at work."

"Is he hot?" In college, her sister always preferred nerdy boys for herself, choosing brain over brawn. Lucky for

Analie, her software developer husband, Scott, exemplified both characteristics.

"Analie!"

"Sorry, old habits die hard. Of course, it doesn't matter as long as he's a good person and treats you well."

She was about to say that she did think Colin was incredibly handsome when Analie continued on. "How long have you been dating?"

"Just a few weeks, but we've been working together since September when he moved here."

Her mind replayed the memory of his eyes lighting up at her pantomiming his order and the lingering warmth of his hands on her arms when he steadied her after she'd slammed into him.

"How's it been going?" She knew the question her sister was really trying to ask.

The lightness she felt momentarily stripped away as pressure built between her brows. "Good. I've been taking it really slow and listening to my internal responses . . . Sometimes I feel guilty, like I'm cheating on Braden—"

"You know you're not, right? Even if it feels that way, you aren't. Braden would want you to be happy again," her sister interrupted.

The bitterness of leftover coffee sat in her mouth as it refused to make words for several seconds.

"It's okay, you know. Everything you're feeling is okay." Her sister's voice was soft.

"I know."

Telling her sister made her relationship with Colin seem more real. When she was with him, his strength seemed to buoy her, but the simple act of having that experience with someone other than her husband was strange and foreign territory.

"Does Mom know?"

"No." She cringed, running her hand over her winter-knotted hair. "I thought you could tell her."

"Mom and Dad would be excited to hear about this too, Emilie." Her sister used her full name for emphasis. "We're all excited for you. There's nothing to be ashamed of."

A deep breath filled her lungs before she intentionally exhaled. "Okay, but I'm not going to make that call today."

Her twin understood sometimes there were limits to the amount of emotional topics she could handle in a day.

"That's fine. I'll keep your secret until then. But really, this is great news. I'm happy for you."

Emilie's niece burst into whatever room Analie was hiding, her high-pitched cries shrieking out of the phone's speaker followed by Scott's voice. "I'm sorry, she wouldn't calm down."

"Em—" her sister started.

"Go," she interrupted. "I love you. I'll talk to you soon."

"I love you too." Penny continued to wail for her sister's attention. "Bye."

"Bye."

She set her phone on the table, glancing out the window when it pinged with a text. Assuming it was Analie, she grinned anticipating what "save me from my four-year-old" message she'd be reading.

Colin: *Thank you, Nurse Emilie, for fixing me up today. Do you think we could have a second chance at a second date sometime next week?*

Her lips curled higher as she looked at the screen. A second message came through.

Colin: *No ice skating.*

A laugh burst from her as she thumbed out a response.

Emilie: *Not good at being pushed out of your comfort zone?*

He responded quickly.

Colin: *Preferably I'd like to stay in a condition to continue working in my chosen profession.*

She felt bad about that. Luckily, he'd said he was in the office tomorrow and would be able to sit down and rest his ankle during his appointments.

Emilie: *Fine no ice skating, what did you have in mind?*

Colin: *How about dinner at L'eau?*

A quick Google search revealed a beautiful waterfront French restaurant. Her stomach flipped just looking at the pictures. Not ready to take their fledgling relationship to amazing French restaurant level, she held her breath as she sent her message.

Emilie: *I'm not quite ready for dinner*

He responded back almost instantly.

Colin: *How about brunch? Everyone loves brunch.*

She laughed at the true statement.

Emilie: *I do love brunch*

Colin: *Thursday?*

Pulling up her calendar she confirmed.

Emilie: *Thursday is good*

Colin: *Perfect. I'll pick you up at 10.*

She smiled at her screen for a long while before setting it on the table and resting her head on the window. Analie was right; everything was going to be okay.

·CHAPTER 24·

Colin stood in the shower longer than he usually would, letting the hot water beat over his skin as he delayed the inevitable. Avoidance usually came easily to him, but there was no avoiding the brutality of a northeastern winter. He'd given himself credit for making it through the last few months with a pretty good attitude, even though it had been completely, ridiculously, and unnecessarily cold all the time.

Now that it was late March, he'd hoped to see some semblance of old man winter loosening his grip. The only thing distracting him from the frigid temperature was the time he spent with Emilie. The last six weeks had been the best of his life. He'd savor the few hours they would get together once a week and then impatiently count the minutes until their next date.

Exiting the revolving doors to his building, an icy wind slapped him hard across what part of his face was exposed. His eyes immediately started watering, and he grumbled, pulling his thick fleece scarf up until it brushed his lower eyelashes. At least the walk to the hospital was short.

Once all his necessary and numerous winter belongings were securely locked away, he double checked his OR assignments for the day.

"Good morning, Dr. Abernan," Kitty sang as she walked past him.

Resisting the urge not to just grunt in response, he said, "Good morning, Kitty. Are you circulating today?" She wasn't wearing her manager's white coat.

"No, just got hot wearing my coat."

He couldn't imagine being hot on a morning like this, but he also wasn't a menopausal woman.

"I'll be in meetings all day. I probably should wear business clothes, but I'm used to living in scrubs." She smiled as she shrugged.

"I completely understand." He grinned back at her, preferring scrubs to dress shirts anyday. "Have a good day."

"You too."

His morning pre-surgery routine went smoothly, and he was halfway through his routine quadruple bypass when his mind began to wander. It went to where it usually did, thoughts of Emilie—specifically the realization that he was in love with her.

He was having a hard time putting words to the way he felt about Emilie. It was so much more than this pulsing need to be near her. Or the feeling of her gorgeous freckled skin under his fingers and her lips on his. Or the way her laugh lit up something that had long been dimmed and dark inside him. Or that her strength made him proud that she'd chosen to be with him when she could have anyone. It was a beat that drummed in his chest every moment of every day, unwavering in its veracity.

He thought he'd been in love his senior year of high school, and foolishly opened the *When you fall in love* letter before understanding what love really was. The way he felt about Emilie was like nothing he'd ever experienced, so he'd pulled out that letter from the bottom of his box last night and read it again to see if it made more sense.

Dear Colin,

I'm happy while I write this letter to you. My heart bursts with joy over the idea of you finding someone that you love. I hope that she's as wonderful as you are, because you, my sweet boy, deserve the best sort of woman. Take heart if this is all a little overwhelming and thoughts of her completely monopolize your day. That's to be expected. You should feel giddy and excited and also a little bit terrified. There's inherent pain in the idea or actual loss of those we love, but that is the price we pay for loving them. One cannot go without the other and the cost of love is so completely worth it, Colin. So let go, love with all of your heart, wildly and unapologetically, and know that if any heartache should come in the future, it is absolutely worth having had this connection with another person. I know that you'll make a good choice and pick someone deserving of a love like this. One who will give you all in return what you give to her. I want you to know that this is possible. The love I talk about is the kind that your father and I share. If it's possible for us, it will be possible for you. I wish you all the happiness in the world and know that whatever happens, I loved you like this and then more.

My whole heart,
Mom

"Dr. Abernan?" His resident, standing across from him brought him back into the OR.

The high-pitched whir of the life support machine running in the background mixed with the expected beeps of the many monitors running simultaneously.

"I'm sorry, Adam. What were you saying?"

"We talked about me closing today. Would that still be a possibility?"

"Yes, of course." He called out to the circulating nurse so it could be marked in the chart, "Wendy, Dr. Barnes will close for me at the end of the case."

"Yes, Dr. Abernan," she replied.

He was reviewing the steps with Adam when she called to him again.

"You're being paged, Dr. Abernan. The transplant coordinator has a recipient who's in need of a direct admission. The office says she's presenting with potential pneumonia." Wendy read off his pager screen.

"Who is it?"

Some of the recent transplant recipients he knew well, others had their hearts for ten plus years and usually followed up with their original surgeons.

"Krystal Reid, sir."

Glancing up at Adam, he stilled his working hands. "You've got this?"

"Yes, sir."

A slight unease flowed through his forearms that he wouldn't be in the OR observing, but Colin trusted this man. Barnes was a good surgeon, and he'd only be upstairs.

After breaking scrub, he collected his pager from Wendy, put on his coat, and dove his hand into his pocket for his cell phone.

"This is Camila," the transplant coordinator answered after one ring.

"Camila. It's Colin. I'm heading upstairs right now. Did you call John?" He climbed the stairs, pulling his scrub cap off and shoving it into his coat pocket.

Everyone at CTSB knew that Krystal Reid was special to John, and that he always personally oversaw her care. John had replaced Krystal's heart at age six and again two additional times. The last transplant she'd received was a year ago, shortly after she turned twenty.

"Yes, he's driving in right now, but I told him I was paging you to take care of her admission in the meantime."

"I'll get her settled until he gets here." He opened the door to the fifth floor. "What room did they give her?"

"510."

"Thanks, Camila." As he hung up, he arrived at 5SW and walked straight into the room.

The hospital room was busy with activity as Ashley placed Krystal on oxygen and Tere, the charge nurse, started an IV line, using it to draw a rainbow of blood tubes. A nurse aide was nearby attaining a set of vitals.

"Krystal, my name is Dr. Abernan. I'm going to get you settled until Dr. Reddington gets here. He's driving to the hospital right now. We're going to get a chest X-ray and probably some IV medications for you but let me start by listening to your heart and lungs." Pulling for his stethoscope, he remembered that he'd just come from the OR.

Ashley wordlessly handed over hers while putting telemetry leads on Krystal's chest.

"Thank you." Colin settled the borrowed stethoscope into his ears. "Take a deep breath for me."

The characteristic high-pitch popping sound of rales entered his ears with each inhale and exhale. Krystal's heart sounded normal except for its accelerated beat.

"Pressure's 170/90, heart rate's 105, and she's febrile at 101.3, doctor," the nurse aide called out from the vital machine as he handed the stethoscope back to Ashley.

"Thank you," he said, making a mental note of the numbers. "Can I get an EKG too?"

The nurse aide disappeared from the room with a nod.

"Krystal, did you take your medications today?" he asked the impossibly small young woman.

She nodded. "Just my morning ones."

Her blonde hair was piled on top of her head and bobbed a bit with the movement. For someone who'd been in and out of the hospital her whole life, she seemed a bit nervous today.

Looking at Tere, who'd finished collecting the vials of blood, he asked, "Can I get a mobile computer in here so I can write at bedside? And can you call for a STAT chest?"

"The unit secretary already called X-ray; they're on their way. I'll grab you a computer." She left the room with the bag of blood tubes to send to the lab.

"What about anything for the fever?"

Krystal shook her head as she coughed into her hand. His fingers found the pulses on her wrist and ankles while the nurse aide obtained a gratefully normal EKG, aside from the sinus tachycardia. Colin was signing the EKG when X-ray walked in.

"This should be online in just a sec, Doc," the X-ray technician said after he pulled the hard plate from underneath his patient and wheeled the portable machine from the room.

Tere returned with a computer on wheels, and Colin signed into the hospital system. The X-ray looked exactly as he suspected with white clouds at the bases of both of her lungs.

"It looks like you have pneumonia. You'll be with us for a few days while we treat you. Do you need to call anyone in your family and let them know you're here?"

She shook her head again. "My mom's already on the way."

"I'm going to sit here a minute and get all your orders in, so we can get you situated for the day." He pulled the mobile computer up to the chair in the room.

"Okay." She seemed to relax as he sat, her heart rate decreasing on the monitor.

"Ashley, can you draw up the IV Tylenol I just ordered? Let's get her comfortable. Also the antibiotics to hang," he ordered while typing into the computer.

"I'll be right back."

"On a scale of one to ten, how would you rate your pain?"

Krystal coughed harder and winced. "A little . . . like a five?"

He frowned. This woman had been through so much in her life and was still putting on a brave face when she was obviously hurting more. He wrote for a small amount of narcotics in case the Tylenol Ashley was getting couldn't reduce her discomfort. As he continued to modify things until the computerized chart reflected the care he wanted her to have, Ashley returned with the medications and explained them to Krystal before hanging the bags.

"I'm going to grab a warm blanket and look for a leftover lunch tray," Ashley said as she exited the room.

Satisfied with his orders, he stood. "I'm going to give Dr. Reddington a call and let him know what's going on. If you need me again, just have the nurses page me."

"Thank you," she managed between coughs.

He rubbed the cold antibacterial gel between his palms as he exited the room. "Ashley, I added 2-4 of morphine to the chart if she needs . . ." His eyes lifted to see Emilie standing next to Ashley and stopped talking mid-sentence.

All the air left his lungs in a quick, stealthy release. It happened every time he saw her. Her scrubs were the pale yellow of a day-old chick with a white long-sleeve shirt underneath. She looked like the fresh promise of spring, and his fingers twitched as he imagined how the fabric would feel against them.

Colin didn't always see Emilie when he worked, but every day in the hospital he hoped she'd be on shift just to be near her. Even to share the same space in the building as her for a short few minutes.

"Hey."

"Hi." Her eyes lit up in that way that made sunshine bounce around inside his ribs before she turned to Ashley. "I'll be back in a few. Thanks for watching my patients."

"No problem." Ashley spoke to her friend but didn't take her eyes off him.

Emilie walked off the unit, sneaking a quick smiling glance over her shoulder before exiting the heavy double doors. The light seemed to change as soon as they closed. Luminosity that was previously hovering just out of consciousness swiftly extinguished. The sudden influx of the rushing noises of the hospital sounded too loud in his ears: electronic pinging, people talking, beds creaking, papers rustling, the click of typing fingers, ringing phones, and Krystal's coughing.

"You love her."

The sentence came as a statement, not a question or accusation.

A simple admission of the facts.

His head turned to find Ashley's focused but gentle eyes on him. Unconsciously, he ran his hand down the front of his scrub top, trying to ignore the burning within his lungs. His thoughts spun rapidly around his mind, trying to reason a professional response to his coworker's statement, but the word "yes" left his lips with a large exhale.

All the tension swiftly left his body with this ordinary three letter word.

Before he let himself evaluate that, he added, "Don't tell Emilie though. We're taking things slow, and I don't want to scare her away."

He glanced back towards the unit doors as if she would materialize at any moment, but they stayed closed.

"Be careful with her."

Nearly responding "I will" automatically before registering the softness in her voice, Colin turned to study her face. Something behind Ashley's green eyes betrayed a knowledge he'd desired from his first encounter with Emilie.

There was some reason that Emilie's smile didn't always reach her eyes, a reason that darkness passed over her face after moments of joy.

"What happened?"

Ashley slowly shook her head. "When she's ready, she'll tell you."

"I really care for her." He felt his heart beat with each word.

Laying her hand on his arm, she gave it a gentle squeeze. "I know."

Ashley continued moving towards the patient food area just as the unit doors opened, and John Reddington walked through in jeans under a large winter coat. Colin quickly shook the interaction with Ashley from his mind and focused back on his job.

"John, I was just about to call you. Let me catch you up on what's happening with Krystal."

·CHAPTER 25·

"5SW, this is Emilie," she answered her nurse phone once she retrieved the ringing thing from her pocket. She stole a small sip of the coffee she'd just purchased and set it next to her computer.

"Meet me in the locker room." His voice was low.

A quick inhale parted her lips. "Okay."

The savory flavor of coffee burned in her mouth as her pulse quickened in her throat. He'd never approached her while they were in the hospital other than to say hello or give an order. Colin was always the model of professionalism. Something in his shade of his words sent a pulsing sensation down her spine, anticipating she wasn't walking into a collegial interaction.

When she opened the door to the locker room, Colin was facing away from her with his hands on his hips. His white coat flared widely at the stance and nicely displayed the strong expanse of his shoulders. As soon as the door clicked closed, he spun and demolished the distance between them with two large steps, his eyes focused on her lips.

Standing in front of her, he paused to gently place one hand beneath her braid before tilting her face to his. Her breathing ceased as the warmth of his hand eased her body into the possession of his mouth. Emilie found herself arching her back and giving in fully to the deep, hungry kiss.

Her tongue raced circles around his as his other arm wrapped around her body. Pushing up against his firm chest, she wove her hands through his wavy hair. His soft moan resonated in her body, and she felt herself climb closer and press firmer to him in search of hearing it again.

The strength of his body was something she sought out in these moments. Something she didn't know she needed until he was before her, holding her so gently but also so resolutely. It thrilled her in places that hadn't stirred in what felt like a lifetime. It warmed and woke her and made her want more.

More touch.

More heat.

More connection.

More *Colin*.

Between them, his pager beeped, and she felt his grip on her loosen unwillingly. She held her grasp tight at the base of his neck, fingering the tendrils of his hair while he traced her lips with a scorchingly soft lick.

"I had to see you." His voice was hoarse against her lips.

A laugh spilled from her mouth. "You'd just seen me."

His smile rose before he started weaving kisses over her ear and then ever so slowly down along her jaw to her neck. This time a moan fell from her lips.

"I had to kiss you then," he whispered.

The pager went off again.

"You should probably look at that." She tilted her head away to maximize the area that he could kiss.

Continuing his path with a series of hot kisses to her collarbone, his rough voice said, "In a minute."

At its third sounding, she knew he could ignore it no longer. They separated just enough for him to glance down at the device. His jaw was set firm in a way that meant he would leave in just a moment, so she took the next few seconds to revel in him.

Today his eyes were more blue than grey, the lighter center ringed by dark ocean circles. His scent was distracting enough when he strode past her in the hall, but this close it was intoxicating. Her thumb itched to trace the sharp corner behind his ear down to the tip of his chin and over his swollen lips. When his eyebrows furrowed, she glanced up to his thick hair, which was a complete mess from her fingers.

"Colin. Your hair." Emilie chuckled.

He ran his hand through his hair, nearly putting it back to perfect. Such an unfair thing for a man to be so handsome with such little effort.

"Better?"

"No," she lied.

He took his scrub cap out of his pocket and placed it over his head, tucking the wayward strands underneath it before tying it behind his head. "I've got to head back to the OR anyway. My resident needs help."

Her head bobbed in agreement. She'd better get back to work too; she hadn't told anyone she was leaving this time.

Taking her face in both of his hands, he tenderly rubbed the thumb of one hand over her cheek before sliding it to her chin, giving her the sweetest graze of his lips over hers.

"*Emilie . . .*"

Her name sounded like a confession.

Like it was breath and water and food and shelter to him, everything he needed to live contained in three syllables. The sound zipped through her muscles, threatening to drop her straight to the floor.

This time his cell phone rang in his pocket.

"Go," she whispered to his lips.

His eyes raced all over her face before he stepped out of the room with his phone to his ear. "Abernan."

◊◊◊

She didn't see Colin for the rest of her shift, but figured he was busy in surgery. After tromping home in the beginning snow, Emilie kicked off her winter gear and changed into pajama pants and a baggy long-sleeve shirt. Her slippered feet padded into the kitchen, and she pulled a large, plastic container of chili out of the fridge. Scooping out a bowl for herself, she was about to put it in the microwave when a sharp knock sounded on her door.

Colin stood on the other side, breathing hard, his face flushed from the freezing fifteen degree night. He had snow in his hair and on the shoulders of his white coat. It took her a second to register that he was wearing his scrubs and running shoes and not warmer gear. What distracted her was the most intense focus she'd ever seen as his eyes bore into her.

"Colin." The surprised word dropped from her mouth. "Wha—"

Her question went unfinished as he pressed all the intensity of his eyes to her mouth with his cold-stung lips.

She responded instantly, lacing her arms around his neck, and he picked her up with one arm, using the other to slam the door behind them. Her legs wrapped around his muscled torso, and a low growl pushed back against her furiously sweeping tongue. His body was freezing from its exposure to the frigid temperature, his hands surprising her with their cold touch as they explored her back.

Colin set her on the kitchen island, never letting his lips disconnect from hers. Pushing her hands against the lapels of his white coat back, he disconnected his arms long enough to pull them behind his body as the coat slipped to the floor. Their lips devoured each other's, and she let her hands roam all over the cold, thin fabric of his scrub top.

"How did y—" she managed against his lips.

"I ran," came the heated answer.

"Wh—" She didn't get to finish that question either.

His tongue played with hers as a hand pulled at the end of her braid. With the hair tie removed, he made quick work of unbraiding before plunging both hands into her hair. She leaned back against his fingers with a pleasurable gasp as he laid hot targeted kisses on the exposed underside of her jawline, making his way down her neck.

"I had to see you." His voice was flaming against her throat.

His words had her needing his lips on hers, and she roughly grabbed his face and pulled it to hers. The heat from inside his body was overcoming the short exposure to the harsh elements as her hands explored his torso. She fisted the fabric of his scrub top and it came free from being tucked into his pants. His hand grabbed behind his head and pulled it from his simmering body in one swift motion.

A gasp escaped her lips as Emilie began exploring his bare skin with her fingertips for the first time. The same need she had earlier in the day came back more forcefully. She didn't realize how much she wanted this, how much she wanted him, and suddenly she couldn't get enough of him.

Her hands explored the strong expanse of his back before tucking under his arms and weaving her fingers through the patch of darker blond hairs over his chest. When both hands settled over his heart, he stilled.

Colin pulled back enough to look at her. "Emilie, I . . ."

His stormy eyes seemed to struggle with the end of the sentence, and she was about to ask him what, but he removed the hand that was behind her back and used it to hold her face ever so gently as he kissed her lips as lightly as he had earlier that day.

She felt a world of possibilities open with that kiss. Secrets and mysteries and things she couldn't grasp seemed available to her if she would just reach out and take them.

"Colin . . ." she breathed against his lips.

Her voice sent him back into a fever pitch. Mouths and hands exploring wildly, she felt his hand dive under the back of her shirt and the pleasure was immediate. She must have groaned against him because he slowly pulled up at the shirt, and she leaned back to allow him to remove it.

His glossy eyes stared at her exposed skin before his mouth led back to hers. "So beautiful."

She felt more than beautiful in that moment; she felt wanted and cherished and safe. He made her want things she didn't think she could dream of again. He made it seem like anything was possible. That this was possible for her again.

Her reverie was interrupted by him trailing kisses down her throat. He placed a warm, broad hand behind her mid-back and she leaned into it as his kisses continued down her sternum and over her heart before lightly tracing the upper edges of her bra. She needed more connection with him so she wrapped her dangling legs back around him.

A guttural sound escaped his throat before he returned to her mouth. Her hands explored his muscled shoulders as one of his slipped under her bra. At her quick inhale, he paused, but her passionate kiss let him know she enjoyed the touch. His other hand teased at the top of her waistband as a few tentative fingers swiped against her belly an inch above her c-section scar.

This time she pulled back. She couldn't let this go any further without telling him.

Before she could speak, Colin gathered her into his arms and breathed against her ear. "This isn't slow."

She softly pushed against his body to look him in the eye. "It's not that. I'm not being fair to you."

When she leaned back even farther, he dropped his arms to his sides. Gathering his hands up in hers, Emilie took a deep breath and let out a halting exhale.

"I want this." She rubbed the back of his hands with her thumbs, looking at how small hers were in comparison. "I want you." Her eyes flicked to his. "I want to be with you."

Saying it out loud solidified what her body had been telling her for some time. Her already rapid pulse jackknifed at her words.

He went to speak, but she lightly laid a single finger to his lips. "Let me finish."

Returning her hand to his, he held it this time, running slow circles over the skin inside her wrist. Even with the comforting touch, her ribs still squeezed inward and her breath trapped in her throat.

"The reason I wanted to take things slow is because I haven't been with a man in almost four years . . ." She paused, gathering her strength, and swallowed against the bitter taste in her mouth before forcing herself to say the words. "The last man I was with was my husband. He and our infant daughter died in a car accident."

She heard his quick inhale and glancing up, found complete compassion in his eyes.

"Oh, Emilie." Sadness seeped into her name.

At his absolute acceptance of her pain, a single tear slipped down her cheek and hit the counter between them. In an instant, his arms wrapped firmly around her. She listened to his strong heart beating beneath his warm chest as he slowly brushed her hair with his hand. Colin never let the strength of his arms waver. After what seemed like an immeasurable amount of time, she felt his exhale as he let go of her.

"I should go."

She couldn't go back to where they'd been only a moment ago, not with the pressure pushing against her spine, but the thought of Colin walking out her door made her chest hurt more than normal.

"Would it be too much if I asked you to stay?"

"No." He kissed her forehead with such tenderness then handed her shirt to her.

Bending to pick his scrub top off the floor, he pulled it over his head. She eased herself off the island and led him to her loveseat. Colin sat and stretched out his arms to her, simply holding her to his strong frame.

Emilie let her face relax against the soft fabric at his shoulder as her hand rested over his heart. The steady beat under her palm and his calming breaths quickly soothed the tension she always felt after talking about her past. That connection, that complete sensation of rightness whenever she was with Colin, flowed through her body as the ticking of the new clock she'd put over the mantle quietly counted off seconds of time.

·CHAPTER 26·

Before long Emilie was asleep on his shoulder, but he stayed on the couch for a long time, working through what she'd told him. Though he'd witnessed his father lose his mother, Colin couldn't imagine losing both your husband and child in one unexpected, horrific sweep. Even over the short few months that he'd spent with Owen at dinners with Max and Kate, the small redheaded boy already held a chubby fist around his heart. Living through the pain of losing your own child seemed incomprehensible, but that was exactly what Emilie was doing every day.

An involuntary shudder ran down his spine, and she stirred slightly with his movement. He held incredibly still, and her soft breathing eventually leveled. Slowly and carefully lifting his arm, he gently stroked the hair away from her freckled face. She was so unbelievably gorgeous, even drooling a little bit on his scrub top.

He could have easily spent the night with her on his shoulder but knew that she'd probably sleep better in her own bed. Shifting in gradual degrees, he lifted her and carefully carried her to the bedroom. He managed to get her under the covers without waking her and leaned in to place a light kiss to her crown.

Colin whispered his truth to her sleeping form, what he almost told her twice that day. "I love you, Emilie."

Walking to the doorway, he heard her twist in the bedsheet before her groggy voice replied, "I love you too, Braden."

His head snapped over his shoulder, seeing her asleep, the words coming from her unconscious mind. Suddenly, all the happiness that flowed through his body abated. A squeezing pain replaced it, gripping him like he'd been punched hard in the gut. His throat tightened, and he swallowed over the excess saliva in his mouth.

This wasn't going to happen.

It didn't matter that he loved Emilie.

She could never love him because she still loved her husband.

Walking to the kitchen, he picked his white coat up from the floor and left, closing the door quietly behind him. Before he knew what his body was doing, his legs were pounding down the stairs and sprinting through the freezing wind. The cold that slashed harshly at his body seemed warmer than the dread that had crept into his chest.

◊◊◊

The next morning, Colin didn't answer her call or call back when he was done with his office appointments. Eventually he texted her, but it was clipped, using work as an excuse. When he worked with Emilie three days later, he was professional but not warm. She texted to ask if he was okay and he ignored it.

After his surgeries today, he strode onto the unit filled with anxiety that he would have to see her again, but relaxed when her name wasn't on the board. A second after he arrived at the charting area outside his patient's room, a flash of bright blue streaked out of the room and aggressively punched him in the arm.

"What the . . ." He looked up to see Ashley's eyes glaring into his own.

Before anything else could be said, she grabbed his ear like a mother with a petulant child and dragged him across the hall to the staff lounge. It was surprisingly easy for her. Although she was thin, she was easily six feet tall, and apparently a force to be reckoned with when angry.

Throwing the door open, she hissed "Out!" to the two nurse aides that were sitting in chairs, and they scurried faster than cockroaches in a light exposed room. She pushed him into the room, blocking the door with her body. Colin opened his mouth to speak, but she closed the space between them with a single step and punched him in the same arm again.

"You're being an asshole!" Ashley's words crescendoed as if she was having trouble trying to control the volume of her voice. "I should know, I *specialize* in assholes. They flock to me like moths to a flame, and I have seen every different variety there is. But you . . ." She pointed a shaking finger at him. ". . . are not an asshole, Dr. Abernan. So why are you acting like one?"

He waited a breath, unsure if she was going to yell or punch him again before defending himself. "I'm not being an asshole."

Wrong answer. She hit him again. His arm was starting to get sore.

"I *told* you to be careful with her. I *told* you, and now you're not answering her calls or texts and being cold to her at work. She bares her soul to you, and you respond with silence? You *are* being an asshole!" She jabbed her hands on her hips.

Colin felt his forearms flex as his jaw tightened. "She still loves him, Ashley. She said so in her sleep. She said *his name* in her sleep. She still loves him and where does that leave me?" His arms swept open. "Huh? There's no room for me in her heart. It's already full."

She made an exasperated sound and flung both her hands up. "That's the stupidest thing I've ever heard! Of course she still loves him. She probably always will, and she will love that sweet baby girl until her last breath, but that doesn't mean she doesn't love you too."

"What are you saying?" he asked cautiously.

Ashley took a deep, steadying breath. "What I'm saying is that I told you to be careful with her. Things are going to be a bit slow, but that doesn't mean she can't love you the way you love her."

He looked her straight in the eye, his words reverberating with conviction. "I've never loved anyone the way I love Emilie."

Ashley scrubbed her hands over her face, nearly knocking off her glasses. "That's exactly my point. You love her, but you're pushing her away? She's not pushing you away, if anything she's letting you in. Have you considered that she might be terrified to lose you? Consider what she's already lost."

The sentence fired off before he could calm down. "I've lost people I loved too."

Her expression softened. "None of us can control when someone leaves us," she paused, "but isn't the chance of love better than none at all? I'd take that chance if I was given it. I haven't experienced love myself, but I *know* with every fiber of my being that it's possible. I've seen it. I see a glimmer of it when the two of you are together, but you'll never find out what could be if you push her away."

The defensiveness that he'd carried just under his collarbones the last four days slowly started to wane. As they stood silent for a minute, the cacophony of the hospital just outside the door creeped into the small space.

"You should call her," she said gently. "Also flowers don't hurt."

The stark realization that his coworker had literally knocked some sense into him washed over this body. He'd been so worried about Emilie rejecting him again that he'd justified blocking her out, even after she took a huge step and told him about her past.

Shit. I am an asshole.

A short breath left his lungs. "Damn it, Ashley. You're right."

Her grin was wide. "I think it's Ash now."

The door behind her opened, and Barbara entered the staff lounge taking a look at the two of them. She continued on to the refrigerator, saying evenly, "Ashley. Dr. Abernan."

Ash's eyes widened pointedly. "I believe you were going to make a call, Dr. Abernan."

"Yes." He nodded a goodbye to both women before he left the room.

He exited the lounge, wanting to rectify the mess he'd made with Emilie immediately, but forced himself to write the orders his patient needed. After speaking to the woman and her family, he walked briskly to the hallway just outside the unit.

Grabbing his cell phone from his pocket, he pulled Emilie's contact up on the screen. How could he not have considered her feelings in his foolish attempt at self-preservation? He couldn't believe he'd been so stupid.

The phone rang several times before her voicemail picked up. She was probably avoiding his call, rightfully so. He raced down the stairs to the OR to change his clothes, hoping that it wasn't too late to fix this.

When he arrived at her building with the flowers he'd purchased from the hospital gift shop, the sun had just set, casting an unnatural glow onto the street. He stomped his boots against the ground trying to free some of the accumulated slush from the walk over and pushed the buzzer for her condo.

There was no answer.

Internally, he cursed himself again for being so idiotic as his finger found the button a second time. Before he could push it, a couple came behind him using their key to enter the building and kindly let him in. As he climbed the three flights to her door, he mentally ran through all the things he wanted to apologize for. Taking a deep breath, he knocked on her door.

Please be home. Please be home.

The door didn't open, but Colin could hear her on the phone.

Her voice was so strained.

Clips of words and eventually, "I love you too, Mom," came before the sounds ceased. His stomach tightened with an unnatural twist as an agonizing resonance hummed in his arms and fingers.

His forehead clunked on the door as he willed it to open. "Emilie?" he called out. "Can I talk to you?"

He heard the reassuring sounds of feet shuffling closer and could feel her presence beyond the slender barrier of wood. "I don't think that's a good idea."

Anguish bounced rapidly around in his body. "Please, Emilie. I'm so incredibly sorry."

A halting exhale came from the other side of the door and what sounded like her leaning against it.

Colin tried again. "Please? Just for a moment?"

The noise of weight shifting off the door and then the click of a deadbolt opening had never sounded so magnificent.

He could fix this.

He just needed a chance.

When the door opened, the look of her almost laid him flat. Her eyes were red and swollen as if she had been crying, though they were dry and eerily blank now. Salted streaks lined her cheeks. Her chestnut hair was wild and disheveled around her shoulders. Shivering in a rumpled tank top and cotton shorts, her bare feet were nearly blue on the hardwood floor.

Even though she probably didn't want him to touch her, he immediately picked her up. He expected her to fight him, but she didn't. She actually dropped all her weight onto him like a ragdoll the minute he swooped her up, lying her head heavy on his shoulder.

After closing the door with a kick of his foot, he carried her to the couch. The flowers he bought crunched under her weight, dispelling their light fragrance into a heavy room. Kneeling on the ground beside her, he shrugged off his jacket and tucked it around her cold legs.

"I am so sorry for being such a complete ass the last few days. You opened up, and I responded in the worst possible way." His hands gripped the microfiber edge of the couch seat, resisting the urge to reach for her. "I know I've been distant and cold, but I want to make it up to you if I can. I'll do anything." He swallowed hard against the lump in his throat. "I was just afraid because when you were sleeping, you said—"

"It's not . . . today is . . ." she interrupted, her voice numb and scarily distant.

Her eyes fluttered from the ceiling where she had been staring and looked straight through him. Suddenly, his words dimmed in comparison to whatever she was trying with difficulty to communicate.

"I should've known better . . . I can't have . . . any . . . again . . ." She waved a hand generally over the room. "This is all too much."

He pushed a hand through his hair, not quite understanding what it was she meant. His heart squeezed wildly in his chest as she silently turned her back to him and buried her face in the pillows on the couch.

This was worse than if she had been crying. She seemed so far away as if he couldn't reach her. His brain was flying with what would be the best thing to say next when she spoke again.

Her voice was muffled, but her sentence was coherent. "I'm sorry I dragged you into this."

A short, painful breath left his lungs. "Why are you apologizing to *me*? You've done nothing wrong. I'm the one that hurt you, and there's nothing more I want than to take away all your pain right now." His arms ached with his own powerlessness. "I wish I knew how."

She turned her head slightly towards him. "I can't be strong for you. Not today."

Reaching out a hand, he tentatively ran it along her tangled hair, rubbing her back in slow, even circles. "You don't have to be anything for me . . . ever. Just be *with* me."

He kept his touch soft and calming, even though it felt as if a pack of starving sharks were fighting viciously to devour his insides. A long time passed, and for a moment he thought she'd fallen asleep, but he heard the words in a low, hoarse whisper.

"Today is her birthday."

His hand froze as every muscle in his body stiffened.

Not only had he abandoned her for the last four days after she'd finally told him about her past, but he did it right before what would have been her daughter's birthday. He wasn't just an asshole; he was the biggest asshole on the planet.

He blinked rapidly as his breath returned to him. "Oh, Emilie . . ." His words halted in his throat.

She shifted on the couch, and her eyes told him everything he needed to know. Sadness circled and hollowed them and would likely reside there in some amount forever. He glimpsed the severity of what she had been carrying around with her for the last four years and knew that she would carry it for the rest of her life.

If he was not prepared to accept her pain, then there would be no chance in truly loving her. Clarity swiftly pulsed through his body as a resounding answer sang in his mind. He'd accept whatever she was able and willing to give and be grateful for the chance to be with her for however long he could. If he could do nothing else in his life, he would love Emilie just as she was.

He yearned to soothe her. "May I hold you?"

A slight nod was all the response Colin needed. Lifting her up so that he could sit next to her, he interwove her body against his. The familiar comfort of having her in his arms vibrated through his veins, and he hoped she was experiencing a similar sensation. If he could absorb all of her suffering through touch, he would have gladly taken it into his body for her.

"It's the first time that I've been alone on her birthday." Her voice had regained most of its usual strength. "Even Ash didn't know about today. When I lived in Virginia, I lived with my parents. There was always someone around on this day. I had," she paused, "some really dark days after the accident, so I lived with them as I got better until I moved here. I thought I could handle today on my own. I've been so strong since moving here . . ."

He felt her shift in his arms, and he glanced down to see her staring at the brick fireplace. "She would have been four."

An image of a miniature Emilie running around learning her ABCs and being tucked into bed each night by her loving family flashed through his mind.

Her shaky exhale vibrated against his body as she rested her cheek over his chest. Ambient street noise hummed beyond the large bay window as he strengthened his arms around her frame.

Colin swallowed against the tightness in his throat. "I know there's nothing I can say, but is there anything I can do?"

When Emilie lifted her face again, her eyes shone with such vulnerability his breath caught. "Don't leave."

His hand traced the outline of her face as he answered her, "Never." He considered his mistake of the last four days. "Never again."

·CHAPTER 27·

Emilie sat on an incredibly comfortable easy chair with a very happy, very chunky, newly one-year-old pulling at the hem of her charcoal sweater dress. He babbled incoherently while nodding his large head. It was covered in sparse, short red hair, with the exception of the center which presented a filled patch of longer hair that roughly resembled a bad baby toupee.

Kate caught her eyes lingering. "I know we should trim the top of his head until the rest of it grows out, but Max here . . ." She poked at her husband sitting next to her on the couch. ". . . won't let me."

"Don't they say not to cut baby hair?" His hand moved over the side of his buzzed and balding head.

"Of course you can cut a baby's hair." A teasing smile laced Kate's lips. "He's going to have many, many haircuts until his falls out just like Daddy's."

Max went to tickle her, and she caught his hand and kissed it instead.

"We have family pictures next week. We can't have him looking like that."

Noticing his mother's attention, Owen furniture walked from the chair, to the coffee table, to the couch, repeating "mamama" on his way over. Kate picked him up and settled him on her lap.

"Traitor." Max waggled a finger at his son before sitting back and looking at his wife. "All right, a slight trim . . . but *I'm* going to do it."

Kate opened her eyes wide, giving Emilie a *Can you believe we have to deal with these men?* sort of look that had her laughing and glancing at Colin in the chair next to her. His gaze was already focused on her and the affection in it was so palpable, her breath almost caught. She glimpsed back to see Kate and Max pass a knowing look between each other.

"I'm going to get Owen ready for bed before we have coffee." Kate rose with her son on her hip. "Babe, why don't you help me?"

"Anything for you, my love." Max winked in Colin's direction before they both left the room.

Emilie could feel Colin's eyes on her face before she turned. "They're wonderful."

He grinned before his gaze swept to the stairs. "They are."

"Thank you for inviting me."

It was Dr. Campbell—Max—that technically asked her to dinner. He'd stopped her in the cafeteria a week ago while she was getting coffee.

"I'm glad that you wanted to come." His eyes fully relaxed as his smile grew.

Reading between the lines, she understood that Max and Kate were essentially family to him.

Baritone singing could be heard through the ceiling, and Colin's face tilted up at the sound. He looked so incredibly sexy in his dress shirt and slacks, the top two buttons of his shirt undone in a casual, but enticing way. She'd failed to consider how seeing Colin's strong jaw and boyish hair over date attire would stir the blood in her veins.

Though they'd had a few day dates recently, Colin seemed to be trying to take everything as slow as he could, leaving her only with a gentlemanly kiss at each goodbye and keeping his strong hands to himself.

Her fingers absentmindedly ran from behind her ear to her collarbone. Blue-grey eyes caught the movement and lingered on her neck. The heat he'd been containing so diligently over the last three weeks quickly filtered into his eyes as his chest rose. When his gaze swept over her snug dress, stocking covered legs, and heels, Emilie wondered if this time it would break free.

Her lips parted, waiting.

"Emilie, how do you take your coffee?" Kate stood at the edge of the room.

"Um." She blinked, collecting herself. "Black, please."

After coffee, they said their goodbyes. The thirty-minute drive to the city passed with easy, casual conversation until she saw that they were close to her condo.

"I'm not used to coffee after dinner, and I feel a bit wired," she lied. "Do you think it would be too much to stop by your place? Maybe we can have a glass of wine or something?"

The car drifted slightly into the other lane before he pulled it back quickly. "My place?"

"Yes." She let her voice darken and watched his handsome Adam's apple bob as he swallowed hard.

Anticipation lingered like smoke, making the short five-minute drive between their places much too long. When he opened the door to his condo and held it aside, she could almost feel the tension reverberating through his muscles. It'd been two months since she'd been inside, and the difference was stark.

The recliner was now nestled into a seating area with a couch, a wingback chair, and a coffee table over a grey-blue patterned floor rug that ironically matched the color of Colin's eyes. A large professional photograph of what looked like a North Carolina beach was hanging on the wall above the piano in addition to other photographs of beach dunes or mountain landscapes on any of the open walls in the living room. A small custom woodwork table resembling a slice from a fallen tree sat under the windows adjacent to the kitchen with two gorgeously constructed wood chairs.

"I've added some things since you were here last." His voice held a shy quality.

"I like them." The condo now reflected his easygoing charm. She walked toward the fireplace and ran her hand over the back of the couch.

Colin seemed to be lost in the sight of her palm flowing over the taut fabric for a breath before he cleared his throat. "I think I have a bottle of wine somewhere."

When Emilie had been here before, she'd seen the pictures on the bookshelves, but didn't really focus on them. Taking her time, she looked at each photo. When she saw one of a younger version of Colin with two adults, her fingers picked it up.

"Are these your parents?" she asked, knowing the answer.

He arrived behind her. "Yes."

Emilie said what was in her heart as she returned the photo. "They are beautiful."

"They were amazing people. I'm lucky to have been their son." He outstretched a mug to her. "Sorry, I didn't think to buy wine glasses."

The sweetness of being offered a mug full of wine tugged at her chest. For as much as Colin was strong and capable, he was also helpless in little endearing ways. "That's okay." She smiled before she took a sip.

He watched her mouth as she swallowed, and she had to fight the impulse to set her mug on the bookshelf and twist her fingers through his hair.

"Would you mind?" She glanced at the couch. "I want to talk to you about something."

She'd thought excessively about it, talked with Nia about it, and knew she was ready to take this step.

Colin cautiously crossed to the couch in a controlled way, and sat as far away from her as he could.

"I really appreciate how much you listen to me. It makes me feel safe and respected."

His gaze focused intently on hers, waiting on her to continue.

"I think somewhere after telling you about my past, we misunderstood each other. Somehow our wires got crossed. I want us to be able to talk to each other honestly. To be able to ask for what we want from each other. What I want . . ." She took an inhale. ". . . is to stay here tonight if that's something you want too."

Desire crept easily into his eyes as the implications of her words were quickly processed by his brain. They searched over her face before settling on her lips. "Are you sure?"

The rapid beating of her pulse throbbed in her neck as she felt the entirety of her skin flush. All she wanted right now was his weight against her, but he hadn't moved from his position, much too far away. She set her wine down on the coffee table, moving to lean a hand onto his knee, giving her leverage to reach his lips. He stayed very still as she barely brushed her lips to his. "Yes."

Any resolve he'd been harboring, she'd obviously broken. Immediately setting his mug down, he leaned back, pulling her body fully on top of his. His mouth passionately explored hers while the very hands she'd been so preoccupied with all dinner swept over her body in a perfectly possessive way. Emilie lost her breath as pressure and heat and connection built inside her.

He hoarsely whispered to her lips. "I've missed you."

"I've been right here." She pushed against his shoulders to sit up and focus on his expressive eyes. "Why did you go back to square one?"

Colin reached a hand up and ever so gently pushed a strand of her hair behind her ear. "I didn't want to chance upsetting you. I never want to hurt you like I did again."

The sincerity in his gaze made her breath catch as vibration ran down her arms to her fingertips.

"Colin." She laid both of her hands over the center of his crisp button-down shirt, and his eyes slowly blinked at her touch. "You hurt me when you stopped talking to me after I was honest with you, not because you wanted this." Her eyes darted between the two of them.

They stared at each other for a brief, tense moment, both of them taking short, expectant inhales.

"I think we need to be better about telling each other what we want." She leaned forward, bringing her lips to his, never moving her hands from his chest. "I'll start. I want this. I want *you*."

This time when their lips met, she knew he understood. His kiss had a slow burning depth that found the far reaches of her and grasped them firm. As his arms wove around her, she noticed something else in his kiss that she couldn't quite understand. Something that hid at the fringes of her mind like a butterfly flitting just out of sight.

Colin slowly leaned his weight forward until she was pushed back into the couch before stepping off of it. Bending down with the softest kiss to the side of her neck, he thread his arms beneath her shoulders and under her knees, deftly lifting her up and carrying her across the room to his bedroom.

◊◊◊

Emilie woke to the strong, rhythmic beating of Colin's heart under her ear. Consciousness returned to her in varying degrees as she registered the warmth of his naked body beside her. Carefully tilting her gaze up a fraction, she saw that he was still sleeping peacefully. A contented exhale left her as she let herself melt into the crook of his arm, listening to the rise and fall of each breath.

Memories of last night filled her mind. Slowly removing each other's clothing while tenderly kissing. The exploratory but gentle way his hands had roamed her whole body followed by his warm kisses. How his lips had affectionately grazed her c-section scar before returning to hers in the most accepting way. He seemed to know her on a level even she couldn't communicate; it was as if their bodies just understood each other.

It felt like a surprise, but if she took the time to converse with her heart, she knew deep down that being with Colin would have been just like it was. Last night was not the quick-paced acceleration like when they kissed. There was an unspoken comprehension that this time should be reverent and meaningful. It seemed fitting that they fell asleep in each other's arms afterwards, not bothering to move or dress or break the connection they'd just built.

Her fingertips sifted through the curly chest hair under her hand, memorizing the feel of his skin with each delicate touch. After a few seconds, a muscled arm wrapped around her body, settling into the dip of her hip with the most magnificent weight.

"Good morning." His voice rumbled deep in his chest.

She lifted her head to see his beautiful eyes, and her lips pulled up on their own. "Good morning, Colin."

His eyes lit up at her smile before they rolled closed in an unguarded expression of bliss as she said his name. When they blinked open, his gaze focused on hers with gentle concern. "How are you feeling? Are you okay?"

I haven't been this okay in a very, very long time.

"I'm good. How are you?"

A chuckle bounced her head a bit as he laughed her name. "Emilie."

She pushed up against her elbow. "What?"

Pulling with his powerful arms, he plucked her right off the bed and settled her on top of him. "You have no idea how long I have been wanting that. How long I've been wanting *you.*"

His words seared into her body, but the intense hunger of his gaze as it dropped to her lips and then to her breasts put her over the edge. She bent at the waist, pushing her body firmly to his as her fingers twisted through his hair. Now Emilie wanted the frantic, heated version of what they'd done the night before.

◊◊◊

She hadn't moved from on top of him, just collapsed, her forehead in the crook of his neck. Colin lazily wove his hands down her back, brushing her hair with his fingers. She didn't want to move, but her stomach rumbled loudly between them.

"We should probably eat something," she said as an answer to it. The rest of her body had been so thoroughly satisfied, it was almost as if her digestive system was pouting at the inattention.

He exhaled into the top of her head. "Probably."

Emilie lifted her face to gaze at his handsome features. His hair was mussed from her fingers, his jaw relaxed but strong, and his color slightly flushed from exertion and euphoria.

"Is there even anything here to eat?" A teasing grin laced her lips.

"I keep milk and cereal stocked along with microwave dinners."

"Good." She laid a kiss on his smiling mouth before rolling off of him.

"I'll make coffee." After momentarily disposing of the condom in the small trash can under the nightstand, he pulled on the pajama pants from the chair by the window. Gratitude flushed through her when he didn't put a shirt on. "If you don't want to put your dress back on you can find something of mine to wear in the closet."

Emilie entered the bathroom and freshened up a bit before stepping into the adjoining closet. Relishing the idea of picking something of his to wear, she took her time looking over all the different options: scrub tops, dress shirts, t-shirts, sweaters. All would fit like a tunic and cover her underwear that she'd put back on.

When she found the blue and grey flannel he'd been wearing when he asked her out—when they'd first kissed—she reached for it. She was snuggling into the soft shirt, buttoning it up over her bare chest, when she spotted a wooden box with a beautifully inlaid top. Her fingers grazed the smooth surface, and she found her hands opening the lid.

The sweet woody scent of cedar lifted to her nose as she gazed at the dozen or so white letter envelopes. The one on the top was face down, the V of the seal looking back at her, but beneath it on another envelope to the left she read in a feminine cursive "*When your . . .*" the rest was hidden under the top envelope. From the other side, tidy block letters of another hand read ". . . *miss me.*" She was contemplating picking up the top envelope when she felt Colin's heat behind her.

Quickly closing the lid, she spun into his chest. "I'm sorry. I wasn't trying to snoop."

His eyes swept her body before resting on hers. "It's okay."

Suddenly, it occurred to her that she knew nothing of his past relationships. It was unmistakably a woman's hand scrawled on at least one of the envelopes, if not all of them. Something nagged at her. She had no right to be jealous, but it bloomed in her chest nonetheless.

"Are those from a woman?"

The left side of his mouth pulled up in a satisfied tug, understanding the implication behind her words, before it promptly fell. Her ribs tightened at the downward turn of his lips as he let out a controlled breath.

"Yes, but not in the way that you're thinking. They're letters from my mother."

She felt her eyes widen, unable to come up with a response to the fact that she had so carelessly trespassed onto something that was beloved to him.

"She wrote them when it was clear she wasn't going to get better." The sadness of his mouth crept into his eyes. "There's a letter for every milestone of my life that she would have . . ." he paused, "that she missed."

Her arms reached for his shoulders, bringing him to her. "I am so sorry."

She was apologizing for the transgression into his personal property, but also for all that he had to experience without his mother as a witness. Something she had and many others likely took for granted.

A deep inhale rose against her. "I'm glad she wrote those for me. It allowed me to feel like she was still with me after she died. I still read them from time to time when I miss her. The milestones I've passed anyway."

Her head tilted up to study his face. "There are letters you haven't read?"

A floppy lock of hair fell into his eyes as he nodded. When he didn't expand, Emilie let her other questions evaporate into the air. Reaching up, she smoothed the tension from his sandy eyebrows with her fingertips. His eyes closed at her touch, letting out a long, halting exhale.

"Let's have breakfast," she said quietly.

He nodded into her hands before taking a step out of the closet. Following closely behind, the smell of coffee met her at the doorway to the kitchen, and she reflexively hummed in anticipation.

"You really like coffee, don't you?" His playful smile was back on his face as he pulled two mugs from an open cabinet and filled them to the brim.

"Doesn't everyone like coffee?" She grinned in response to the outstretched mug.

His laughter filled the kitchen as he shook his head. "What are you going to do today?" he asked, lifting his mug.

At dinner last night, they'd discovered they were both off today.

Feeling buoyed by his laugh, his tenderness last night, and his honesty this morning, she took a chance and ventured into new territory. "I don't know. What are *we* going to do today?"

His eyes glinted with mischief when they glanced up from over his lifted coffee cup.

Suddenly, she wasn't very hungry for food anymore.

·CHAPTER 28·

Colin didn't know how he was going to make it through the day. He didn't know how he was going to make it through the whole day without telling Emilie he loved her.

Already he'd barely kept it to himself as they made love for the third time in twenty-four hours, drunkenly inhaling her honeysuckle scent while her coffee-stained tongue played with his. Last night he nearly burst with it, especially since being with Emilie was so much more than physically satisfying. It was like nothing he'd ever experienced.

Now as she unabashedly bit into her chicken, mushroom, and swiss sandwich, juice dripping freely from her chin, he didn't think he could take the pressure building in his chest. When he reached to brush the liquid away, she just stilled with a grin on her lips and let him. He loved her even more like this, when confidence and happiness radiated from her, even with a mouth full of chicken.

"Is your lunch good?" The corner of his mouth picked up.

After coffee, Colin had driven her home so she could shower and change into different clothes before they at last got something to eat.

"Mmmm-hmmm." She put the back of her hand over her mouth. "How's yours?"

He was holding the burger he'd ordered, but he'd been so distracted by how she seemed to look even more stunning with a post-orgasmic sheen, he hadn't taken a bite.

"Good," he said, sinking his teeth into what was a delicious burger.

Has food always tasted this good?

She took a long sip of her soda as Elvis's voice crooned in the background. "So what do you want to do after this?"

Thinking he'd already accomplished what he wanted to do most twice this morning, he let his brain stretch to other activities but came up short. "I don't know. Do you have any ideas?"

"It's almost sixty today and sunny, which is a miracle. We could go for a walk in the Commons." She bit into the crinkle cut fry she'd pulled through ketchup.

"Oh no!" he answered quickly, stretching his fingers out in a handmade stop sign. "No Commons. We both know what happens to me there, and I don't want anything to ruin this day."

She laughed loudly and carelessly, and a bit of his resolve not to tell her slipped away. "A different park then. We can walk Esplanade."

"Maybe. I run there a lot though so if you jinx it for me, I'm going to be pissed."

"I can't Eagle Scouts honor it, but I can promise that I won't intentionally try to maim you." Those lips pulled into that flirty twist he adored.

"I suppose that's a start." His cheeks were starting to hurt.

"I was thinking." Her gaze fixed on her plate for a few beats, her long hair falling in front of her shoulder. "Maybe afterwards you can come over to my place, and I'll make us dinner."

"I'd like that."

Her gorgeous brown eyes lifted with light behind them. "Okay, good. You sitting at home eating a TV dinner tonight would make a sad end to this day."

"As long as I got to spend the day with you, it wouldn't matter how it ended." He swore the skin beneath her freckles flushed. When he reached across the slick formica table to hold her hand, Emilie gave it to him easily. "I'd love to come over." Lifting her hand to his mouth, he kissed her knuckles.

Releasing her hand, he was picking up his burger again when Shannon appeared behind Emilie's shoulder.

"Dr. Abernan, I wanted to thank you for seeing dad on such short notice this week."

He watched Emilie glance over her shoulder to see who was speaking, as he answered, "Of course. Anytime you need me, I'll be available."

The two women registered each other's presence and their different emotions displayed easily on their faces, concern on Emilie's and surprise on Shannon's.

"Is Bo okay?" she asked at the same time Shannon said, "Oh . . . Hi, Emilie."

Emilie's eyes swept over the restaurant observing for the first time that the ever-present patriarch was not here. He should have considered that she'd notice Bo's absence when she suggested they'd eat here for lunch. The worry that scrunched her freckled brow sat like a large rock in his stomach.

Shannon fiddled with the lowest button on her cardigan. "Yes. He's just home resting today."

He could see Emilie resisting the urge to ask for more information before her eyes flitted to his, knowing he wouldn't betray his patient's confidentiality.

Shannon's stress-ridden face broke into a slow smile. "Mom would have liked this."

Even though they were not currently touching each other, it was apparently obvious that they were together. It dawned on him that everyone in the restaurant might be able to easily see the truth that he was carefully trying to hide from Emilie.

A young twenty-something man in a double-breasted white cook's jacket rushed to Shannon's elbow. "There's a problem in the kitchen."

"Excuse me." She strode off as quickly as she had appeared.

Without speaking about it, they both fell into thoughtful silence. Colin wasn't sure what was running through her mind, but his was momentarily thrown back into work.

After paying the bill, he helped Emilie into her duffle coat and stepped into the crisp but truly lovely spring day. She seemed recovered from the interaction with Shannon and began telling him another story about her spirited niece. When they reached the pathway on the Charles River, the high sun was sparkling off the water, ebbing and cresting as the river flowed. Many other people were taking advantage of the warmer weather—parents pushed children bundled up in strollers, runners were abundant, and several walked like them.

Emilie's eyes watched the water, and they strolled in companionable silence for a while. A double scull being pulled through the water by two athletic women passed them. Colin liked their conversations, but also found that being next to each other like this, without words, was just as enjoyable. Reaching down, he laced his fingers in hers, and she smiled up at him as he did so.

"What do you want me to make for dinner when we get home?"

It felt as if his heart was trying to escape via his collarbones; it was so light and soaring in its ribcage. What a simple little question, but she asked it in a way that made it feel like they had been doing this for ages. That they were just out taking a walk on this beautiful afternoon, and soon they would head back to *their* home, *together*. He wondered if she noticed the ease of which the day, this first day of them being together, was going.

"Food." Honestly, as long as she was with him, he'd eat bugs.

She huffed a bit. "What kind of food?"

"Good food," he said, needling her.

She let out an aggravated growl that had him smiling so much, he pulled hard on the hand he was holding and spun her into him. A high surprised sound escaped before he covered her lips with his, and it melted into a quiet sigh. He moved his other hand to the side of her face, sliding his fingers into her hair at the nape of her neck.

Emilie gasped against his lips, and he knew that his fingers were probably cold. He'd chosen to forgo gloves, and his reward for facing the elements was the soft feeling of her beautifully freckled skin under his fingers. If she gave him the opportunity, he would spend the rest of his life memorizing this delicate map of points. He kissed her slowly, tasting every reach of her mouth with tender, unrushed strokes of his tongue.

Pulling her back into an easy walk, Colin tried to conceal a smirk. "What would you normally make today?"

"On my days off, I try to make something that I can reheat for the rest of the week. I was thinking of making lasagna."

"That sounds delicious."

"Okay. We just need to stop by the market to pick up a few things on the way home."

He wondered if she knew she was doing it again, speaking in that simple way that made his pulse and thoughts race. There was no way he was going to make it out of this day alive if those beautiful words kept falling from those beautiful lips.

They walked quietly for a few moments before she asked, "What made you want to be a doctor?" He realized that with all their conversations, they'd never discussed the topic.

"Because of my mom," he answered. "Before she died, I was thinking about becoming a math professor like my dad. After seeing the different oncologists and how wonderful they all were with her, I decided that was what I wanted to do.

"I was pretty singularly focused on that career path until my second year of medical school when a faculty member and mentor gently suggested that perhaps I choose a different field of medicine. That way I wouldn't be reliving her death with every patient I lost to cancer.

"I'd been interested in cardiology and with her suggestion, it was like I was given permission to pursue something else. Something that I just liked instead of trying to make up for what I'd lost."

She was nodding faintly beside him, her eyes looking out over the water as the slight breeze pushed her wavy hair. "Professor. Your father taught college math?"

His eyes strained involuntarily, and he swallowed against the bitter taste in this mouth. "Yes."

Emilie's gloved fingers tightened around his. "What was he like?"

Tension ran down his arms and he stopped, letting go of her hand. "Emilie, I don't . . ."

She turned to him, squinting and shielding her eyes against the sun with her hand. Almost automatically, he stepped closer to cast a shadow over her face.

Her hand dropped from her forehead to his arm. "I'm sorry for asking."

He felt his chest pull against his coat with his inhale as he looked at the water. "No. It's okay. You're allowed to ask. It's just . . ." The words caught in his throat, scratching against the inside of his neck. "I . . . I couldn't save him."

Her sharp inhale drew his attention. Darkness flashed quickly in her eyes before she pushed them tightly closed. Her other hand flew to his bicep as if she was about to lose her balance.

"Emilie?"

Her eyes snapped open. "How did he die?"

It was a strange sensation that flowed through his body as she asked that question. In that second, it became more important to him to answer her than it was to conceal the pain of how his inactivity played a role in his father's death. He became hyper focused on the tension in her eyes and his pulsating need to relieve it.

"My father had AFib but never told me about it. He'd been on coumadin therapy when he got a late spring flu going around campus. I came and took care of him for a few days, brought him cans of chicken soup and crackers." His gaze flowed to the moving water. "I didn't think anything about how he didn't eat the spinach salad he always had everyday with dinner.

"His INR spiked with the shift in his diet, and when he returned to campus a few days later, he fell in his office and hit his head on the side of his desk. He'd already taught his classes for the day, and I was on call that night, so it wasn't until someone checked his office the next day that they found him on the carpet."

He glanced to see that the previous agitation in her eyes had soothed, only concern remained in them.

"At the time, I didn't know about any of his medical history, so I didn't understand how my father was fine one day and found dead on the floor of his office the next. The autopsy showed a massive intracranial hemorrhage. The thing . . ." His breath caught.

"The thing is that this is what I *do*. I've spent my life dedicating myself to my career. Had I known, I could have titrated his medication, or gotten his cardiologist on board, or *something*."

His hand flew through his hair as itchiness swelled in his body again. "But I didn't know anything. He never told me, and because he didn't trust me enough to tell me about his health, he died of something completely preventable."

Her fingertips on his coat sleeve tightened. "He probably didn't want to worry you after all you'd been through with your mom."

"On some level I understand that." A heated exhale left his lungs. "But I was thirteen then. I'm thirty-eight now and a *goddamn* cardiothoracic surgeon. If I'd known, he'd still be with me."

Her gloved fingers pushed a stray hair from his temple, reminding him she was right in front of him. When Colin glanced down, her eyes were filled with such empathy that his head bowed on its own accord. His eyes fluttered closed at the pressure of her forehead against his, her hand sliding to the base of his neck, holding him to her. Her touch was comforting in a way nothing prior had ever been.

"I'm sorry, Colin."

His resigned exhale was wisped away with the breeze riding off the river.

◊◊◊

After a very long walk and a stop by a small market in Beacon Hill, they arrived at her condo. Colin revealed his limited abilities in the kitchen and was given the task of chopping vegetables for their salad. Sizzling and the smell of browning beef and onions filled the room.

He stopped chopping from his assigned station at the kitchen island to watch her body as she worked over the range. The late daylight streamed in through the large bay window and bathed everything it touched in a warm golden glow. She was adding tomato sauce to the cast iron pot when he crossed to her, swept the hair from her shoulder, and kissed the side of her neck. As he knew she would, she hummed and melted into his kiss.

"How do you know that's my favorite?" Her voice was breathy.

He gave the answer that burned in his chest. "I just know."

Emilie leaned back into him, and he wrapped his arms around her waist, holding her as she continued adding ingredients to finish the sauce. Once the lasagna was assembled and in the oven and the salad cooling in the refrigerator, she poured them each a glass from a bottle of wine and led them to the loveseat.

They sat facing each other—the light from the window encircling Emilie's head. It reminded Colin of the first time he'd been in her condo after she was nearly mugged in the Commons. He'd never experienced anything like his vision slowly returning and seeing her concerned eyes searching his.

He set his wineglass on the ground and gathered her free hand in both of his. "Emilie." He took his gaze from her hand to her eyes. "Did you mean what you said last night? About us being honest with each other?"

Setting her glass on the ground as well, she wove her second hand in his. "Yes. I think it's important. I think I hurt you by not telling you the truth sooner, and then we didn't talk for days."

He winced internally at the memory of trying to shut her out of his heart and the pain he caused her. "That wasn't your fault," he countered quickly. "It was mine."

"Still, I should have been up front with you." Her words only strengthened his resolve that he was going in the right direction.

"I need to talk to you about something and I need you to understand that I don't expect anything from you. I know it would be asking too much." His pulse thrummed at his words, knowing more than anything he did want her to feel the way he did.

"What is it?"

A suppressed smile teased at his lips as he looked into her focused brown eyes and saw the slight crease of bewilderment between her chestnut eyebrows.

"I love you, Emilie."

Her lips parted in an audible gasp.

Rolling his thumb over her wrist, he continued, "I've loved you for some time actually, but I was afraid if I said anything, I would scare you. I didn't want to do anything that would make you push away. I don't expect you to feel the same way or say anything in return, but I had to tell you."

He knew it was unfair of him, but his eyes searched her face.

"I . . ." she began and then the words were caught in her open mouth.

A tentative hand moved to her cheek, and she didn't shy away. "I just needed you to know."

He leaned into her and kissed her with all the love he felt for her. It was enough for him to love her and to let her know, if that was all he could have. When she kissed him with the same intensity he gave, hope soared in his chest, but fell as soon as he gazed into her eyes after their lips separated.

"I can't . . ." She struggled.

His insides felt as if they were being slowly and painfully shredded, but he gathered her into his arms. "It's okay. Do you want me to leave?"

She shook her head against him, and he took comfort in that action. Then she nestled into his arms the way they fit so perfectly together, and placed her hand hesitantly over his heart. Colin tried not to let his breath catch at her touch, controlling his breathing was so hard right now with everything he'd said.

Smoothing out her hand, she pushed her palm fully to his heartbeat. "Please stay."

Certain she could feel the jackhammer of his muscle beating beneath her hand, he made her a promise, pulling her closer and silently breathing it into her hair.

Always.

·CHAPTER 29·

The metallic clang of her locker door resounded in Emilie's mouth, like chewing on a piece of aluminum. This oddly acute perception had followed her all week. After Colin had told her he loved her, the reality in front of her eyes didn't make sense. Light played off objects differently, scents that she usually ignored presented themselves for her evaluation, and textures against her fingertips intensified.

Existence was varied and unusual to her, but Colin seemed relaxed and unburdened after he said three little words that tilted her axis. Since then, they worked together once and texted a few times. It was almost as if the words she'd undoubtedly heard hadn't been said as he patiently waited for her to draw her own conclusion.

Everything was the same, but everything was completely different.

Her brain went into overdrive trying to process this new information, making her tired. She'd lost sleep lying in bed staring at the ceiling, her hands pressed firmly over her sternum. Logically, loving another person shouldn't diminish the life and love she had with Braden, but a weight still sat at the base of her spine.

It was one thing to be intimate with another man again, but it was entirely different to be in love with another man.

That, of course, was the hitch in the first place.

He wasn't just another man.

He was *Colin*.

After pushing through the unit doors, she moved towards the charge desk to pick up her assignment. The buzzed back of Max's head was hovering nearby and rotated when the night charge pointed her direction. Relief flowed over his face as he strode towards her and tucked them into a charting alcove.

"There you are."

Pressure built between her brows, but she forced her mind to be sensible. "Do you need help with a patient?"

He ran his hand over his auburn beard. "No. It's Colin. He was running this morning and . . . he's downstairs in the emerg . . ."

She didn't need to hear the rest of that word. Adrenaline surged through her veins as her heart jumped to the ready in her chest. The muscles of her calves and quads fired immediately as she pushed her weight against the floor and sprinted through the double doors.

"Emilie, wait . . ." Max's voice sounded as if it was underwater.

Her hands hit the steel handle of the stairwell hard before she flew down the five flights of stairs to the ground floor. Rounding the corner to the back entrance of the Emergency Room, she rushed through the open double doors.

The familiar pinging of medical equipment, the static of the EMS radio, and staff working and talking through open trauma bay doors made her freeze for a nanosecond pause. Bile rose in her throat, and she resisted the overwhelming urge to double over and throw up.

Not again. Please, not again.

Forcing her muscles to move, she dodged into the opening of three rooms before she found him.

Colin's eyes were closed as he lay on the emergency room gurney. Blood soaked the right side of his scalp and the pillow beneath his head. Where his brow met his hairline there was a line of tidy stitches about an inch long. His left pinky and ring finger were wrapped in gauze lying on top of the hospital's green checkered gown.

Her vision narrowed to the side of his neck as she watched his chest rise and then fall. An inhale rasped in her throat as she felt the shaking start in her fingertips and move up her arms.

As she silently crossed the room, the barely functioning medically trained part of her brain read the telemetry, the blood pressure machine, and the pulse oximeter. The pounding in her ears was louder than the beeping of the IV pole running fluids into this arm. Every machine showed that his vitals were strong, but disbelief smacked strongly in her chest.

Stopping beside him, she reached a trembling hand to touch his brow below the line of blue sutures.

Colin's eyes flew open. "*Emilie.*"

The timber of his voice should have bought her relief, but it did the opposite. A strangled sound came out of her mouth as her fingers united the ties at his neck, yanked at the snapps at his shoulder, and ripped his gown down to survey the damage herself. Her vibrating fingers ran the length of his chest. The right side was bruised badly, but it was whole.

He was not completely broken.

The legs that had so steadily brought her here gave out beneath her, and she felt Colin's arm wrap around her. He pulled her onto the gurney, her cheek falling to the left side of his chest as uncontrollable tears streamed from her eyes onto his warm skin.

Max stomped to the entry of the door, breathing heavily.

"Damn, she's fast," he said at the same time Colin shouted, "Jesus, Max! Didn't you tell her I was okay?"

"I tried to," he heaved. "She was like . . ." Another breath. ". . . a rocket."

Colin swore under his breath, and with a slight groan of discomfort, he pulled the pulse ox off his right hand to hold her tighter.

"It's okay," he murmured. "I'm okay."

Her entire body shook as she sobbed. She was no longer in control of her actions. Somewhere in her brain, it shouted at her to get off him, that he was obviously in pain, and she was making it worse, but her hands clung to him unwavering.

He's alive. He's alive. He's alive.

"I'm sorry, man. I had no idea."

"It's okay." Colin soothed both of them.

Footsteps sounded at the door before Max's voice said, "Just a minute," turning someone away before closing the curtain behind him with a mumbled, "I need to do more cardio."

Time seemed infinite before she registered that it was Colin's heat beneath her body, his scent encompassing her, and his warm breath on her face. When she lifted her head, his worried eyes surveyed her face, the greyness in them making her stomach twist.

"I thought . . ." She winced. Her insides seemed to disintegrate with the idea of what she thought had happened.

"I know." He held her face in his damaged hand. "I know, but I'm okay. Emilie, look at me. I'm okay. I'm right here with you."

She nodded slowly, understanding on some level, but knowing she was nowhere near believing it wholly. Her lip trembled. "What happened?"

He took in a painful inhale. "I was running through a crosswalk when a cyclist decided not to stop at the red light. I guess he didn't see me run from behind the truck parked at the curb. I helped him until EMS arrived. I think he broke his hip."

When her eyes drifted to his right side, he said, "I got lucky. A few broken ribs and a small lac on the head. Everything will heal."

"Your hand."

"Road rash on the back of my fingers."

She pushed against the bed railing to sit up and look at him, this time paying attention to every wound. There were small cuts and scrapes on his forearms she hadn't noticed before, and he probably had some on his legs beneath the blanket. She consulted the telemetry and blood pressure monitors again.

His eyes pleaded with her. "I'm okay. I promise."

The breath that left her tight lungs took all the energy she possessed with it. "Okay."

◊◊◊

Emilie never went back to 5SW to start her shift; Max coordinated with the charges to have a float nurse take over. Instead, she stayed with Colin, moving to the small hard chair next to the gurney until he was discharged home. Fortunately for her, it wasn't much longer.

Every second she spent in that room listening to the sounds of the ER around her was agonizing, but she wouldn't leave his side. She focused on counting her breaths and synchronizing them with Colin's as her thumb ran circles over the rest of her fingertips. The ER doc had given him a hefty dose of morphine for the rib pain, so he was breathing nice and slow.

Max came back and offered to drive him home, but that would have meant canceling his office hours and rescheduling appointments. Colin insisted he could walk, but she assured Max that she'd request a car to get Colin home safely, and he could come and check on him this afternoon.

It was mid-morning when Emilie helped him into fresh scrubs since his running clothes had been cut off with trauma shears. The entire time she helped, moved, breathed, she felt completely numb. The weighing sensation pulling at her shoulders and ribs doubled with every anxious second she spent watching his heart beat on the telemetry monitor.

When they broke into the fifty degree sunshine waiting on the sidewalk for the Uber she requested, it was the first time she drew a full breath. She let her eyes linger on the naked maple tree on the street across from the hospital, tracing the tiny buds on it's stretching branches.

"Thank you for doing this." Colin's words brought her back to him. "You didn't have to miss work for me."

She forced her voice to sound light. "This isn't the first time I've had to play nurse to you."

His beautiful eyes searched her face, not quite believing her tone, but his lips curved into a slight smile regardless. "That's true."

His un-bandaged hand found her cheek, the warmth of his fingers light and soft. Every little touch steadied her, but also tormented her in a new way. Her eyes watered almost instantly.

"Hey." His voice was so incredibly tender. "I'm okay. I'm standing here right next to you."

"It's not . . ." Emilie couldn't finish the sentence.

Her eyes pulled towards the curb when she heard her name being called from the street. As they sat in silence on the short drive to his condo, Colin reached across the seat and held her hand. The solidness of his fingers around hers should have been a comfort, but instead a shock ran up her arm.

The jolt of the truth hit her chest so hard, her eyes darted to the road ahead to see if they'd been in an accident. It felt as if the steering wheel slammed straight into her.

There was a reason she felt as if her world had changed all week, because it had. She'd been avoiding the truth, but it pulsed with every beat of her heart.

Nothing spoke louder than her actions.

She swore she'd never step foot in an emergency room again, but she'd *run* there to see that he was okay.

She undeniably loved Colin.

And now she was terrified of losing him.

·CHAPTER 30·

The tension that radiated from Emilie was almost palpable. Her hand had been fidgeting ever since she slid off the gurney in the ER. Colin's drug inhibited mind clumsily fumbled, thinking of how to make her feel better, to convince her that he was fine.

Well . . . mostly fine.

His head and flank were already starting to throb severely with that last dose of IV morphine wearing off. The three of his largest injuries hurt the most, but soon bruises would show up where he'd hit the ground and rolled after the initial impact. When they reached his condo door, he drew in a large breath and his ribs retaliated against the movement, making him groan involuntarily.

Emilie's still shaky fingers reached up and traced his brow, her eyes darting from his forehead to his matted hair. He resented being the cause of that subtle tremor. Catching her hand with his, he gently kissed her fingertips. Her body visibly relaxed, eyes fluttering closed as she slowly exhaled.

Better.

When her soft brown eyes blinked open, he pulled her captured hand to the center of his chest and wove his bandaged one under the braid at the base of her neck. Her lips parted before they even touched his. The swelling in his chest and euphoria he felt had nothing to do with the lingering effects of the narcotics dissipating from his system.

It'd been a week since he'd kissed Emilie—entirely too long. After everything that happened today, he wanted to be with her more. Be able to touch her more. Be able to *love* her more. As their tongues wove together, she pulled at his sides to bring him closer, and a painful grunt left his lips. Immediately, she dropped her hands and stepped back.

"I'm sorry."

"It's okay. I'm just getting a little sore." He dug his keys from the paper bag of medications given to him by the discharge nurse. "Let's go inside and I'll take these."

Emilie brought him a glass of water as he carefully changed from the OR scrubs to his soft pajama pants and cotton T-shirt. The action of stretching and moving was probably stupid to do now instead of waiting until the morphine tablets kicked in, but he felt more comfortable in his own clothes.

"Why don't you also take ibuprofen?" She was already in his medicine cabinet, pulling out the correct dosage.

He liked the sight of her in his bathroom, knowing where things were. Her aqua scrubs reflected off the mirrored cabinet as she closed it, giving him dual Emilies. The more this image played in his mind—her in different colored scrubs, putting her toothbrush away before walking with him to the hospital, a quick but stirring kiss outside before they started the day—the more he liked the idea of her here with him.

She lowered her head in that shy way of hers as she approached, and Colin knew he must have been staring too intently.

Her hand held out the burnt orange pills. Letting his fingers run from the inside of her wrist to the center of her palm to collect them, he watched the delicate skin over her throat as she swallowed. Damn it if he didn't want to push through all the pain and press her to bed right now.

"You should lie down." She moved past him to adjust his pillows and pull back the comforter.

"Only if you lie with me." He heard the gruffness in his voice and didn't care.

"*Colin.* You've broken ribs and had quite a morning already."

"I told you I was fine."

Her finger pointed to the opened covers with a stubbornness he'd only seen in spurts. "Rest."

The first thing on his mind was presumably out of the question right now, but one way or another he wanted her in his arms.

He softened his voice. "Please lie with me."

Her chest lifted and fell quickly as her lips opened. "Only if it won't hurt you," she whispered.

Three large steps brought him to those lips, sealing them with his own. This time her hands carefully wove around his neck, avoiding all his injuries.

"You could never hurt me." His words came out hoarse.

Emilie stepped back, toeing off her sneakers as he settled himself into bed. She crossed to the other side and tucked up under his left arm, hesitantly putting her hand against his side. He collected her hand and settled it where it belonged, deeply exhaling at the feeling of her palm over his heart.

He probably shouldn't have felt so much satisfaction lying fully clothed in bed with Emilie after being beat up by a speeding bicycle, but it hummed in his body nonetheless. When the morphine kicked in, it hit him harder than he expected, and he felt himself doze in and out of consciousness. Every time he came back, Emilie grabbed at his senses first: her honeysuckle scent, the softness of the back of her hand under his fingertips, her quiet and peaceful breathing.

When he returned again, he felt the absence of her warmth along his side. Turning his head, his vision swam a little. *Next time half a dose*, he thought. Emilie was sitting up against the headboard, not touching him. Her thumb was tracing each of her other four fingers in turn—pinky, ring, middle, index—again and again.

"Hey," he said.

Her brow remained furrowed, but her fingers gently pushed through the hair on the left side of his scalp. His eyes closed at the touch and when she repeated the action, an incapacitating peace ran through his arms and legs.

"You should stay." He forced his eyes open against the medically induced drowsiness.

She was gazing at the triple canvas panoramic photo of the Appalachian Mountains on the opposite wall. "I will for a while." Her voice sounded distant, but everything was a little fuzzy right now.

"No, you should stay. Here. I know not all the time would make sense, but maybe between shifts."

The hand in his hair froze, and he felt the energy shift immediately.

"I can't."

Stupid morphine. Immediately, he remembered they hadn't even gone on a proper dinner date without his friends there. He was pushing things again because *he* was ready, instead of waiting for her to be.

"That's okay. I understand."

She shifted on the bed and pulled her hand from his head. "I need to go."

Colin pushed up and almost immediately regretted that action as a painful groan left his mouth. "Emilie, don't. I'm sorry. I'm just . . ." He blinked. "The morphine is hitting me hard, and I'm losing my filter. Don't leave."

She got up and stood at the end of the bed. "It'll only get worse. It'll be too hard."

The narcotics flushing through his system made him groggy and inaccurate. When he pushed the covers back from the bed, he missed the first time. "What? You're not making sense. Please sit down and talk to me."

"I can't."

A new pain pierced through his body. "Why?"

Her mouth opened, but nothing came out. She moved briskly to the side of his bed, crouching to pick up her shoes. "I can't do this anymore."

He swung his legs over the edge, but in an instant her hands firmly pressed down on his shoulders, preventing him from standing.

Blinking up, the look in her eyes shattered what was unbroken in his body. They were haunted with sadness, fear, and ringed with something else he couldn't place. "*Please*, Colin. Let me go."

Before he could answer, she covered his mouth with hers in the most exquisite and excruciating kiss of his life. When his eyelids finally opened, her shoes were in one hand and the other swiped at her cheek before she sprinted out of the room. He registered the slam of his front door before he could stand enough to stumble into the kitchen.

I'll never catch her like this.

It took two attempts to pull up her contact on his phone once he found it plugged into the charger on his nightstand. He collapsed on the edge of his bed when the call went immediately to voicemail. Hanging up, he called again, this time waiting to the end of the message, her happy voice punching him in the stomach as it played in his ear.

"Emilie." His breath heaved. "Please. I'm sorry. You told me and I didn't listen and I'm so sorry. I promise I can do slow. I can back everything up. Just . . . just come back. Please come back and let's talk about this." He almost added that he loved her, but then remembered that was what got him into this mess in the first place.

His hand nervously ran over his head, his pinky snagging in his blood-matted hair. She probably went home, but what if she didn't? How could he find her?

He was pulling up the Uber app when a knock sounded on the front door.

"Thank God," escaped his lips.

After half stumbling, half walking to the front door, he opened it quickly. Kate—not Emilie—stood on the other side in a streamlined navy pant suit. As she took him in, her friendly grin immediately fell as her eyes widened.

"Max said you were okay. You don't look okay."

His head hung heavy as a painful breath left his lungs. "No . . . I'm not okay."

·CHAPTER 31·

Emilie was still breathing heavily when she found what she was looking for on her laptop. The idea that crystallized in her mind on the quick run home now seemed like the only sensible thing to do. Colin would see through her when he came over once the drugs wore off, and there was not a doubt in her mind that he wouldn't forgo taking another dose in order to talk to her.

She had to leave.

It was the only solution and the only way to save them both in the long run.

Powering up her phone, she typed a quick message to Ash.

Emilie: *You said that you'd take a shift if I needed it. Would you be able to work for me on Monday?*

She turned to pull the large canvas overnight bag from the bottom of her closet and heard her phone ping on her bed. The voicemail icon had popped up. A sob racked her body at the sight of the tiny icon, knowing Colin's voice was there on her phone, confused and upset. Her hands started shaking as Ash's response flashed over the screen.

Ash: *You got it. Are you okay?*

She pushed tears aside.

Emilie: *I want to go home and visit my family for a few days.*

Ash: *Everybody okay at home?*

Emilie: *Yes. I just need to be there for a little while.*

She knew she couldn't ask for Ash to cover her shift and not at least partially explain why.

Ash: *Okay. Fill out the shift switch request online and I'll accept it.*

Emilie: *Thank you*

Ash: *Let me know if you need anything else. ANYTHING.*

Emilie: *I will*

After powering her phone off again, she returned to her computer, navigated both webpages, and started feverishly throwing clothes into the bag.

◊◊◊

The gravel crunched under the tire's wheels as the cab drove away. With her bag on one shoulder and her purse on the other, Emilie moved slowly through the grass, stopping at two well-maintained, flat lying granite slabs.

Her knees gave out from under her, and she collapsed to the ground between them, lying a hand on each one. The late afternoon sun had warmed the stones, and heat radiated through her fingertips. As she always did, she let her fingers trace the small etched footprints on Lucy's headstone.

"Hi." Her voice came out strained and high as the tears she'd been holding in the entire flight splashed to the earth.

She'd forced herself not to think about her actions, just sit in a state of immobile numbness over the last few hours. If she focused on the devastated look on Colin's face as he asked "why," she'd never have gotten on the plane. The memory of their last kiss fried all of her nerve endings as every muscle in her body refused to relinquish its stranglehold.

She didn't want this, she didn't want to destroy him, but what was the alternative? She wasn't strong enough. She always told herself she was, but in the end she just wasn't.

Sunlight continued to shift as the wind blew the loose strands of her hair around her face until they stuck to her wet cheeks. The sour taste of her stomach mixed with the salty taste of her tears as she licked her lips. Analie's lilac perfume preceded the arm that draped over her shoulder as her sister's pencil skirt covered legs carefully folded themselves beside her. She tucked her head onto her twin's blazer covered shoulder and stained the fabric with salt.

Long minutes passed before she felt collected enough to lift her head. "How'd you know I was here?"

Emilie hadn't told her family after impulsively buying the plane ticket, knowing that when she showed up on her parents' doorstep, she'd be welcomed with open arms.

Her sister's body tensed, but her voice remained calm. "It doesn't matter."

Sitting up, she pushed at the wetness on her face. "How'd you know?"

Her twin blew out a breath. "Don't be mad." Tucking a loose strand from her tiny chignon behind her ear, she said, "It's not really my fault. You've had the same password since college, which isn't very cyber secure."

"What are you talking about?"

Analie's fingers delicately wiped away a straggling tear. "You know I worry, right? It's out of love, but I *might* check your email every once in a while."

Her mouth fell open, unable to respond.

"I know. I know." She spread her hands. "But Em, you almost died once. I worry, and sometimes checking up on you makes me feel better; less helpless, less out of control."

An exhale left her lungs as she laid her head back on her sister's shoulder. She understood completely how Analie felt and couldn't hold it against her.

"I saw the airline tickets and called Mom, and when she didn't immediately say you were home, I knew you were here." Analie laced her fingers through hers. "What happened?"

For a few breaths, the sounds of traffic from the nearby busy street and the wind whipping through the trees was all that could be heard.

"I love Colin."

Saying the words out loud to Analie sent an odd sensation sprinting through her veins. Her brain spun for a few hurried seconds before she understood that it was remorse.

She wanted Colin to have been the first one to hear those words. She wanted to see his eyes smile before she felt his breath on her lips and his body surrounding hers.

She wanted to but she couldn't.

"Okay." Her sister's voice slightly extended the word, like she was waiting for more information. Seconds passed before she said, "Help me see why that is bad."

Her breath caught in her throat. "It just is."

She could almost feel her sister's brows pinching. "Does he know you love him?"

"No. I broke it off this morning."

"Why?"

"*Because* . . ." Emilie lifted her head to stare into matching eyes. "I can't be *here* again. I can't do it. Like you said, I barely made it through the first time. I won't make it through again."

Analie's pragmatic irises stared back at her. "The chances of that happening again are incredibly slim."

"The chances of my husband and child dying in a car crash were incredibly slim the *first time*." She heard the snap in her voice.

Her twin's hand rubbed Emilie's shoulder before pulling her into a hug. "You're right."

An inappropriate laugh tumbled free of her mouth. With every emotion in her body fighting with each other, she'd start crying again if she didn't laugh. "You never admit when I'm right."

"I do too," her twin quipped.

"Sure. Believe whatever fantasy you want to believe." Part of this seemed easier. She was just bickering with her sister, not completely dismantling what was left of her heart.

"I admit when you're right. It's just that it happens so *infrequently*, you probably don't remember."

She pushed a jabbing finger into her sister's ribs.

"Hey! Don't poke at me. I'm the one missing my last class to console you."

She sobered. "I'm sorry, An. I didn't mean for you to be here."

Her sister waved her hand. "I sent out my slides electronically, so at least the good students will review them. Don't worry about it. Emergencies happen."

The sound of the word sent a sharp shudder through her. Her mind projected a disfigured mash-up of the scenes that always played, but now Colin's face replaced Braden's, his blue-grey eyes piercing hers. She shoved a hand against her sternum and dragged in a breath.

"What?" Analie's eyes tensed. "What is it?"

Swallowing against the bitter taste in her mouth, she just shook her head.

"It's okay." Her twin rubbed her back. "It's okay. You're okay. Everything is okay."

After several rounds of focused breathing, her voice came out pitched and tight. "This morning . . . Colin had a collision with a cyclist when he was running. He's okay. But I . . ." She swallowed with difficulty as the tears streamed on their own. "I didn't know. You know? I thought it was all happening again like some sick twisted deja vu. I ran downstairs . . . to the emergency room to see him. To see if he was okay, and then I lost it."

"Oh, *Em*." Analie's arms were around her again.

They sat there for a long time, Analie rocking her while she tried to let go of the anxiety vibrating through every cell of her body.

"He doesn't know, does he? About what you saw when Braden was in the ER?"

"No." Her voice was less than a whisper.

Time stretched between them again. Her sister's knuckles lightly stroked her forehead, just as their mother used to do to help them fall asleep as children. The wind blew across the cemetery and pulled on the empty branches of the trees that dotted intermittently across the vast space. Her jeans were damp from the moist grass, and she was sure Analie's cream skirt was ruined from the dirt. Eventually, her sister's gentle touch lulled her, and the exhaustion of the day dragged her eyes closed.

She had no sense of how long they'd been like that when she heard her twin's voice again. "Emilie?"

Rousing herself enough to answer, she said, "Yeah?"

Analie drew in a long inhale and released a careful breath. "Does Colin love you?"

For the hundredth time that day, her body felt unimaginably heavy as she exhaled a simple word. "Yes."

·CHAPTER 32·

Leaving Max and Kate's house usually left him emotionally bolstered, but tonight Colin felt drained. It had been an excruciating six days. Six days where he had nothing to do but think about how badly he'd screwed up again. Even the adorable way Owen toddled from one side of the room to the other, showing off his new ability couldn't pull Colin out the negative fog he'd been in since the accident.

The scenic single lane road opened up to a double, and he found himself accelerating around the car in front of him, gripping the wheel forcefully as he did. His forearms tensed, and he blew out a long, painful exhale. The nagging, persistent throbbing at his right side was a constant reminder of his mistake. How if he'd had any sense, he'd have restrained the words that came out of his mouth.

When Kate had showed up at his door last Friday, he'd begged her to take him to Emilie's with a desperation he didn't know he could possess. Kate made him sit down, drink a glass of water, and explain what had happened. It was betraying Emilie's trust to tell Kate about her past and the reason why they'd been taking things so slow, but he felt like he'd been navigating their tentative relationship in a vacuum, and now he really needed a woman's wisdom. Kate had listened and then told him what he didn't want to hear—that Emilie was probably spooked by the "move in with me" innuendo and to give her some space.

Clearing his throat, he merged onto the Northern Expressway and rolled down his windows, letting the cold night air push against his skin. The dashboard thermometer said forty-eight degrees, but he didn't care. Numbness already fought the twitch of apprehensive itchiness that he couldn't resolve by running. His outlet had been stolen from him the same day as his happiness, so his unrest sat thickly in his chest alongside his rib pain. At least in the car, he could feel the force of his movement against the world around him.

John had reasonably taken him off the surgery schedule for the week. Even though long hours whittled away in the OR would have been a welcome distraction, Colin understood it was best practice to let him heal before returning to surgery. Gratefully, he'd been able to keep his office hours twice this week, so every day he wasn't just sitting at home thinking about what he'd done.

Every time he left the large office building adjacent to the hospital, he stared at the multi-storied behemoth, and willed his feet to walk home instead of to 5SW to see if Emilie was working. As a substitute, he looked for her elsewhere, in less conspicuous places. He found himself weaving the paths of the Commons for hours, hoping to run into her.

In the end, all of his searching was pointless.

The skin around his eyes tightened as yesterday's memory flashed fresh.

As he and Max walked towards Bo's, the bouncy music piped out of the speakers increased. A crowd of people were waiting outside, and Max went inside to put their name down for a table. A few seconds later, Ash bounded down the stairs in jeans and a loose sweater with a to-go bag in her hand.

"Ash." The word escaped his mouth in a rushed exhale.

"Dr. Abernan, hi." She smiled as if she had no idea that his life was completely falling apart.

"Having lunch with Emilie today?" He kept his voice very even.

The white bag looped over two long fingers looked like it might contain two styrofoam boxes. Her phone rang at that moment, and she glanced at the screen as she answered offhandedly. In retrospect, it felt as fate had intervened to distract her with a call. Her eyes looked over her phone as she replied.

"No, she's in Virginia visiting . . ."

The end of the sentence hung in the air as her head snapped up. He could see all the pieces fall into place behind her green eyes as they enlarged. The strumming guitar music was too tinny as he swallowed against the burnt taste at the back of his throat. Her mouth opened, but no words came out.

"The wait's only twenty minutes." Max appeared at his side. "Hey, Ashley. Having a good day off?"

Her eyes darted from his to Max's before a forced smile laced her lips. "Sure am, Dr. Campbell. Just grabbing some sustenance." She lifted her bag before her surveying gaze flashed back to his face. Colin knew he looked like he'd been hit by a Mack truck, not a simple bicycle. "Well . . . I should be going."

"See you later." Max's voice held a smile.

Ash's legs pulled her away from the two of them in long quick strides, glancing over her shoulder once. His friend's eyes flicked from the sidewalk to his face.

"Shit, Colin. What is it?"

Rubbing at the eyebrow just below his sutures, he made himself say the words. "Emilie's in Virginia."

"Oh," Max said slowly.

Virginia.

Not only had he scared her away from him. He'd sent her fleeing the state.

"Maybe she had a planned visit and failed to mention it."

Colin put his hands on his hips and stared at the grey asphalt beneath their feet, willing himself not to give into the bottoming out feeling that dropped in his stomach. All the hope he'd harbored up until that point that maybe she just needed some time and they could work through this evaporated. Max's thick hand clasped his left shoulder.

"I'm sorry, man."

"Yeah." His vision memorized the color of the various small pebbles trapped beneath him, trying to ignore the fact that his chest felt like it had been cracked open by a sternal saw. "So am I."

After parking his car, Colin took the elevator to his condo and fiddled with his keys. He knew what would be behind his door when he opened it.

Memories.

The ghost of Emilie everywhere.

Mementos of a different time when things were all possibility.

Hanging up the keyring with his wallet, he walked into the darkened main room. His piano sat silently in front of him, bathed in moonlight. He pushed a hand through his hair as he forced himself to drag in another deep, uncomfortable breath. Generally, he only played during the day, but a song pushed itself into his mind, resonating down his forearms to his fingertips.

Light danced off the white keys until they were cast in shadow as he gently compressed them. The melancholy dissonance of the mild melody against the harmony pulsed in his veins. Somber chords filled his silent condo and hovered in the air. Unlike when he tried to play earlier this week, his fingers didn't stumble or hit incorrect keys. Tonight, the slow pulsating ebb and flow of the pianissimo tones sang out the misery that beat in his chest.

His head hung heavy after the final keys were pressed. When a drop fell against the bench between his legs, he pushed the back of his hand over his wet eyes and stood. He needed to get to bed, or at least lie in bed and maybe sleep would actually come to him tonight.

Tomorrow, he was back on the surgery schedule. Tomorrow, he could do what his body and mind were trained to do. He would help others. He would save lives. He might not be able to repair his own, but he could put back the pieces of other peoples' damaged hearts.

·CHAPTER 33·

Walking on to the floor to gather her assignment, Emilie ignored the rising dread pulsing through her body. It had been a week since she'd systematically dismantled her relationship with Colin. She didn't know if he was still recovering, but she knew eventually they would be working together again. After writing down her four room numbers, she sat at a computer to look up her patients' names.

Her mouth gaped open at the first one.

Killian O'Connor.

Bolting from her chair, she hurried to the assigned room, barely pausing as she rushed through the door.

Bo's wrinkled, weary face looked up and smiled, but there was no happiness in his eyes.

"Hello, Emilie."

She gingerly sat at the side of his hospital bed and reached for him. Bo gave his life-weathered hand to her, and she relaxed a bit at its warmth.

"Hi, Bo," she said, holding back the tears that threatened at the corners of her eyes.

She didn't even know why he was here—hadn't taken the time to read the chart or even the diagnosis once she recognized his name. Giving herself a firm internal shake, she told herself she had to be what he needed today, and that was his nurse.

"Are you okay with me taking care of you today?"

"Yes, my dear." He used his other hand to pat hers lightly. "It's always better to be surrounded by those who care for you."

Her lips lifted at the corners as Gian, one of the night nurses, stood in the doorway. "Oh there you are, Emilie. Can I give you report?"

She squeezed Bo's hand as she said, "yes," and followed him into the hall to the charting area. Her shift started off in its normal busy fashion, and it wasn't until early afternoon that Barbara found her in the medroom.

"How's Bo?"

Glancing up from the injections she was preparing, she said, "His EF is low and his sats keep dropping. He's stable right now though. They're starting him on all the heart failure medications to try and improve things."

Gian told her Bo had come in overnight having what the ER doctors thought was a heart attack and was sent immediately to the cardiac cath lab to clear the potential blockages in his heart. Only after they were inside his heart, guiding wires into his arteries beneath fluoroscopy imagery, did they see that all his vessels were clean. The catecholamine surge that led to what looked like a heart attack was caused by stress. It was under echocardiogram that they saw the telltale ballooning of Takotsubo cardiomyopathy.

"I'd say I couldn't believe it but I can." Barbara's shoulders deflated. "If anyone could have 'Broken Heart Syndrome' it would be Bo. He loved Mary so much."

"I know." Sorrow echoed in her words.

"I'd tell you to take good care of him, but I already know that you are." Her manager patted her back before leaving.

After giving her other patients their IV medications, Emilie headed back to Bo's room. Any extra time she had today, she intended on spending it at this man's bedside. She was placing a warm blanket over his legs when his words caught her off guard.

"Shannon told me that she saw you and Colin having lunch at the diner."

The day came flooding back to her. The touch of his hands and mouth as he made love to her again right in his kitchen. The sloppy grin that wouldn't leave his face over lunch. The way his eyes pierced hers after he told her he loved her.

She tried to stifle the strident gasp that dragged into her squeezing lungs and focused her attention on perfecting the tuck of the beige blanket around Bo's feet.

"He's a good man," Bo said.

The fingers of her right hand curled over her chest, and she used them to push the fallen braid from her shoulder in an attempt to cover her reaction.

She *knew* Colin was a good man, but being a good person didn't protect you from being inexplicably wiped from the earth.

"I know right now life seems long, but let me tell you, it's over in an instant. Even lying here at eighty-two, it seems like just yesterday that Mary and I were having lunch at midnight together in that cafeteria downstairs."

This was a topic she could talk about without feeling like she was unraveling. "You never told me the story about how you met," she said, moving to the IV pump to check the titration of his pressors.

Half expecting him to go into one of the long, lovely stories Mary often shared with her, the shock of his next words sped down her spine.

"We fell in love a lot like you and Colin did, working together at the hospital."

Her fingers tightened around the cool steel bar as she ignored the pulsing in her throat.

"Oh?" The strangled word was released in hope that he'd continue to talk about the woman who she still loved and missed.

Her nurse phone rang in her pocket, and relief thumped in her chest. Never looking Bo in the eyes, she murmured that she needed to answer the phone and walked outside his room. Once tucked into the charting area, she answered the simple call, notifying her that MRI was coming to take another patient to their scheduled exam. Rubbing the knot between her brows, she tried to push down her tense shoulders.

She felt Colin before he uttered a word. His familiar scent fully encapsulated her, making it hard to keep her breathing even. All-encompassing pain vibrated through her veins at his presence behind her. She struggled against the immediate, intense impulse to lean back into the heat of his solid body. Pressing both hands flat onto the charting desk in some febrile attempt to ground herself, she took a halting inhale.

She wanted to ask if he was okay, to ask if his ribs were better, if he could sleep at night because she couldn't, if food tasted like chalk and metal mixed together, but that would defeat the whole reason she was torturing the both of them in the first place.

"Emilie." His voice was low, the usual timber of it running a shiver down her spine. This time, however, there was a guttural sadness in her name that crushed her immediately. She pressed her eyes closed tightly. "Can we talk? *Please.*"

The pleading quality of his words made her want to spin and wrap her arms around him, but she forced herself not to move. If she turned around and he saw her eyes, he'd know this wasn't what she really wanted. Then he'd fight for her.

No. She had to keep this going. She wasn't strong enough to be with him, even if she wanted to be.

Her steely voice came out cold, even to her ears. "Is there a patient you need to discuss with me, Dr. Abernan?"

The short, painful exhale that blew over her neck hit her *hard*. Her fingertips gripped the edge of the counter to lock her body into place as her eyes pressed closed again.

I'm sorry, Colin.

"No."

He hovered behind her, and she felt every tormenting beat of her heart in her ears.

"I'm sorry about Bo." It felt like he was going to touch her, that he would lay his hand on her shoulder, but he didn't.

"Thank you," she whispered.

She felt his warm breath flow against her skin before the space behind her emptied. Her hand slid over her back, half expecting it to be naked. A tear ran down the outside of her cheek, and she quickly whisked it away. The call bell pinned too loudly as the laughs of the patient care aides joking from the nurse's station pushed into her consciousness.

How could anyone be laughing right now?

·CHAPTER 34·

Listening to the loud drops of water on the umbrella above him, Colin watched as the water fell around his black oxfords. It made sense to him that it would rain today.

It seemed right.

Appropriate.

After he'd discharged Bo home with his family two weeks ago, he'd made himself available if Shannon needed him, even for a house call. As days lingered on, gratitude bloomed that Bo had that time with his family before they found him lying peacefully in his bed a few mornings ago. He'd needed that time to say goodbye to his mother so many years ago and was glad Bo's family had those extra days with him.

A sea of umbrellas surrounded the two and a half by eight-foot hole in the muddy earth. At the service, he'd never seen a church packed so tightly. Bo had meant so much to the community, and it was fitting that everyone was here to say goodbye.

The priest could barely be heard over the pounding water, but eventually everyone shuffled from their positions in the grass to their cars as Bo's body was lowered into the ground next to Mary's. This was always the hardest part for him, the part when it became real by returning the body to the earth. It was when Colin spread his parents' ashes in the sea that he understood they were truly gone.

Through the ocean of black dresses, black suits, black shoes, and black umbrellas, he knew Emilie was here somewhere. He knew she was huddling under a flimsy plastic canopy, weeping much softer than the sky did above them.

The past three weeks had been more agonizing than losing either of his parents because Emilie had *chosen* to leave him.

A halting inhale pulled against the numbing ache that sat between his right ribs and his sternum. Part of him felt like his bones would never heal, that it was his penance for scaring the love of his life away. Running his free hand through his hair, he walked away from the gravesite, the wet ground squishing under each step.

A lot of the people were already driving away, heading to the wake at the diner. Looking back over the cemetery, he saw Emilie huddled under a large tree abloom with fresh spring leaves. His breath caught in his throat as she pushed her hands against her cheeks and her umbrella tumbled to the ground.

Everything was too intense, like a photo's saturation had been pushed to the limit. The bright green of the new leaves almost matched the neon grass. The deep teal of the umbrella somehow perfectly encapsulated Emilie's essence: laughter, strength, beauty, and sadness.

He had to fight the immediate urge to run towards her and pull her into his arms. Seeing her at work a couple times a week had been hard, but he firmly kept his mind on his job, and minimized his time on the floor. The sight of her standing under a tree wearing the same dark hose and black heels that she'd had on before he'd been inside her the first time was tortuous.

"Hey, Dr. Abernan." A familiar voice stepped up behind him.

He turned to see Ash standing eye to eye with him in her black dress and heeled boots. "Hey, Ash."

"I just wanted to say that I'm sorry." Her eyes flitted over his shoulder and then back.

He cleared his throat. "Bo will be missed."

She opened her mouth as if to say more, but no words came out. Instead, her lips pressed into a slight frown as she squeezed the sleeve of his suit jacket, her arm getting splashed by rain as it slipped between their umbrellas.

"Thanks." His word came as an exhaled whisper.

Ash walked away towards the road, and his body turned on its own to the tree, which now stood by itself, its leaves shaking with the force of each accelerated water droplet. He blinked against the hollowness in his chest and started towards his car.

◊◊◊

The right thing to do would probably have been to attend the wake, but Colin couldn't bring himself to do it. The idea of seeing Emilie again, at a closer proximity, intensified the stiffness he felt in all his muscles. He scratched at his throat and then pulled to loosen the black silk tie from around his neck. After laying it and his suit jacket on the kitchen island, he slumped into his father's recliner, staring out at the grey, wet sky.

The same thought filtered through his head as it often did over the last few weeks. *I'm not going to get over this.* This loss was going to sit like a little black scar over his aorta for the rest of his life, and there wasn't a surgeon alive who could remove it.

Maybe it would be best to move somewhere he could work more, have more hours, get back to his old way of living. Since he'd only been with CTSB nine months, he'd have to wait until he'd finished a year at least for professionalism's sake. Or not. Maybe he should just tell John he'd love a good recommendation, but he couldn't be here anymore.

If seeing Emilie now was difficult, someday walking onto 5SW and finding an engagement ring on her finger would be excruciating. All the air left his lungs as he pushed both hands through his hair, cradling his head.

A knock sounded at his door. Probably Max to check on him. Since he was called in before the funeral, he'd promised to come by once he'd finished up at the hospital. Pushing against his knees, Colin rose, every fiber aching with the movement.

When he opened the door, it felt like the bicycle had hit him in the chest again.

Emilie's chestnut hair was plastered to her scalp and clumped into long, wet strands. Leftover raindrops fell from her thick eyelashes and streamed in rivulets over her delicate freckled face. Her drenched black dress clung tightly as her lower lip quivered.

"Emilie." His shocked first word freed the rest of his brain to process the shivering sight of her and follow with more pragmatic ones. "You're soaked. Let me get you a towel."

His torso began to rotate into action, but the serious tone in her voice stopped him.

"I need to tell you something."

The desire to hear her words warred with his need to get her warm and dry, but she took the decision away from him by continuing.

"I . . ." She stopped and took a shaky breath, hugging her waterlogged cardigan-covered arms tight around herself.

It was one of the hardest things not to gather her to his chest.

She exhaled as strength glinted into her eyes, her brows set with determination. "I was an emergency nurse before I worked here. The day of the accident, when Braden's car was hit by a powerline truck head-on, he and Lucy were brought to my hospital. I was in my manager's office when EMS rolled them in." She drew in a rasped breath. "I saw everything. Braden's broken chest. The horrific code as they tried to save him. Lucy's tiny lifeless body. Everything. After that I swore I would never set foot in an ER again."

His throat felt as if it was closing off. His mouth opened, but only strained air came out.

"That's why I pushed you away. I couldn't have that happen again. I couldn't lose you the way I lost them."

"*Emilie* . . ." He stepped forward, and she didn't pull back, just tilted her head up to pierce his eyes with hers. "I'm so sorry." And he was, for everything. For everything that she'd had to endure in her lifetime. For the mountain of grief she had to climb after not only losing her husband and child, but watching them die in such a graphic way. For any distress he'd caused her in their time together. "I would've never had Max tell you I was in the emergency room if I'd known. I would've kept you away from there. I'm sorry. I'm so sorry."

His hand drifted up on its own, his thumb brushing the residual rain off her cheek. Her dewy lashes closed for a moment before her eyes focused back on him.

"If I had to, I'd run there again. I love you too much not to."

His heart thundered as he drew in a long breath. His fingers traced her jaw as his eyes searched her face, unable to believe the words she'd just said. "You love me?"

Her hand gently settled over the center of his chest. "More than anything."

Light resonated and bounced behind his breastbone as he wrapped his other arm around her sodden body and covered her lips with his. Emilie wove her arms around his back, pulling them even closer together. This kiss felt different. His entire body hummed with a vibration that didn't feel entirely contained to him, that felt only possible with them together.

Pulling back to graze his lips to hers, he whispered, "I love you."

Her face tilted back until their eyes met. "I love you."

If hearing his name fall from those lips was exquisite, hearing those words was infinitely better. A smile tugged at his mouth as he lowered it to kiss her again, but she leaned back slightly. He lifted his head, crossing his arms behind her lower back.

"I also need to tell you that I'm sorry. I'm sorry for not telling you the truth and then shutting down. I just . . ." She took a deep inhale. "I was so scared, and I thought I wasn't strong enough. But then I stood watching Bo being lowered in the ground and realized that the pain of not being with you when you're right in front of me is so much worse than any future pain of losing you." Her fingers pushed the hair from his temple. "I'm sorry for hurting you."

His eyes closed as he turned his jaw to kiss her palm as it moved down his face.

The elevator dinged in the background, and footsteps thumped into the hall until Max's voice said, "Oh, hey."

Almost groggily, Colin looked up, never loosening his grip on Emilie's body.

"Hi, Max," she said.

His friend ran his hand over his beard. "I was going to check on you, but it looks like everything's good so . . ." He gestured to the elevator. "I'll just be going."

"Thanks." They answered in unison, and then Emilie's pearlescent laughter began to fill the hallway.

Max poked twice at the button. "You know if you invited the completely drenched woman into your condo, you wouldn't have to kiss her in the hall."

Colin lowered his voice as he tugged at her waist. "That's true."

Emilie's laughter ceased as heat flushed over her skin and settled in her eyes.

He bent his head until he heard. "Still here. Still standing right here. Come on! This thing is taking forever."

"Goodbye, Max!" he called, leaning back to slightly pick up Emilie and pull her into his condo before kicking the door shut.

He loved the little high-pitched surprised noise she made when he lifted her from the ground, but right now he was only interested in hearing a different kind of sound from those gorgeous lips.

·CHAPTER 35·

Emilie took a deep breath of early fall air, relishing the sensation of the cool breeze on her skin. After unlocking the entry door to her building, she climbed the three flights of stairs to her condo. The scent of tomato sauce and pasta water filled her nose as soon as she pushed her way through.

Colin stood at the stove in a blue graph-check collared shirt tucked into his grey slacks. He looked up from the pot he was stirring and gave her the sexiest smile. During the day, she'd almost forgotten how breathtakingly beautiful he was.

"Smells delicious." She grinned as she crossed into the kitchen.

He gave her a quick peck before his focus was back on his task. "Don't get too excited. I boiled pasta and warmed sauce from a jar."

"Still. It's nice to have dinner made when you get home for work." She placed her hand over his, encouraging him to drop the wooden spoon in the pot. "Especially when it's made by such a handsome man."

Weaving her hands over the smooth fabric of his shirt up his muscled biceps and into the hair at the nape of his neck, she pushed an appreciative kiss to his lips. With his hands free, Colin wrapped his arms around her waist and held her tightly as their bodies and mouths reunited after a long day apart.

Slightly breathless, he joked, "If anything burns, it's your fault, not mine."

"I'll take that risk," she whispered to his lips before pulling back. "Let me get changed, and I'll help you finish dinner."

"No, I've got it. Everything is almost done." His thumb found her cheek for a delicate brush of his lips to hers. "Get comfortable and relax."

She changed out of her burgundy scrubs into her most comfortable pair of jeans and a light long-sleeve sweater before joining Colin at the table in front of the bay window. The streetlight bounced off her elm's spectacular yellowing leaves, making a luminous backdrop for their dinner. Since they didn't spend much time talking last night after he'd flown home from a long week away, she asked about his trip with Max.

He flipped through the pictures of them backpacking in the Smoky Mountains. Emilie looked at them, but her focus kept being pulled to the lift of his eyebrows, the tugging corner of his mouth, and the excited tone of his voice as he detailed each image to her. The remnants of the summer sun still warmed his skin to a slight tan and lightened his sandy hair, making his eyes more striking.

After clearing the dishes, Colin took her hand and led her to the loveseat. She settled against him, breathing in his intoxicating scent, and laying her hand against his strong chest.

"I just realized I spent all dinner telling you about my trip." His voice reverberated against her body. "How was your day?"

"Good. Busy, but good," she said.

"Nothing crazy today?" He rubbed her arm lightly.

Her mind quickly recounted her shift. Other than counting the minutes until she could be back here in his arms, nothing stood out. "No, not really."

"Nobody asked you to hose a guy's chest out?"

Her body pulled up on its own as a gasp fell from her mouth. His eyes held a mischievous glint, and he had the slightest smirk on his delicious lips.

"Was that today?"

He nodded. "Thinking back on it, the second you pantomimed inserting a shower head into a man's chest, I was toast."

She went to playfully kiss the smirk off his face, but his arms wrapped tightly around her, pulling her deeper into a kiss that reached every cell in her body. When his lips finally fell from hers, his warm breath tingled the wet skin that still resonated from his attention.

"I have something for you."

Colin leaned forward and pulled a letter from his back pocket. She glanced at the plain white envelope for a breath before flitting her eyes back to his. His gaze held such focused sincerity that her heart hammered in her chest.

Her hand trembled slightly as she took the envelope from him and turned it over. The front had no writing on it, and as she gently broke the seal, she saw the lined, college-ruled paper inside. Unfolding it slowly, she instantaneously recognized the scrawling handwriting as the same she'd seen in his box of letters.

A fluttering flash swung through her belly. "Is this a letter from your mother?"

"It is." His voice was deep with emotion.

"Shouldn't you be reading it?" She was slightly confused now since she'd broken the seal to the envelope.

He nodded to the letter. "It's addressed to you."

To the woman who holds my son's heart,

She glanced up at Colin with tears beginning to brim in her eyes. His steady gaze contained such concentrated affection that her already ragged breath caught while she struggled to swallow.

I am so incredibly grateful for you. You are someone who I will never meet, but who will be such a vital part of my Colin's life. I love my son more than you can ever know, or rather I hope with my entire heart that you love him as much as I do. I wish that I could meet you. To hug you and hold your face in my hands with the appreciation I feel for being there for him when I cannot be. I ask that you not only take care of him, but give him

the love he deserves because if you are reading this letter, then he
has already given his heart to you. I love you, even though I don't
and will never know you, I love you and so does he.

My whole heart,
Helen

A tear trickled down Emilie's cheek as her subtly shaking hands held the letter. She was so overcome by his mother's words that she hadn't noticed Colin slip from beside her. As she lowered the letter to her lap, she found him kneeling with an open ring box in his hands. A surprised inhale filled her lungs.

His eyes were as moist as hers. "Emilie, I love you more than anything in life. All I want is to spend the rest of my days loving you. Please let me love you forever. Will you be my wife?"

"Yes, Colin. Yes." She reached for him as she squinted hot tears from her eyelids.

The look of relief and happiness on his face as he rushed to her lit up her chest as their lips met. He took her face in both of his hands, and she felt as if he was pouring his soul into her body, making silent promises to her.

When they separated, she said what vibrated in every cell in her body. "I love you."

He looked deep into her eyes. "I love you."

Taking her left hand, he gently slipped the stunning diamond ring on her finger. The large center diamond was surrounded by a halo of tiny ones.

"Colin, it's too much." Her voice was raspy.

"Nothing is too much for you." He kissed her hand. "Whatever you want, you can have. I want you to have everything your heart desires."

She set down the letter to push her fingers over his temple. "All I want is you."

The joy behind his eyes made her whole body effervescent. "You have me. I'm yours."

A question brewed in her mind. "The envelope wasn't addressed. How did you know it was for me?"

He pulled a second envelope from his pocket and turned it over in front of her. *When you meet the woman you want to marry* was written on the outside. He opened the envelope to show her a yellow post-it note inside. It read simply, *I am so incredibly happy for you, Colin. Have your love read this letter from me. Congratulations on your life together.*

"Your letter was inside this envelope with this note."

A sob caught in Emilie's throat when she thought of his mother writing this letter for her thirteen-year-old son during her last days on earth. How much she must have loved the younger version of the man still kneeling before her. Emilie hoped that somehow his mother knew how much she loved her son, and how she intended on spending the rest of her life cherishing him.

Carefully folding the letter back on its creases, she handed it back to him. With all the stripped honesty that had passed between them in the last few moments, she was amazed when a laugh bubbled up in her throat.

"Analie and my parents are going to be so surprised."

He glimpsed at her from the corner of his eye. "No, they won't."

"What do you mean?" Her brows furrowed.

The grin that broke across his face was so wide, her own lips automatically followed suit. "I didn't spend the whole trip with Max. The last day I spent in Virginia asking your family for your hand."

Her mouth dropped open. "They know?"

"They know and they happily gave their blessing."

Though Colin had only spent time with her family during their visit over the summer, she understood that they saw what she saw—his incredible character and that he meant everything to her.

The confident twist returned to his lips.

"It seems you thought of everything."

"I *am* an Eagle Scout," he reminded her.

"Don't get too cocky, or I'll have us married in the Commons."

His eyes slid into a playful glare. "You wouldn't."

"You just told me I can have whatever I want."

"Whatever you want that doesn't cause me bodily harm."

Her lips raised, glancing from his eyes to the ring that sat on her finger. Sadness washed over her like the slight fall breeze flitting through the leaves of the tree outside the window.

At a different time, in a different life, there had been a different ring on that finger. The tightness she usually felt between her shoulders and around her ribs gave a little quick grasp, then released.

"Emilie . . ." Colin's voice was serious. "If you don't want to do this now, I'll wait. If you never want to do this, I'll happily be a part of your life however you'll have me."

Her fingers lifted to his jaw, fixing her gaze on his. "I want to marry you. Sometimes in happiness, little moments of sadness seep through, but it doesn't diminish the love I have for you. They are separate in my chest, but occasionally I feel them both at the same time." She wove her fingers over his ear and into the unruly hair at the nape of his neck. "Most of the time I just feel the happiness being with you."

Colin gave a small single nod. He always seemed to recognize her pain and accept her in spite of it. His warm thumb traced her cheek as he lifted her lips to his in a kiss so affirming, she felt wholly, completely, absolutely, understood and loved.

·EPILOGUE·

Colin stood in the corridor next to the surgical suite, tying the strings of his scrub cap behind his head and tucking the loose strands of his hair beneath. He placed the paper into his chest pocket before grabbing a gown from the cart nearby.

It was amazing how much life had transformed in the last two years. How the instant that Emilie said yes to marrying him, it set forward a chain reaction of one change after another. It turned out that she hadn't been kidding about being married in the Commons.

He remembered protesting that the weather might not cooperate with an outdoor venue, or rather it was more likely that lightning would strike a nearby tree downing a large branch that would cleave him in half. Emilie had laughed it off and once he could see that she had her heart set on the idea, he conceded.

In the end, she'd been right. It had been the perfect place to have a wedding, especially in mid-October with the fall leaves ablaze as the altar behind them. The only thing more stunning than the venue had been his bride. The way the blush lace wedding dress hugged her body before cinching at her waist and flowing ethereally to the ground had taken his breath away. Her chestnut hair had been swept into a relaxed gather of curls at the base of her neck with a few loose strands grazing the paleness of her freckled skin.

He'd never seen anything more gorgeous in his entire life than Emilie at their wedding.

Kitty pushing open the swinging door to the surgical suite broke him from his revere.

"We're ready for you."

◊◊◊

A few hours later when things had calmed down, he stood next to Emilie and kissed her forehead.

"You are so incredibly strong," he whispered to her.

Her eyes were tired but happy when she looked into his. "I love you."

"I love you." His heart seemed too big for his chest, the way it thrummed against his sternum.

She glanced down to the small, soft wonder wrapped snugly in her arms. "I love you too."

He immediately amended his earlier thought—he'd never seen anything as beautiful as his gorgeous wife holding their newborn son.

Sitting in the chair next to her bed, Colin wrapped his hand around her crossed arms and beamed at the pale, wrinkly newborn baby held within them.

Their baby.

It was incomprehensible at times how he got this lucky. He remembered lying in bed two months after their wedding, loosely brushing Emilie's hair with his fingers when "What do you think about starting a family?" had startled him out of his relaxation.

He'd wanted to have children, but understood with all that she'd been through, it might not be something she would ever be ready for. Her head had tilted up as she told him that she'd been talking extensively with Nia about it, and if he would like to try for a child, she was ready. He'd kissed her, and they started that very evening.

Emilie's deep breath pulled him back into the room. The slight frown at her lips and tug of her brows told him that memories were running through her mind. When she glanced up, he rubbed his thumb over her cheek and lightly brought his lips to hers.

Her mouth lifted into a smile when he pulled away, and he let his fingers delicately run over the inch of dark brown hair on their son's head. "He looks so much like you."

"Except his eyes. I hope they stay blue."

"I hope he gets your freckles."

His wife and the mother of his child grinned shyly.

As Colin watched the marvel of their child breathing peacefully, he felt her attention on his face. "Have you read it yet?"

The *When you become a father* letter was still situated in the chest pocket of his flannel shirt.

"Not yet."

Emilie's affectionate gaze made his whole body light up. "Why don't you take him, and I can get a little rest while he sleeps."

She held their son out, and he took him into his arms. They'd yet to put him down in the bassinet the Nursery nurse provided.

"It won't be just the three of us soon." Her grin was teasing, but soft.

They'd decided to have the first few hours of their son's life to themselves before friends and family joined in their joy. Analie and her parents would be arriving from their flight in a few hours, and Kitty even promised not to tell anyone until a few hours after Emilie's planned c-section. With so much "family" in the hospital, it was hard to keep a secret.

Colin leaned over, carefully holding their son, and kissed her softly on those incredible lips. She smiled before shifting slightly to a more comfortable position to rest. He switched the lights off over the bed and went to sit on the bench by the window, lying his sleeping son very gently in his lap.

Lightness pulsed over his entire body as he gazed over the little life nestled on his legs. Opening the envelope, he lifted out the paper beneath to read the last letter his mother had written him.

ACKNOWLEDGMENTS

First, always first, I want to thank AJ for always believing in me and supporting this dream. It is not an exaggeration in saying that this book would not be here without your help. Thank you for *usually* never minding when I talked a bit too much about the book, and being a good sport about me spending our evening hours typing away.

Thank you to my wonderful children, Brooke and Alex, for understanding when I needed to work and being the perfect cute distraction when I needed a break.

A huge thank you Rachel Garber for being my incredible developmental editor and proofreader. You not only fully understood my vision, but were so enthusiastic about it, thank you. I am also grateful for my Line and Copy editors, Mandy Ballard, and Rebecca Jaycox. A big thank you to Diren Yardiml whose beautiful art graces this cover.

Thank you Jackie Fulcher for being THE best friend a person could have, my twice through beta reader, eternal optimist, and cheerleader. Thank you to Chelsea Kaczmarczyk for being not only the alpha reader, but an amazingly supportive friend, and Stephanie Bedell for betaing not once but twice.

Thank you to my Mom and Dad for being pleasantly surprised when I told them late into the process that I was writing, and for being encouraging as I trudged through the publishing stages.

Other wonderful people I'd like to mention who helped with this book are Chris, Madison, Ollie, Mary, and the helpful fellow authors at The Writing Gals group.

Last, but not least, thank YOU, the reader, for picking up this book. I truly hope that you enjoyed this story. For me it was simultaneously sad and joyful to write. I cried at times when writing it and was giddy during others. I hope that Emilie and Colin's story brought you some of those emotions as well. Thank you so much for spending time out of your life with them and with me. I am grateful for you.

ABOUT THE AUTHOR

Laura Langa is a lover of trees and all things green, drinks tea-not coffee, and relishes the pull of the ocean. As a former medical professional, she uses her experience in the field to inform her writing. You can visit her website at www.LauraLanga.com or follow her at @LauraLangaWrites on Instagram and Facebook.